Princess of the Everglades

Princess of the Everglades

Charles Mink

Pineapple Press, Inc.
Sarasota, Florida

Inquiries should by addressed to:
Pineapple Press, Inc.
P.O. Drawer 16008
Southside Station
Sarasota, FL 34239

LIBRARY OF CONGRESS CATALOGING-IN-PUBLICATION DATA

Mink, Charles, 1951-
    Princess of the Everglades / Charles Mink. — 1st ed.
    p.   cm.
    ISBN 0-910923-98-1 (hardcover) : $16.95
    I. Title.
PS3563.I467P75   1991   90-24998
813'.54—dc20   CIP

First edition
10 9 8 7 6 5 4 3 2 1

Composition by Sherri Hill

For Elizabeth Arthur

Childhood shows the man
as morning shows the day.

— John Milton

1

Two days before the hurricane, in September of 1926, Kirk Quintaines's Progressive Mandolin Orchestra played at the home of Thomas Edison in Fort Myers, Florida. The orchestra played outside on the verandah while the guests danced and slapped mosquitoes. Mr. Edison himself sat on the railing around the verandah and watched the orchestra. He wore a white linen suit. His blue-veined hands rested at the top of his walking cane. Over his shoulder, silver moonlight bathed the crowns of the royal palm trees on MacGregor Boulevard.

Mr. Edison watched two little girls in the second mandolin section. They sat at their chairs and played their mandolins among stern, bearded men in tuxedos and solemn women wearing bustles and bifocals. The girls' feet barely touched the floor.

The great inventor rose and walked closer to the orchestra. With growing enchantment, he watched the two children. Their small, sturdy fingers traveled up and down the fretboards of their instruments like synchronized spiders. Their jaws were clenched in determination. Their eyes moved between the music on their stands and the conductor's baton at the podium.

When the orchestra's first set came to a close, Mr. Edison

approached the podium.

"How old did you say your daughters are, Mr Quintaine?"

"Ten."

"Ten years old," he repeated. "I'd like to shake their hands."

"Sheila, Skeezix. Come meet Mr. Edison."

The next morning found the orchestra on an old bus en route to their next engagement in Moore Haven, Florida. The bus was taking them as far as LaBelle. At LaBelle, they would meet a boat which would take them up the Caloosahatchee River to Moore Haven on the southwest bank of Lake Okeechobee. Mr.Edison had sent the entourage off with a breakfast of thick bacon slices and turtle eggs. The turtle eggs were cooked sunny-side up. They were saltier than chicken eggs and the girls refused to eat them. Mr. Edison also donated a half barrel of ice which was put in the back of the bus for the bottles of Coca-Cola.

Skeezix wandered up and down the aisle of the bus with pencil and paper. She was making a list of things people didn't want to know about. So far this was her list:

1. What is in your large intestine
2. How elephants reproduce
3. What caviar tastes like
4. What people look like after a year in their coffins

At the front of the bus, her sister Sheila sat with her mandolin case at her feet, staring out the window. She might make a list of things people didn't want to know about but she wouldn't go up and down the bus soliciting contributions as Skeezix did.

The musicians had begun to practice. Mandolin melodies darted in and out of the open bus windows on the wings of dragonflies. Mandolin, mandola, and mandocello cases lay littered about the interior of the bus like fallen soldiers.

The bus came to a sudden and abrupt halt. The tires

moaned and buried themselves into the marl road. A mandolin string popped. The barrel of melting ice and Coca-Cola slid forward. Winthrop Ethridge DuQuesne clutched his Gibson Style U harp guitar to his chest. The instrument had cost him $450 in 1923. Skeezix tumbled to the front of the bus, holding her pencil and list. Suddenly, the air was absolutely still. The slight circulation created by the forward momentum of the bus ceased.

Sheila leaned her head out the window. There were five alligators stopped in the middle of the road. Their spiked hides were as black as coal against the white marl of the road. One of the alligators had its jaws apart and was hissing at the bus. Sheila saw hundreds of crooked teeth in its mouth. The teeth gleamed in the sunlight. She saw the color of its throat. Pinkish-white. She saw the alligator's sides expand and contract in respiration.

The bus driver jabbed at the horn, cursing under his breath. His name was Theddo and he was a Negro. His black face glittered with perspiration.

Skeezix followed her father out the door of the bus, keeping a safe distance behind. She watched her father pick up a chunk of limestone and hurl it at the hissing alligator. He missed it. A blood vessel thumped against the starched collar of her father's shirt. The aura of heat from the bus engine was suffocating and she stepped away.

Theddo and some male orchestra members jumped out of the bus and joined her father. Soon the grinning lizards retreated under a barrage of projectiles, loudly slithering into the underbrush. A kingfisher sat in the top of a cabbage palm, watching them. His pompadour waved under the darkening sky.

"Skeezix," her father said. "Would you like for us to wait while you tie your shoe?"

The girls accepted the tacit commandment that twins shall dress alike and today was no different. They had on the white cotton dresses their mother had ordered them from the Sears catalogue, red satin sashes, silver charm bracelets on the left

11

wrists, and ivory hairpins. Their mother had taken the dresses out of the trunk this morning, washed them, and hung them out to dry from a mahogany tree in Mr. Edison's back yard. Pummeled by the Gulf breezes, the dresses had smelled fresh and of lye soap when they put them on. But now, after an hour in the bus to LaBelle, the dresses were glued to the girls' backs with perspiration and the pristine whiteness was blemished all about with specks of blood from where they had squashed mosquitoes.

Sheila's sartorial air had always been more correct than Skeezix's. Sheila's outfits always looked clean, neat, and geometric. On Skeezix, clothes never looked right. They looked limp and awkward. The girls' bone structures were nearly identical so that was not the cause. The cause was Skeezix's attitude about clothes. She regarded them as a necessary evil, a tolerated encumbrance. Skeezix was caught sitting in an unladylike fashion much more often than Sheila.

Three miles down the road, the bus came to another grinding halt.

"Surely they're not *hostile* Indians," remarked F. W. Clancy.

F. W. Clancy was one of two mandobassists in the orchestra. His large instrument was in a wooden crate wrapped in canvas in a special storage compartment underneath the bus; thus he was unable to practice en route. F. W. lived two blocks away from the Quintaines in Bismarck, North Dakota, and had written the definitive instructional manual for the lowest member of the mandolin family.

The Seminoles lined the road in front of the bus. There were no visible guns, knives, arrows, or tomahawks. The leader was holding up a huge snapping turtle with one hand and waving with the other. He had a big grin on his cider-colored face, exposing the disintegrated fragments of his teeth. Skeezix thought he looked like an Eskimo she had seen in a story book. She wasn't afraid of the Indians as long as her father was here.

12

"Do you know how to speak their language?" her father asked the bus driver.

"I don't speak no Injun!" Theddo snapped in contempt. It was clear to both of the twins that Theddo had had his fill of their father's mandolin orchestra and this trek to LaBelle.

Half of the orchestra filed out of the bus to see the Indians. Skeezix and Sheila were the seventh and eighth in line. Their father brought his mandolin to scare the Seminoles with his playing.

The Indians, men, women, and children, wore garments that had many bright cloth strips sewn onto them, in colors of every hue. The strips of cloth were highlighted here and there with rickrack trim. The Seminoles were a riot of color. Sheila thought they had the most beautiful clothing she had ever seen on Indians until she got close enough to smell them.

"I don't think they bathe," she confided in a whisper to Skeezix.

"Or brush their teeth either," Skeezix said.

Several children of their age or younger were running about, kicking up sand and giggling. Sheila noted that even the youngest of the girls wore the long strip skirt. The hems were soggy and muddy. The Indian children ran barefooted. The bottoms of their feet were a different color from the rest of their skin. They were yellowish-white with deep, chiseled lines in them, like the tributaries of rivers.

"If one of them touches me, I'm whackin' 'em," said Skeezix.

"And Mr. Edison thought *we* should be in school," said Sheila.

Overhead, the sky rumbled. The Indians did not look up. Only the white people looked up. In the east, a gang of vultures floated like swirling ash. The vultures did not flap their wings. A tiny rivulet of perspiration raced down Sheila's side from under her arm. She slapped it, fearing it was a bug.

The Indians wanted to hear the mandolin so their father took out his instrument and played "Nola" by Felix Arndt for them. The Indians had no reaction whatsoever to the melody

13

and, to heap further insult, failed to applaud at the end.

The girls then watched in amazement as their father handed his mandolin to the Indian.

"He's not going to let him *try* it," Sheila said in horror.

"That's his new Gibson F-4 Artist's Model," Skeezix said.

The Indian set his turtle down and accepted the instrument with great respect. He seemed, however, more fascinated with the mandolin pick than the mandolin. He put it in his mouth and tasted it. The Indian seemed to know that the pick was made from tortoise shell. Sheila and Skeezix watched him bite on the mandolin pick with his soft, leathery teeth.

"We have Indians where we come from," Eugene Gaylord Smith said helpfully. Eugene, at twenty-eight years of age, was first mandocellist with the orchestra. He had thin, delicate fingers that raced across the copper frets of his instrument, winning the admiration of audiences throughout the land. Eugene was a pale man with dark, penetrating eyes, a sparse moustache, an omnipresent satin-backed vest, and a disinterest in the female gender that even the twins knew about. The turtle eggs at Edison's house had given him a case of dyspepsia and he had gulped down an entire bottle of stomach bitters since breakfast. He said to the Indians, "Perhaps you've heard of the Mandans. Or Sioux."

A little Indian girl walked up to their father and tugged at his pant leg. She stood very close to him and looked up at his face. She was younger than the twins and her ebony hair was clotted and discolored with sand and dirt. She had the foot disease.

"What is it, little girl?" Kirk Quintaine asked.

"Coca-Cola?"

Sheila and Skeezix looked at each other. It was the first English words they had heard spoken by an Indian.

"Coca-Cola?" the Indian girl repeated.

"You want Coca-Cola?" their father asked.

For the next quarter of an hour, the girls helped pass out Coca-Colas to the Indians. The men in the orchestra pried the caps off with bottle openers and the twins passed them out. Sometimes the Indians grabbed the Coca-Colas before the caps were even off. Then they broke the necks of the bottles on a rock or a stump and poured the foaming brown liquid down their throats from the jagged opening in the bottle. The Indians guzzled their Coca-Colas. They often drank a half or even a whole bottle in one big swallow.

Then they belched. It was *belching*, not burping. The twins thought they belched in the most heathen manner. They never said "Excuse me" or tried to squelch it. They belched openly and with great joy. In fact, they tried to outdo each other. All the Indians participated in the belching activities, from the children right up through the elders.

Skeezix watched an ancient squaw place her ear to the mouth of a Coca-Cola bottle. The squaw listened intently to the fizzle of the carbonated water. Skeezix estimated the old woman had twenty pounds of necklaces on. They were heaped in piles from her collar bone to her chin. The old woman picked up the bottle and tipped it to her wrinkled lips. In a moment, she let forth with a prolonged belch that resonated her body cavity like a drum. During the atrocity, she looked directly at Skeezix. There was an impish look in her wasting, Indian eyes.

"Makes you never want to drink a Coca-Cola again," Skeezix said.

"I know," Sheila said.

The twins watched a boy shake a bottle of Coca-Cola with his thumb plugging the top. Next he shocked them by jamming the glass base of the bottle against his privates. When he let his thumb off the bottle, the brown foam spewed into the air like Old Faithful. The boy had the foot disease like the other children and his ebony hair looked as though it had been hacked off with a machete.

The Coca-Cola flying into the air got the biggest laugh of the morning, not only from the boys and girls but from the adults as well. Skeezix thought the Indians' behavior was shameful. The hardest part was accepting the fact that these

15

savages with their gruesome manners and grimy fingernails were God's children too and were assured a place in His kingdom. Sheila did not think about the Indians as God's children. She thought: If they think they're getting their filthy fingers on my mandolin, they've got another thing coming.

The barrel of ice had been reduced to water by the heat. Only a few Coca-Colas were left.

"I'd like to spring a gin rickey on one of them," Valentine T. Peck said.

Valentine T. Peck was concertmaster. He was a clean-shaven, handsome man with a penchant for gin. He liked Florida better than North Dakota because it was easier to get booze. Valentine was sweet as sugar to the twins but he had a mean streak in him. He had been dethroned from the Boy Scouts for whacking a tenderfoot with a board. He was a ladies' man and had been married so many times even his best friends stopped coming to the weddings. Last night he had created a minor scandal by making an advance on Mrs. Edison.

"We're not giving gin to the Indians," their father warned Valentine T. Peck. "We leave that stuff on the bus. Do you understand me, Peck?"

"Sure, boss," Valentine T. Peck said. "Did you see the sky? I don't like the looks of it."

The Indians wanted to pay them back for the Coca-Colas with livestock. They offered the orchestra their turtle, some curlews, and a bag of fresh alligator meat. The orchestra opted for trinkets instead, little souvenirs they felt would not give them diseases. By the time everyone had decided what trinket they wanted, Theddo was jamming the horn of the bus in despair. Sheila and Skeezix each got a palmetto fiber doll. The doll was a foot high with layers of tiny bead necklaces and two stitches of crimson thread for its mouth.

The twins' mother was finally forced out of the bus when the cry went up for a group photograph with the Indians. The orchestra needed the banner out of the trunk. The banner was made of gold satin with navy blue lettering, professionally done in Chicago. It was hung from the back of the piano if there was a piano where they played; otherwise it was hung from the xylophone. The twins knew their mother was not pleased to have to get it out. Her anger, however, paled in comparison to Theddo's, who was no longer keeping his mouth in check even in front of them.

"I ain't gonna be in no goddam picture with no goddam swamp dwellers!" he cried.

They posed in front of the long side of the bus, facing north. They had to keep squeezing together to all fit in the picture. It was all the girls could do to keep from pinching their nostrils. The smell was overpowering.

Some of the orchestra members let the Indians hold their mandolins. The Indians held them out proudly, squeezing their necks as if the little musical instruments might get away. The ones that didn't have mandolins held out their Coca-Cola bottles. The turtle took advantage of its captor's inattention and scrambled to the sawgrass alongside the road. It made a sustained scraping noise on the marl bed beneath its carapace.

"Sheila, Skeezix," called the photographer. "Hold the banner up higher. We can't see it."

The twins looked at each other and sighed. They obeyed.

KIRK QUINTAINE'S
PROGRESSIVE
MANDOLIN ORCHESTRA

The rain began in huge splats that made marks the size of saucers on their clothes.

2

Kirk Quintaine was born in 1884, during the last era of the American Indian. He was six when Sitting Bull was shot to death at Wounded Knee. He was a teenager when Geronimo appeared in sartorial mockery at Teddy Roosevelt's inauguration. His wife's grandfather had fallen with Custer at Little Big Horn. Kirk could remember family picnics west of town where they would have to clear away bleached rib bones from the Great Northern Buffalo Herd before dining.

His father was a grain dealer who had a government contract with the Sioux and Mandan reservations. As a boy, Kirk would accompany him and help him unload dusty bags of chicken feed from a horse-drawn cart. He remembered the old squaws with their weather-beaten faces staring at him from outside the tepees. Some of them were murderers, his father said. Later, long after the chicken feed had been washed from his hands, he would hear their drums, the tribal melodies, the impassioned chants. The music would often visit him at night alone in his room and he would think of old people who had died.

Kirk's mother called the Indian music "noise." She was a fanatical devotee of the new Missouri ragtime music and bought every new piano roll that came on the market. In 1902, they traveled to Sedalia and heard Scott Joplin premiere a new composition at the Maple Leaf Club. The great Negro musician nodded off while playing his new composition, creating a pianistic cacophony that dumbfounded the patrons. The *St. Louis Globe-Democrat* later wrote, " ' The Entertainer' is a jingling work of a very original character, embracing various strains of a retentive character which set the foot in spontaneous action and leave an indelible imprint on the tympanum." On the train trip back to North Dakota, Kirk's mother talked about Scott Joplin falling asleep at the piano. She ordered the sheet music of the new piece from John Stark and Son of St. Louis. The inscription above the title read: "Dedicated to James Brown and His Mandolin Club."

Kirk's first mandolin was a $2.50 special from the Sears catalogue, the "Illinois" model. It had nine ribs in the bowl-shaped back, alternately maple and mahogany wood, and an inlaid tortoise shell pickguard. He learned to play the music of Mozart, Haydn, Beethoven, Schumann, and Tchaikovsky as all good little boys did. He also learned the new music of Richard Wagner from Germany. He played for every great aunt and uncle who came to the Quintaine house and was first chair in the Bismarck Mandolin Club.

The turning point in his musical career came when an eccentric furniture maker in Kalamazoo reinvented the mandolin, using violin construction principles, and a famous Bohemian composer moved to New York.

The unlikely combination of two men's lives, Orville Gibson's and Antonin Dvorak's, had a powerful impact on young Kirk Quintaine. He was captivated by Mr. Dvorak's views on American music. Kirk adopted his views and went around town quoting Mr. Dvorak as if he had invented the words himself. "American composers should draw on their own folk music to create an indigenous, serious art form, not perpetuate derivative and watered-down European models." Kirk had never considered himself a composer, but now, inspired by Dvorak's message, he became one.

At the same time, he was mesmerized by Gibson's new mandolin. It had a flat back, a carved top, f-holes, a high bridge with a staggered saddle, and a metal tailpiece to secure the instrument's strings. The mandolin looked different, it played different, it sounded different. It was loud. But most of all, it was an American instrument, not an imitation of a European model.

Suddenly, Kirk had a purpose in his music. He had a musical statement to make, a statement that no one had made before. He made the discovery that within him he had the tools to make the serious American music that Dvorak had spoken of so eloquently, the music that was the real voice of America. It was the music of his childhood. By combining the melodies of the Plains Indians with the structure and the syncopations of ragtime—played by an orchestra of American mandolins—he would create a music that had never been created before, a serious music that only Americans could produce. By age twenty-five, Kirk was a fanatic about a music he labeled "Indian jazz."

The townspeople of Bismarck conjectured endlessly about Kirk's transformation from dutiful mandolin soloist to grandiose artiste. The consensus was that Kirk's mother and father were to blame. They allowed him to run his extravagant course unchecked.

Now the rain was a vertical river between heaven and earth. Kirk had the feeling that if the boat had a special gear they could take it straight up to the sky!

They were on the Caloosahatchee River, a few hours from Moore Haven. The orchestra was trying to keep dry by huddling together in several small groups away from the leaking spots in the roof of the boat. Many of them had their Seminole trinkets out and were busily gazing at them or feeling them or exchanging them.

Kirk looked out at the Everglades on either side of the river.

He didn't see it. He saw a single vibrating sheet of water between the boat's roof and railing, completely obstructing any view.

Skeezix was walking between the groups of musicians, trying to finish her list of things people didn't want to know about:

5. What lives under rocks
6. The Russo-Japanese War
7. The bacteria in saliva

Sheila was at the lavatory facilities beneath the deck, standing guard for Violet May Cooper, mandolist. The lavatory facilities consisted of a red bucket in a dark, airless room.

Skeezix walked up to her father and said, "How does he know where he's going, Daddy? You can't see anything."

"WHAT, HONEY?"

Kirk couldn't hear her over the pounding of the rain.

"I SAID, 'HOW DOES HE KNOW WHERE HE'S GOING?' "

"HE SAYS HE KNOWS."

The captain was a superannuated Huck Finn, complete with pipe and straw hat. His ninety-year-old bones were endowed with a simulacrum of boylike musculature. His skin hung off him in tawny, parched folds—the mark of a Florida Cracker. He spoke knowledgeably on the *Titanic* and *Lusitania* as if being the pilot of this floating junkyard made him an authority on all boats. His teeth were brown fragments, he claimed to know Edison personally, and he attributed his cheery personality to the resurrected Christ. He also claimed to play the mandolin.

"It ain't no lie," hooted the captain. "I used to play up a storm on that thing. Read them damn notes off the page like they was goin' outta style."

What I need right now, Kirk thought, is an ignorant yokel trying to impress me. He glanced at his wristwatch. It was a 21-jewel Elgin he had paid $37.60 for in February. It was a quarter to two. Where were they?

The orchestra had an appointment tonight with a Mr. Broadus Gantt in front of the Riverside Lodge at six P.M. At that time they would be informed of the particulars of tonight's engagement. As he understood it, it was a reception for the Moore Haven public school faculty. Mr. Gantt was responsible for paying the orchestra upon the completion of four hours of satisfactory dance music. The fee was $150, six dollars per musician. H. Russell Truitt, first chair second mandolinist who doubled as stage manager, received eight dollars. Sheila and Skeezix's money went into a trust fund for their college education at Northwestern University in Evanston, Illinois.

Kirk viewed tonight's engagement as a vital one. It would serve as a dress rehearsal for tomorrow: Saturday night's extravaganza at the Breakers Hotel of Palm Beach. The Breakers was having a grand reopening after the fire that had destroyed it, and Kirk Quintaine's Progressive Mandolin Orchestra had been invited to perform. The list of luminaries rumored to attend the event was enough to turn his hands to ice. Henry Ford, Frank Lloyd Wright, Rudolph Valentino, Robert Frost, Maurice Ravel, and even Herbert Hoover were scheduled to attend. Edison had been invited, of course, but had a prior commitment. Kirk had Edison's formally written letter of regret in his mandolin case.

They would share the stage with the finest musical organizations in the country, including Paul Whiteman's orchestra, Duke Ellington and the Washingtonians, Moten's Blue Devils, and the New Orleans Rhythm Kings. That a mandolin orchestra had been invited to the gala event in Palm Beach was a miracle, let alone *his* mandolin orchestra. Kirk was the first to admit that his selection was due in part to his musical twins, and he was grateful for them. Still, it was an honor and his first chance for national recognition. He had the firm conviction that when people heard Indian jazz on the mandolins they would know instantly that this was the real voice of America.

However, along with the glittering banners of hope came a ghastly parade of problems. Keeping seventeen double-stringed instruments in tune was a major undertaking in itself, especially in the Florida heat. The harp guitar alone had sixteen strings, six standard and ten sub-bass, and each one had a malicious inclination to go flat. The mandobasses required constant adjustments in their giant bridges with the slightest error in placement creating inaccuracies in pitch somewhere in the fretted scale. The mandocello's A string often slipped from the notch in the saddle and moved too close to its unison partner for free vibration. Then, if he filed the saddle notch too deep the string would come down too close to the fretboard and touch the high frets. What a fine line he walked with those mandocellos! With the mandolins, their E strings were often strung so tight that a quarter tone sharp in tuning would break the string. Then there was *that* money down the drain.

Perhaps the most difficult task for him as leader, though, was maintaining the morale of the musicians. The majority of them were not convinced of the profundity of Indian jazz and preferred to play two-steps, fandangos, and Charlestons. And most of them were homesick for the northern plains. They hated Florida, with its bugs and heavy air.

Another problem was keeping the uniforms clean. And keeping the music organized in everyone's folder. And repairing the music stands. And keeping track of the outdoor clips for the music stands. And replacing worn-down and cracked plectrums. Every potential glitch had the certain ability to destroy a performance if not thoroughly checked and rechecked in advance.

The boat edged up the Caloosahatchee River to Moore Haven. Sheila returned from beneath the deck where she had been standing guard at the toilet facilities for Violet May Cooper.

"Did she go number one or number two?" Skeezix asked.

"Number two," Sheila answered. She pinched her nostrils with her thumb and forefinger.

Violet May Cooper walked to a corner of the boat where she

joined Adeline DeVekey and Beatrice Templeton, the remainder of the mandola section. The twins watched her walk and glanced at each other.

Sheila said, "There's something else down there."

"What?"

"I don't know. I heard little feet."

"Rats!"

The twins went below deck, listening for rats. Skeezix decided she needed to use the toilet so she sat down on the bucket in the dark room. Sheila fanned Skeezix's face with a music folder. The bangs of hair on Skeezix's forehead rose and fell on the rhythmic puffs of air. The rain wasn't so loud down here.

"Do you think we're going to drown?" Sheila asked.

"No one seems too worried about it."

"I know, but there's just so much water!"

"Drowning is a good death," Skeezix said. "You go under water. You take a big breath. And it's over. No pain."

"How do you know that?"

"Daddy said."

"Do you float or sink?"

"Sink."

"Thank you, Miss Walking Encyclopedia."

"You're welcome, Sheila."

"Listen. Do you hear it?"

"Yes, I do."

"Here comes Mother."

"Hello, Mother. I'm almost done. Tell Daddy there's rats on this boat."

The rats were the least of Kirk Quintaine's problems.

He was short. He was short and he had an abnormally large head. His hats had to be custom-made. The latest haberdasher wound a measuring tape twenty-five and a half inches around his skull and meekly indicated that perhaps a medical problem was at the source of the anomaly. Kirk also had a voice that was irritating to many people. It was high-pitched and whiny. He rarely made announcements on the bandstand. He couldn't sing either.

Where most people would size up a stranger by their clothes, the shape of their body, their hairstyle, or their eyes, Kirk would immediately focus on their hands, inspecting the fingers, palms, and wrists for adequacy in mandolin performance. The children would often find him lost in thought, sitting on a favorite rocker under a paddle fan. When they spoke to him, his response was mixed up with little bearing on reality. "Go to the mother with your Piggly-Wiggly," he might say. When he slept he slept on his back with his hands across his chest, fingers intertwined. The girls could almost see the notes flying by beneath his eyelids. The notes were black and wiggly, like worms.

"I saw Lloyd Loar in Havana," the captain was saying. "Now there's a good mandolin player."

"Uh-huh."

"Plays a good saw, too."

"Could you estimate at all," Kirk asked, "what time we might be in Moore Haven?"

"Moore Haven? Five o'clock. No later than six."

"I don't know how you can possibly see where you're going," Kirk said. "Anybody know where Sheila and Skeezix are?"

He had a feeling about his children sometimes. He thought they were the inevitable consequence of married life, a consequence that did not entirely meet with his approval.

They were born on February 26, 1916. He was there for the birth. He felt in his heart that it was something never meant to be witnessed by the male of the species. The violence and bloodshed could only be compared to war. Kirk stood trembling

25

at the operating table, coming to grips with his culprit status in regards to this horror and learning that there were grave consequences for all things done and not done in this life. He was 32. Mrs. Quintaine was in a chloroform daze for nearly a week afterwards. Sheila, emerging three minutes after Skeezix, had nearly kicked out her mother's bladder.

Their infancy left him in a perpetual state of exhaustion. Worse yet was the mindlessness of the maintenance chores. A baboon could easily be taught to do them: Stick a bottle in a mouth, rinse a diaper, restrain flailing little arms and legs, flush out urine-soaked scalps. He hated every last little detail and, all the while, his manuscript paper lay on his desk, devoid of the little black lines and dots that were his work.

Then came the jabber: a rude assault on language and decency. And the dining room table with its extended radius of flung oatmeal and applesauce. Kirk could recall the look of biblical agony on Skeezix's face when she got soap in her eyes. He could recall Sheila waking after a deep slumber, darting her eyes around the room in confusion, lost in reality.

He was indifferent to their fantasy world. He would often carry their dolls by their feet, their heads bouncing against his knee as if they were turnips. He told them there was no such thing as Santa Claus when Skeezix still believed, assuming they already knew. He once bought them a kaleidoscope before they had the coordination to close off one eye.

His daughters grew to become members of the human race, due to or despite their parent's efforts, he wasn't sure which one. If there was one memory most vivid from this period of their emergence, it was their grand entrance amid the sunflowers in their front yard on Sunday morning before church, absolute pictures of health and excessively careful tailoring, leaving in their wake, hidden safely behind the doors of the white house on Main Street, a heap of wet towels, clotted hairbrushes, and half-empty cereal bowls.

It was from the beginning, however, that their personalities began to diverge. From infancy, Sheila was more distant. Her attention was more easily diverted. She was less concerned who cared for her. Her crying was more ferocious and demanding, less pitiable, so that when she started up in the hellishness of three A.M., Mrs. Quintaine and he, in defiance, were slower to get up and appease her. It was true that she would laugh heartily when tickled or thrown up over the shoulder, but it was a strangely empty joy. Rare was that instant when she would share the joy with warmth and affection. At lullaby time, she simply didn't melt on him the way Skeezix did.

Then there was the matter of her physical appearance. Her facial features were more severe; she had a pointier nose. She had more body hair. She had unattractively short and muscular forearms. How could he help not favoring Skeezix?

One of the great mysteries of his life was that Sheila turned out the superior musician. They were both given equal training and encouragement, yet, from week one, Sheila could play circles around Skeezix. Sheila also kept exemplary care of her instrument, a Lyon and Healy Style B mandolin from Chicago. She polished it often and without being told and kept her case free of foreign material. Kirk would open up her case to the odor of furniture polish and moth crystals. With Skeezix's, the smell was of sweaty palms and Crackerjack.

The rain continued in uninterrupted sheets. Kirk was talking to the captain. "I still don't see how you can tell where you're going."

"Come again, sonny?"

"I said, 'HOW DO YOU KNOW WHERE YOU'RE GOING?'"

"Shoot, mister," the captain said, "I know this river like the back o' my hand."

It was then, with a horrible groan, the boat slid into the west bank of the Caloosahatchee, sending alligators and wood storks racing away in a panic. Emily Jackson, a weary North Dakota musician with underarm stains she no longer cared to hide, slid across the deck on her mandobass case, bowling over everything in her path. Three or four healthy rats scrambled up the steps, the first ones to bale out. Beneath the deck, Sheila shrieked and Skeezix tipped over on the makeshift toilet. The contents spilled out to foul the floor.

"We're shipwrecked!" Skeezix said with delight.

3

In 1910, Kirk bought a Gibson F-3 mandolin with the money set aside for Lily's wedding ring. Lily had sighed. It was the first of many times she would yield romance to art.

Born Elizabeth Howser in 1890, she was the fifth of a North Dakota wheat farmer's five daughters. Because of her grandfather's gruesome end at the hands of the Oglala, tales of Sioux savagery were a part of the house, imbedded in the woodwork like termites. To this day, the very sight of an Indian would start her heart pounding in terror. It happened again when they encountered the harmless Seminoles on the way to LaBelle.

Lily was the prettiest of the five daughters, with luxurious chestnut hair and gentle eyes. She started piano lessons at age six with the preacher's wife, who discovered that Lily's real talent was a sweet and pure singing voice. In the parlor room, Lily would sing "Thou Art Mine All" for deaf old buffalo hunters who didn't know when to applaud.

She met Kirk in the church choir where he sang tenor and was already establishing a reputation as a budding mandolin virtuoso. They fell in love and got married. The YMCA Mandolin Club performed "Ballabile Cappriccioso" by M.A. Bickford at their wedding and many of those in attendance were parents

29

of the young musicians. Her father smiled witlessly throughout the ceremony, his beet-red head erupting from out of a new blue suit from the Sears catalogue. He liked Kirk because he got one of his daughters out of the house.

Kirk and Lily exited the church doors onto a meadow of sunflowers that bobbed cheerily under a Dakota sky. They took the Model T to Minneapolis for their honeymoon, sitting absurdly close in their rice-sprinkled formal wear. When they got to town they checked into their hotel, had supper, and then went to hear a mandolin orchestra. Afterwards, Lily sat in her hotel room gazing out the window. They were on the ninth floor and it was hot, ninety degrees. She stroked the air about her face with a five-cent Japanese folding fan. She had never been so nervous.

The consummation of their marriage was a disaster. It was so poorly done that they didn't try again for two weeks. He wanted the bathroom light on so he could see what he was supposed to do. She would have no part of that perversion!

Five years later, they were still uncomfortable but the twins were conceived nonetheless. The births were wretched but Lily expected it to be wretched since age nine when she had found out her sex was responsible. Infant care was not as bad as Kirk proclaimed, especially in light of her unmarried sisters on the homestead threshing wheat and slopping hogs.

Lily was not as surprised as Kirk about the divergence of the twins' personalities, and she was quicker to accept it. What her husband perceived as their merits and faults, she perceived as their differences. She loved her twins equally. The most bothersome difference was Sheila's singing voice. It was harsh and raucous and continually fed the gossip mill at the Grace Methodist Church. When Lily was out of earshot, the old women would murmur. How could a canary produce such a crow? By contrast, Skeezix had a wonderful voice, much like her mother's. The women in their choir robes clutching their music folders and smelling like roses on Sunday morning favored Skeezix though they tried not to let on.

When the twins were two, the Quintaine family made a

pilgrimage to the Wall Theater in Fremont, Nebraska, to hear George Hamilton Green, the xylophone virtuoso. Lily sat in the darkened vaudeville hall, her pretty face blanched by the stage lights, arms twisted towards the baby carriage in the aisle, hands clenching two glass milk bottles. The xylophonist's technique was dazzling, but Kirk did not like the sound of the instrument. He felt, however, it was time to put his personal feelings aside and to expand his market in recognizing the enormous popularity of the xylophone. A progressive mandolin orchestra ought not be without one. Naturally, *she* would play it since she had the most keyboard training. Kirk decided to bestow another title upon her in the orchestra, along with that of vocalist, pianist, and librarian. She would be Lily Quintaine, xylophonist-in-residence. Kirk ordered a "Drummer's Special" from J. C. Deagan in Chicago. Its portability was the key factor in the purchase. The xylophone had a full three chromatic octave range, a triple-plated metal resonator for each bar, and a hand-carrying case with steel-reinforced corners. The cost was $75. Lily heaved the case up onto the dock at Moore Haven, thinking how that money might have been spent on a new screen door, a vacation in Canada, or an occasional Porterhouse steak.

"We're here."
Kirk went up to the captain.
"You know what gets my goat?"
"What is that, Mr. Quintaine?"
"It's Crackers like you who pretend you know everything. We're lucky we made it here alive."
"Come along, Kirk," Lily said. "Nobody could see in that downpour. He did the best he could."
"Look at that, Lily. He still won't admit he didn't know where he was."
"Sir, you oughta take some geniality lessons from a person of Lloyd Loar's stature," the captain said. "Big Head."

"Excuse me? Did you say something to me?"

"I didn't say anything."

"You didn't say anything to me?"

"No, I didn't say anything."

She was tugging at his arm now.

"He called me a 'Big Head,' honey. Did you hear that?"

"All right. Calm down."

"If we get an idiot like this to Palm Beach tomorrow," Kirk fumed, "I'll guide the God-forsaken boat myself!"

It had stopped raining but the streets of Moore Haven were flooded so that it resembled Venice, Italy. The orchestra was escorted to the Riverside Lodge in several small fishing boats. The mandobass cases had a boat all to themselves. On the way, Skeezix counted the colors of the rainbow on her fingers.

"There's seven," she announced.

"But look over there," Sheila said.

In the distance, towards the Atlantic Ocean, the sky was as black as the night. It slowly approached across the green glades.

In their boats, they passed trees and electric poles with posters advertising tonight's performance.

ANNOUNCING
CONCERT AND DANCE!
WITH
KIRK QUINTAINE'S PROGRESSIVE MANDOLIN ORCHESTRA
FEATURING LILY QUINTAINE ON VOCALS
AND XYLOPHONE
AND THOSE "AMAZING MANDOLIN TWINS"
DON'T MISS IT!
THIS IS ONE OF THE FINEST ORCHESTRAS IN THE LAND!
WHEN? FRIDAY NIGHT, THE 17TH OF SEPT. 8:30 P. M.
ADMISSION: 25¢ FOR TOWNSPEOPLE, 50¢ FOR
NEGROES, $1.00 FOR INDIANS
SPONSORED BY THE WOMEN'S SOCIETY OF
MOORE HAVEN

Sheila and Skeezix peered at the photographs of themselves on the posters. The water in the street was up past the wheel hubs of the Model T's stranded alongside the store fronts.

"Sheila?"

"What?"

"It's fading."

"What is?"

"The rainbow."

Their performance was postponed until 9:30 so the orchestra could have supper. They had catfish and mangos. Skeezix made an announcement every time she came across a bone in the fish.

"Another bone," she said.

When Sheila found a bone, she said nothing. She quietly withdrew the translucent fiber from her mouth and deposited it on the rim of her plate with her finger.

They both thought the mangos tasted like peaches with something wrong with them. The mangos were cut up into squares in a bowl with a giant serving spoon. The orchestra was seated at one long table in the hotel's dining room. At dessert time, Kirk rose with a pad of scribbled notes for the nightly inspirational message.

He was a zealot, and only Lily knew how difficult it was living with one. Last night, he argued with Thomas Edison. Fortunately, at age 79, the great inventor was too deaf to actively spar with Kirk. Still, she could tell he was annoyed that the fine mandolin music, for which he had paid them well, was tainted by Kirk's portentous sermon on American music.

"This man," she said later, "this man has three hundred and fifty patents in the field of electricity alone! He is *this far* from a Congressional Medal of Honor."

"So?"

"So how can you compare Orville Gibson's flat-backed mandolin and Lloyd Loar's mando-viola with Edison's inventions?"

"America needs a cultural identity more than some incandescent lamp."

"Oh my God! Am I really hearing what you just said?"

"What?"

"I want to tell you something, Kirk. If it wasn't for Sheila and Skeezix, our orchestra would be on Thomas Edison's black list. Does that matter to you?"

Lily had come to the conclusion that her husband was an excellent musician with delusions of grandeur. This was to take away nothing from his accomplishments: Their orchestra probably was the finest in the land—how else could she explain the invitation to Palm Beach?—and this was due, for the most part, to Kirk's iron will and hard work. Still, she thought his Dvorak obsession and his magisterial stance as the discoverer of the real American music was misguided and a little silly.

The worst part was the costumes. In their performances she became "Red Wing," "Blue Beads," "Minehaha," "Shanewis," "Iola," and any other Indian maiden from their repertoire. Every night, she painted her face with brown dye. She put on the buckskin dress, the knee-high moccasins, the war bonnet. She strapped on the rubber tomahawk and sang preposterous lyrics about noble savages, the same kind of noble savages who had outraged her grandfather's lifeless form at Little Big Horn. Last night at Edison's, it must have been a hundred and fifty degrees under that buckskin! As usual, Kirk called far too many Indian jazz numbers, to the predictable chagrin of their audience. When the whole thing was over, Lily, desperately overheated, jumped into Edison's swimming pool, nearly naked. Her makeup floated off in tiny waxy beads.

Lily, however, was not as tolerant of Kirk's excesses when it came to the children. She took a firm stand when he bullied Sheila and Skeezix. In Bismarck, practice hour was every night between 7:30 and 8:30. Friends were sent home, the radio was turned off, and the toys were put away. One winter night, Lily stood in the cellar practicing her xylophone under a single, dangling incandescent lamp. Her hands, still hot from the dish water, clutched the bamboo handles of her mallets. Her apron quivered with the vibrations from the xylophone's wooden bars. From the dark corners of the ceiling, daddy longleg spiders peered out from their cottony webs. Screaming from upstairs gradually infiltrated and destroyed her arpeggios. Lily dropped her mallets and bounded up the steps. Skeezix had put some jacks in her mandolin case which had made several nicks and gouges on the back of her Lyon and Healy Style B. Lily stood at the bedroom door, panting, gazing wide-eyed at the petrified faces of her daughters as Kirk howled.

"My God, Kirk!" she wailed. "They're only children!"

It was the most defiant her voice had ever become.

Lily had a secret from Kirk. She didn't like the mandolin. She didn't like the xylophone either, but she especially didn't like the mandolin. She preferred a French horn or a singing voice, something more mellifluous.

In the dining room of the Riverside Lodge in Moore Haven, several hunting trophies adorned the walls: a black bear, a bobcat, the yard-long skin of a rattlesnake, and the stocky black head of a wild boar with ivory tusks and ferocious, cold-blooded eyes. Lily glanced at the trophy then glanced back at her daughter. Skeezix had fallen asleep during her father's pep talk and her skull lay limp on the dining room table, clear drool oozing from her parted lips. Two Negro waitresses stole about the table, collecting silverware as silently as possible in deference to the orchestra leader. They were heavy black ladies and breathed loudly as they worked. Their maid uniforms were cuffed at the elbows and their bare forearms were covered with droplets of perspiration. A Seminole dishwasher stood at the kitchen door and surveyed the women in the orchestra. He had abundant ebony hair, unclipped yellow fingernails, and chipped teeth lined with decay. It occurred to Lily that the two racial types in the dining room were at the source of her husband's musical obsession. She wondered if this had occurred to Kirk. Most likely, he had more noble and credible exotics in mind.

"Yes F. W.?"

Kirk was taking questions from the orchestra members now.

"When is the polishing party?"

"It depends on what time we get to the Breakers tomorrow," Kirk said. "But I do plan to devote an entire hour to polishing. Our instruments have to look the sharpest they've ever looked. And I will expect the mandolinists to help with the bigger instruments when they're done with their own."

The screen door slammed. It kept slamming during their meeting. The townspeople of Moore Haven could not resist a visit to the Riverside Lodge to catch a glimpse of the highfalutin mandolin orchestra from North Dakota. Unfortunately, every time one of them opened the screen door, droves of flies entered. Finally, the manager, exasperated, locked the doors.

"A word about featherdusters," Kirk went on. "I think we all know that they're the best thing for cleaning that tricky area between the strings and the headstock without completely removing your strings . . . ."

Lily had a chunk of catfish wedged between two upper molars. She tried to dislodge it by sucking it out with her tongue. The kissing sound this made was partially obscured by the whirring of the paddle fan overhead.

"I know that not all of you *have* featherdusters, but I trust that those of you who do will be kind enough to loan yours out."

"I'll loan mine out."

"Thank you, Emily."

Emily Jackson, mandobassist, sat with her hands folded on top of the table, fingers intertwined. She had been nodding her head respectfully throughout Kirk's speech. Emily was a serious musician and only nineteen years old. She wore a countenance of solemn purpose when she played that helped achieve an artistic, collegiate legitimacy in the orchestra's performances, a quality that Kirk desperately sought. Unfortunately for the gentlemen, she was engaged. Her fiancé was

36

an undertaker in Bismarck who had fashioned a case for her instrument out of spare coffin materials. The case was either morbid or humorous depending on the temperament of the viewer. Like Kirk, Emily had an appreciation for fine wristwatches and owned a 17-jewel Ladies' Elgin with imbedded ruby chips that twinkled in the stage light as her delicate fingers traveled about the bass fretboard. Emily was a frugal woman and kept nearly every cent of the six dollars a week Kirk paid her, storing the money in a special compartment of the mandobass case.

The other young woman in the orchestra was Ella Griffith Bedard in the mandocello section. Ella was twenty-four years old and had a fondness for the latest flapper fashions. She sat in the second row behind Eugene Gaylord Smith and played her parts joylessly, holding down her oversized instrument as if it were some recalcitrant mule. Last night at Edison's house, she had a menstrual catastrophe that everyone knew about. Lily helped her wash out the dress in the morning. Now Ella leaned back in the dining room chair with mango juice on her chin, daydreaming. She was pretty and charming and, unlike Emily, enjoyed flirting with the men. Lily had to keep an eye on her with Kirk. Her husband was not the unfaithful kind, but who knew what any man would do when opportunities availed themselves?

Lily took secret pleasure in the likes of Emily Jackson and Ella Griffith Bedard, young women who would become thirty despite their unreasonable doubts they ever would. Nearly thirty-eight years old herself, Lily had come to realize she was in for a long haul. Images and places from her childhood seemed so distant and foreign as to have become the property of some strange, dead person. Their wedding portrait, fourteen years old now, was a photograph of two dopey and forgotten teenagers. Kirk and she had simply accumulated too many memories to call themselves young anymore.

Kirk sat down and drank a half glass of ice water. He then put the cold glass to his forehead and held it there. He glanced at Skeezix asleep with her head on the dining room table amid heaps of fly-covered catfish bones. A sudden thunderstroke rocked the hotel. The boar's head toppled off the wall, shattering the left tusk. F. W. Clancy stabbed himself with a toothpick. Skeezix, lost in dreams, awoke with a start. At nearly the same time, a disoriented barn owl crashed through the dining room window in a shower of glass. Sheila screamed. Lily leaped from her chair. The kitchen staff was suddenly in the dining room, flushed from their sanctuary by the commotion. They were mostly male Seminole Indians and they surveyed the upheaval with dim, uncomprehending grins.

The owl hopped silently to the southeast corner of the dining room where it turned with its tail feathers to the wall. Blood dripped from a hidden wound and collected in a pool beneath its wing.

"It's hurt." Skeezix said. She approached the bird slowly with Sheila close behind.

"GIT DAT BIRD OUTTA HEE-UH!" yelled one of the Negro waitresses.

She came after it with a broom. When she got too close, the owl raised the feathers on the back of its neck and began to scream like a banshee. The girls threw their hands up over their ears, their faces frozen in delight.

The waitress scolded the bird to be quiet. "SHUT YO MOUF!" she yelled. But, broom in hand, she stood her distance. Mosquitoes poured in through the hole in the window.

"You didn't see the way it came in," Sheila said to Skeezix.

"Why?"

"It came in like a . . ."

"Like a what?"

"I don't know. Like a ghost."

4

The evening's performance began promptly at 9:30 at the Glades County Courthouse. It began with "The Star-Spangled Banner" from Walter Jacob's *Patriotic Sampler*. The arrangement featured, on the next-to-last fermata, the first mandolins sliding up to the twenty-eighth fret of their instruments! The note was so high it made dogs howl.

Lily stood in front of the bandstand trying to get the crowd to sing the National Anthem. She made large, sweeping gestures with her arms, snapping the buckskin fringe of her Indian jacket. Nobody sang. They gawked. The tomato farmers, the catfishermen, the cane cutters, the teachers, the preachers, the pharmacists, the salesmen, the Indians, and all the public officials from the mayor to the councilmen, stood and stared at Lily and the orchestra.

To many of the people in the crowd, the mandolins seemed too small. The mandolins only looked right in the hands of the two children in the second row.

Lily noticed several Indians staring at her. She imagined that they had impure thoughts. They stood in the back near the punch table with evil smiles. She averted her eyes from theirs and sang so loud her lungs ached. The Indians ogled Violet May Cooper too. Violet May was twenty years older than

Lily but had enormous breasts. They jutted out so far that she could nearly rest the back of her mandola on top of them, Hawaiian-style.

One man kept staring at Sheila and Skeezix. The twins were accustomed to public scrutiny but this man was too close and he wouldn't keep his eyes off them. Skeezix, least likely to concentrate on her music, was more distracted than Sheila. The man had a banjo case.

"Can I help you, sir?" Skeezix asked after they finished the first number.

"You play very well for children."

"Thank you," Skeezix said. "Mister, we're not allowed to talk to people until intermission."

"Unless it's Thomas Edison," Sheila corrected.

"Right. Unless it's Thomas Edison."

"Does your dad allow people to sit in?" the man asked. "I can play any banjo obligato part."

It happened in every town. Even the tiniest of hamlets had their local virtuoso, someone who played the banjo, the concertina, the mandocello, the harp guitar, the marimbaphone, or the ukelele. And these local hotshots or their agents never failed to approach the bandstand at some point during the evening's performance. Sometimes they had their own music. Sometimes they had a complete orchestral score. Kirk's policy was strict and unbending. No one was allowed to sit in. Period. The orchestral sound he had worked for so many years to achieve was a single voice, a poetic voice of integrity in the American wilderness and he would not have it sullied. The display of individual virtuosity was antithetical to the orchestra's existence. So, no sit-ins. That was Kirk's policy and it had gained him many enemies throughout the United States. Last week in Valdosta, Georgia, at the Orpheum Theater, the father of a seven-year-old banjo wizard threw a punch at Kirk during intermission, narrowly missing his left ear.

"The Star-Spangled Banner" was followed by "Egyptian Princess" by Joe Morley and "Marche Militaire" by Franz

40

Schubert. Lily then stepped onto the conductor's podium to deliver her prepared speech to the Moore Haven crowd.

"Ladies and gentlemen, I have the privilege tonight to speak with you briefly about our music."

She turned to Kirk.

"Those Indians in the back," she said. "They keep . . . They keep . . ."

"They keep what?"

"They keep looking at me."

"Let them look," he said. "Remember: Palm Beach. This is a dress rehearsal."

Lily nodded and turned back to the crowd.

"Many of you may have wondered why I'm dressed in this Indian attire . . ."

During Lily's speech, Kirk stood with his back towards the audience. He thought angrily how this was the motliest collection of backwood boors he had ever played for. He held his baton down between his knees. Skeezix started talking to Sheila. Beatrice Templeton, mandolist in the second row, shushed them with a finger to her lips. In the back, a lady with a purple dress and flapper beads poured unlabeled bottles of gin into the punch bowls. At the windows, the wind rattled the Venetian blinds.

"We, as Americans," Lily continued, "would like to think that we have a music that is our very own, that is not some second-rate imitation of European music. As Americans, we would like to think that we have a voice of our own, a voice so distinctive and so American that no doubt would be left in the mind of the listener. People from all over the world could hear this voice and say: 'That is the sound of the New World.' I'm Lily Quintaine of Kirk Quintaine's Progressive Mandolin Orchestra and I believe we have discovered our uniquely American voice. It's a voice unlike any other. A voice we can be proud of. It's the sound of the New World. We call it Indian jazz, played on American mandolins."

"Well, let's hear it then!" somebody shouted.

Kirk bristled. He gave the orchestra four free beats and they broke into "Big Chief Battle-Ax" by Thomas Allen.

At intermission, the man who had been watching Sheila and Skeezix came up to them and put his banjo case on stage. He opened it and the girls gasped. It was the Leedy Egyptian, the most ornate and expensive fretted instrument in the world! From Sioux City to Seattle, the instrument was a legend among banjo and mandolin orchestras. The tone ring was solid fourteen-karat gold, the headstock was imbedded with rhinestones, the heel was hand carved to imitate the bow of a slave galley, and the entire fretboard, from the nut to the resonator, was engraved with mother-of-pearl figures of camels, pharaohs, and pyramids.

"It's loud, I bet," Kirk said.

"And heavy too," Skeezix said.

"It took me seven years to save the money to buy it," the man said.

His name was Broadus C. Gantt and he was the classics teacher at the Moore Haven public high school. He was a thin, frail-looking man with spectacles and a walrus moustache. He spent the majority of his days in a broiling schoolhouse drilling the ten tasks of Hercules into the heads of sullen Indian braves who stared at the floor in his classroom. His other students were Caucasian ruffians who came to school barefoot and longed to be on the banks of Lake Okeechobee, dynamiting catfish out of the water. At night, Mr. Gantt practiced his Leedy Egyptian banjo under a lightbulb swarming with moths. He was in charge of tonight's dance. "You know, Mr. Quintaine," he said, "I think people are enjoying the Indian jazz . . ."

"Mmm-mm?"

". . . but, occasionally—every once in a while—"

"Yes?"

"—you probably ought to . . . you know . . ."

"What?"

"Throw in something else."

Kirk opened the next set with "The Stars and Stripes

Forever" with Lily playing the piccolo descant on the xylophone and the mandocellos playing the trombone part. The audience cheered wildly at the end. It did not discourage Kirk. These were ignorant people who did not recognize significant musical expression. They were satisfied with the crass sensationalism of brass bands.

Gantt was gone during the number. When he returned, he had a somber face.

"Let me make an announcement," he said. "Ladies and gentlemen, can I have your attention please?"

The audience got quiet for Gantt like they did not for Lily. Many of his students were in the audience and they paid him public respect they did not show in the private confines of his classroom.

"I have just received a telegram from the Miami Weather Bureau. A hurricane is due to hit the coast in the vicinity of Miami this evening."

Sheila put her mandolin on her lap. She began to nibble on her plectrum. Skeezix watched a cockroach by Gantt's feet. Its long antennae waved in the air.

The twins' knowledge of hurricanes was limited to what they had learned in their fourth grade social science class in Bismarck. One cool afternoon in May, their teacher, Mrs. Watkins, had stood by her desk at the front of the classroom and spoke of the Galveston hurricane of 1900 while they squirmed on their hard chairs daydreaming onto sunny wheatfields outside the windows. Skeezix remembered. They were wearing their sailor suits with the single, hard pleat down the middle. A hurricane was like a tornado that formed over the ocean. It had an eye, which tricked you. It had winds that could blow you off a tree and send you sailing up into the air like a bird. It could send the ocean up to reclaim whole islands and peninsulas.

Hurricanes killed people too, people meaning adults. To Sheila and Skeezix, children did not die awful deaths. If they died, they died quickly and easily without struggle. In their fantasy, death was the instant transition from life to heaven. When Sheila envisioned her own death by drowning, she sank under the waves and took one gulp of water, then drifted away on angel wings where, high in the sky, she looked down on herself. The little body floated peacefully in the water, face up. The face had the unchanging expression of a rag doll.

The hurricane announcement had little effect on the crowd in the Glades County Courthouse. Nearly everyone stayed to drink spiked punch and dance to Indian jazz. A few of the older residents left early to secure their homes. When they opened the doors, the wind blew in thousands of mahogany leaves, soiling the punch and dismantling the ladies' hairdos. Kirk called "Blue Beads." In a quick jerk, Lily arched her neck to stretch her vocal cords then sang:

> In the forest shade
> Dwelt an Indian maid,
> So the story runs that I was told,
> And a paleface gay
> Stole the maid away
> From a brave whose love was true as gold;
> And at evening in the shadows gray
> To himself this lonely brave would say:
> Every breeze is sighing 'Blue Beads' . . .

Before the song was over, the sheriff started throwing some of the Indians out. Many of the Seminole braves, stumbling drunk, had begun to get boisterous at the back of the room. They yelled things in the Hitchiti tongue that were in reference to Violet May Cooper's cleavage and Lily's private parts. The sheriff bloodied the nose of one of the Indians in forcing him out the door and everyone gathered around to look at the splashed blood on the floor.

Kirk was enraged. He was losing his orchestra to the distractions. Lily was the first to see he was enraged; then Sheila saw it. They knew he would soon begin to howl. The howl would be far beyond what was called for. The blast of fury would freeze every human form within earshot and turn faces towards him in walleyed shock. Red-faced, he would slam his baton down on the conductor's stand, breaking it in two. They had seen it only last week in Chattanooga. The broken piece of baton had gone sailing into the air like some cockeyed arrow. Young girls had cried.

Kirk thought: Did I not make it clear that tonight's performance was not a throwaway on farmers in small-town Florida? Maybe I did not make it clear. Tonight's performance was supposed to be a serious dress rehearsal, the final rehearsal before Palm Beach tomorrow night in which the President himself will be in attendance! And just look at the mess he had.

The mandobasses had let the tempo run away like sows in a garden; his concertmaster, after a dozen gin rickeys, was a quarter of a beat behind the rest of the orchestra; and nobody was heeding the dynamics anymore so that the music was a monotonous gray wall of mandolin noise. And Skeezix! Damn her especially! He could forgive the lackluster tremelo, the going out of position on high notes, the sloppy care of her Lyon and Healy Style B, but he could not forgive her nose buried in the music. It was the ultimate display of contempt to him as the conductor: to have his baton ignored. She had not so much as glanced at him in the last ten minutes.

Well, young lady, Kirk thought fiercely, you are FINED! 25 cents! 50 cents! 75 cents! Keep it up! You and the rest of the orchestra . . . you're all fined! And Mr. Valentine T. Peck, I have some news for you. Jacob Schwartzendruber is the new concertmaster. So put that in your pipe and smoke it, you drunk!

"Watch Daddy!" Sheila said under her breath to Skeezix. "He's getting mad!"

Even Adeline DeVekey succumbed to the distractions of rattled blinds and tossed Indians. Adeline was in the mandola section next to Violet May Cooper. A dauntless champion of universal notation and a pillar of responsible musicianship, Adeline had served three faithful terms as vice-president of the orchestra and was now treasurer. But Kirk thought without mercy: She's fined too. Every time a blind rattled, she jerked her head in the direction of the noise, away from her music and his baton.

Kirk had Broadus C. Gantt to blame. The orchestra's concentration had quickly dwindled after his hurricane announcement.

At eleven o'clock, the weather had become too fierce to ignore and the remainder of the dance was called off. The orchestra members rubbed down their mandolins with cotton rags and returned them to their cases. Emily Jackson and F. W. Clancy retracted their endpins into the huge cavities of their mandobasses. Lily went from seat to seat in her Indian costume collecting the music folders. She placed them longways in a heavy wooden crate.

The lady who had been pouring the gin into the punch bowl approached the bandstand. She complimented Kirk on his Indian jazz. She and her dance partner had created a quirky two-step to go along with the music. Though it did not catch on with the rest of the audience, Kirk thought it was rather nifty. The woman's dance partner was a thin man in a tuxedo who stood with his hands in his pockets as she talked to Kirk, smiling dimly and saying nothing. The single compliment altered Kirk's entire view of Moore Haven and cooled his anger towards his orchestra and Broadus C. Gantt.

Sheila and Skeezix shook a lizard out of the KIRK QUINTAINE'S PROGRESSIVE MANDOLIN ORCHESTRA banner. It was their job to fold it after every performance. They faced each other with the banner a bridge between them. Usually Skeezix held it tight while Sheila folded.

"You should have watched Daddy, Skeezix," Sheila said. "He's going to fine you. Probably all of us."

"Well, Daddy's crazy," Skeezix said, glaring at him on the podium. "How is anybody supposed to concentrate on notes when the wind is blowing the courthouse down and all these Indians are getting beat up in the back?"

"He'll still fine you."

"Well, I'm going to ask him," Skeezix said. "I'm not afraid."

When Lily finished collecting the folders, she took the xylophone down, starting by detaching the raised wooden bars that corresponded to the black keys of a piano. Gantt approached her with the banjo case.

"Have you ever thought," he said kindly, "that maybe the girls ought to be in school playing with their playmates and learning to conjugate? I mean, rather than playing Indian jazz on their mandolins for a bunch of flappers and drunks."

"I think they're getting a wonderful education, Mr. Gantt," Lily said. "Besides, they'll be back in school by Thanksgiving."

Kirk stomped across the stage with his baton.

"All right. What's he saying to you?"

Lily sighed. "Just talk."

"What's he saying to you?"

"He thinks the girls should be in school. That's all."

"Oh, he thinks the girls should be in school, does he?"

Gantt eyed him nervously, squeezing the handle of his banjo case. He wondered if this tyrannical orchestra leader was insane enough to punch him.

"I want to tell you something, Mr. Gantt," Kirk said. "Leave my wife alone! That's the first thing. The second thing is if you have something to say, you say it to me. Are you clear on that, banjo great?"

"You've made yourself very clear, Mr. Quintaine," Gantt said. "Now who do I give this to?" He had a check for one hundred and fifty dollars even made out to "Kirk Quintaine's Music Orchestra" drawn on the First National Bank of Moore Haven, Florida.

"Dandy," Lily said after he left. "Just dandy. You start a fight with the man who's paying us."

"I'm sorry, but he's been causing us problems all night. You know why?"

"Because you wouldn't let him sit in?"

"That's right."

5

At two A.M., the town fire siren sounded. It summoned all able-bodied men to fill sandbags. A portion of the dike around Lake Okeechobee had given way a half mile east of town. Kirk put on his coat, then his hat, then his gloves. The girls sat up in their beds in the hotel room, the sheets on their laps, and peered at him through the darkness. They had on their matching peppermint-striped flannel pajamas.

"Bye, Dad," Skeezix said.

"Bye, Daddy," Sheila said.

Lily sat up in her bed, warm in her flannel gown under two sheets and a chenille bedspread. She had a horrible taste in her mouth that told her she had been asleep. The xylophone melodies she had played hours earlier repeated themselves over and over and over again in her head. "Kirk," she said, "be careful."

"Go back to sleep," he said. "I bet when you wake up the hurricane will be over. What is it, Sheila?"

"Oh, nothing."

"You want to say something. Now say it."

"Daddy, I wish we were at Mr. Edison's. He would invent something—a balloon or an aeroplane that would carry us away from here."

48

"Mr. Edison's not *God,* honey," Lily said.

"I would feel safer there too," Skeezix said.

After Kirk left, Lily got up and locked the door. She shuffled across the wood floor in the darkness, careful to avoid the twins' mandolin cases which Sheila had set neatly next to the chest of drawers. The flounced cuff of her nightgown brushed the black enameled doorknob.

"There's Indians around here," she whispered to the girls.

Lily heard the clatter of shoe soles on the staircase which led down into the lobby and outside into the storm. She considered the owners of those shoes, the men in the orchestra: her husband, Valentine T. Peck, D. E. Lichtenfels, Leroy Fink, and Jacob Schwartzendruber of the first mandolin section, Eugene Gaylord Smith and H. H. Pickering of the mandocellos, F. W. Clancy and Winthrop Ethridge DuQuesne in the back row, and H. Russell Truitt and Xavier Tesch in the second mandolins. She loved Xavier Tesch for keeping his music folder in perfect condition. His music was always in order and he never allowed his second mandolin parts to become dog-eared. He was a neat person. She, however, could not imagine Xavier Tesch doing manual labor, *any* of them for that matter. She could not imagine them filling and lifting sandbags in the rain. She hoped they all had gloves to protect their fingers, especially Eugene Gaylord Smith who was probably the most delicate of them all.

She went back to bed and adjusted her pillow about the headboard. "Now go back to sleep," she told the girls. "Daddy's right. You go back to sleep and when you wake up the hurricane will be all through."

"But we *can't* go to sleep, Mom," Skeezix said.

"Well try."

There was a knock at the door.

"Who is it?"

"It's Evelyn."

It was Mrs. Evelyn Thompson Witt, the lone woman in the first mandolin section. Evelyn boasted of thirty-five private mandolin students in Bismarck and had a chicken farmer for a husband. Lily turned on a lamp and let her in. Evelyn stood at the door in a blue union suit that accentuated every lump and bulge in her fifty-five-year-old body. The union suit ended at her ankles so the twins could see her bare feet, pale and chubby with discolored, hooflike toenails that they felt vaguely they should not be viewing. Evelyn had her mandolin.

Within ten minutes, the remainder of the women in the orchestra had congregated in their room, afraid to face the storm alone. They brought their instruments with them, wary of leaving them unattended in their rooms with Indians lurking about. They placed their mandolin, mandola, and mandocello cases in every available corner, limiting where they themselves could be.

Beatrice Templeton in the mandola section had a box of licorice-flavored cough drops and she passed them around the room. When the box got to Sheila and Skeezix, they quickly passed it on, knowing they were not allowed any candy after they had already brushed their teeth. The ladies, with their hair down or up in switches, in union suits or nightgowns, sat, stood, and laid about Lily's hotel room sliding cough drops around in their mouths. The cough drops made gentle clicking sounds against their teeth. They discussed Lady Line suppositories, Egyptian pile cures, dropsy of the womb, and forty-seven-cent sanitary protectors as the rain hammered the window panes. Try as they might, the twins could not stay awake for long. They did not have the adult capacity for staying awake when exhausted, and exhausted they were from a long day that had begun with turtle eggs for breakfast at Thomas Edison's house. Sheila and Skeezix fell asleep now with the hefty rumps of wheat-fed North Dakota women weighting down their beds.

Lily watched the sleeping faces of her children. She smiled ruefully. They had inherited the large skulls from their father, a condition that—though it had made their birthing worse than most—had had its own distinctive charm when they were toddlers as it gave them a certain miniature woman, doll-like appearance. But now, as they grew to maturity, their heads seemed slightly odd and unattractive. People would call them big-headed. Like Kirk. Skeezix's two permanent top teeth protruded dryly from her upper lip as she slept. A sudden fury of rain slammed against the window, threatening to break it, and Lily thought maybe Gantt was right. Maybe the banjo-playing high school teacher was right. Maybe Sheila and Skeezix should be at home. There they would awaken to golden wheat-fields full of hidden pheasants and an English springer spaniel named Lady carrying a rolled copy of the *Bismarck Herald-Tribune* up the dewy lawn. Then off to school with their lunch buckets full of cheese and bread and apples, charm bracelets jingling, to sit at desks and learn the things school children learn. No flappers, no drunks, no hurricanes. Lily's heart beat faster with the violence of the storm. She looked down and saw her heartbeat move the Egyptian cotton of her gown above her left breast. Her chest felt light. Kirk was gone and the storm was worsening.

Ella Griffith Bedard, the young and pretty mandocellist, looked carefully at the sleeping faces of the twins. "Good. They're asleep," she said. "Listen, everyone. Guess what I found out today?" Her green eyes were sparkling. "You're going to love this."

All heads leaned forward. Violet May Cooper's face turned stern and her eyes focused on Ella's lips like a hawk. Her mouth dropped slightly and Lily could see the fillings in her lower molars. Two of the women were now sitting on one of the twins' beds. Adeline DeVekey stood near the corner with her arms folded across her nightgown. She moved in on Ella's words. Emily Jackson, mandobassist, lay on the floor between the two beds, staring up at the ceiling.

"You know our good friend Eugene?" Ella asked. "Musician extraordinaire?

"Yes. Yes."

"Guess what *he* does?"

"Tell us."

Ella leaned in, making a creaking sound on Sheila's bed.

Her eyes were wide and full of wonder. She whispered, "He practices the secret vice."

"Speak up, child!" Violet May bellowed. "You're competing with that God-forsaken rain!" She motioned towards the window.

"I said, 'He practices the secret vice.'" Ella said it as loud as she could with the twins sleeping so close.

Emily Jackson winced on the floor and readjusted her shoulder blades. "Forgive my ignorance, Ella darling," she said, "but what's the secret vice?"

"Oh Emily! You are so sheltered!" Ella said with loathing.

Emily sighed. "All right. I'm sheltered. Now what's the secret vice?"

"He brings up the vital fluid with his hand."

"MY WORD!" Violet May roared, nearly choking on her cough drop. She lunged at Skeezix and cupped her hands over her ears. She supplicated, "What happens if they're not really asleep?"

"They're asleep, Violet May."

The older women in the orchestra, Mrs. Evelyn Thompson Witt, Beatrice Templeton, and Adeline DeVekey, cast their eyes towards the floor and shook their heads solemnly. Only a woman of the younger generation with a weak Christian upbringing—a flapper!—would dare give voice to such a topic. Ella was a flapper, Adeline DeVekey thought. A low-class flapper.

Lily said, "How do you know this, Ella? Did you *see* him?"

"Of course I didn't see him. But somebody did."

"Who? H. H.?"

"Somebody."

H. H. Pickering sat in the front row of the orchestra in the mandocello section, next to Eugene and directly beneath Kirk's baton. He had been to Florida in 1906 with his parents and had seen a herd of manatees in the Peace River. In Bismarck, he worked in a sporting goods store where he devised duck calls in a dim storage room. He was a short bull of a man with powerful arms and a scarlet neck from frequent hunting expeditions into the Yellowstone mountains of Montana. As a mandocellist, he was fair, awkward and graceless compared to Eugene. His meaty fingers lumbered about the fretboard of his instrument like a crab out of water. H. H. and Eugene normally roomed together on tour and sat beside each other in the dining rooms in the homes, boarding houses, and hotels that hosted them. H. H. had been caught on more than one occasion stealing a kiss from Ella Griffith Bedard. He had turned forty in June and was a bachelor.

The ladies in the room were not shocked so much by Eugene's secret vice or even by H. H. catching him in the act. They were shocked by a discussion of the sordid subject which had to have occurred between H. H., a male member of the species, and Ella Griffith Bedard, a female of the species. It was Ella Griffith Bedard who troubled them the most for she had shown a wanton contempt for the deportment of her gender. She had sold out the modesty and discretion that should be the virtue of every woman, as if it were a nickel Coca-Cola at the drug store.

The night dragged on, and, as the men in the orchestra piled sandbags on the dike of Lake Okeechobee in a horizontal rain, Ella Griffith Bedard sat with the women of the orchestra in the Quintaine's hotel room directing the conversation towards titillation. Sheila and Skeezix slept. Sheila lay on her back with her eyebrows twitching and dreamed of mistakes: of going out of position on the high notes, of playing F's for F sharps, of missing second endings and codas, of wearing stockings with runs in them, hair switches that clashed with her sash, snow-stained shoes and holey underdrawers, of spelling "occasion" wrong on a test at Thomas Jefferson Elementary in Bismarck. Skeezix lay on her side in the fetal position. With each new surge of wind and rain, she grimaced and tucked herself together more tightly. She slept a dreamless sleep, a dead and silent sleep, devoid of rhythm and music—but still she heard the rain. A Seminole janitor wearing a strip shirt

53

stood in the hallway with a broom. He placed his ear to the door and, his ebony eyes full of wonder, listened to the clean, foreign women inside. He breathed silently through his nostrils. He walked away on his moccasins and then came back. When he listened very closely, he could hear the mandolins humming inside their cases.

"I'm going to ask you something, Lily," Ella said at three A.M. "You don't have to answer if you don't want to. But I'm going to ask anyway."

"Go ahead."

"Do you and Kirk . . . Are you able to . . . I mean . . . Are you able to fulfill your conjugal duties? Oh please, ladies, don't gasp on me. You know you all want to know."

"I don't want to know!" Emily Jackson said. "I really don't, Ella."

"You do too, Emily," Ella said with scorn. "You just won't admit it."

Lily smiled and got another cough drop from Adeline DeVekey. She popped it in her mouth and began to gently knock it against her teeth with her tongue.

"Don't answer her," Violet May admonished.

"It's all right, Violet May," Lily said. "It's an honest question."

"The children," Beatrice Templeton said.

"Oh pipe down, Beatrice," Ella said. "Even if they're awake, they don't know what 'conjugal duties' are."

"In answer to your question, Ella: We don't; we haven't; we probably aren't going to. Are you satisfied?"

Ella looked surprised. She was not convinced that Lily would evade the question; still, she was unprepared for the direct and unhesitating answer. With those few words, so confidently expressed, Ella realized she did not know Lily. Ella said, "I don't see how you could. I mean, with this hectic touring schedule, we barely have time to sleep, let alone . . . Why is everybody looking at me like that?"

Ella sat at the foot of Skeezix's bed. Lily looked at her. She had never felt so old. Ella was a child. A babe-in-the-woods.

How could she hate her as a woman, as an equal, as a threat to her life, or as competition for her husband? She couldn't. She could only be annoyed at her misbehavior. Fifteen years of marriage and motherhood had made her different from Ella. Much too different. Lily felt she had grown up far more than she had ever wanted.

She had fulfilled her conjugal duty seven months ago. That was the last time. It was impossible on a tour. Kirk was nervous about his mandolins. All kinds of things could happen in the night: a string could pop, a bridge could slip, a neck could crack, a sounding board could cave in, a roach could chew the notes off a music page, a thief could take the harp guitar . . . . It went on and on. On the night before an important engagement, Kirk would not sleep at all. In the shadows, he would flop around like a fish on the strange hotel bed, worrying, worrying, worrying, and keeping her awake too. It was on these nights that she wished she had never married, that she had stayed on the farm in North Dakota with her sisters, and, there, with her feather pillow, gaze out onto the moon over the plains, to drift off to the music of crickets and wind whistling high in the poplars.

A blast of wind rocked the Riverside Lodge and Skeezix whimpered in bed.

"It's getting worse," said Adeline DeVekey.

"I know that."

It was Lily.

"Ssshhh," Violet May said with her finger over her lips. "There's somebody out there. Listen."

"Out where?"

"In the hallway."

"I don't hear anything."

"Yes. There's somebody eavesdropping on us."

Violet May marched to the door, huge breasts swaying under the nightgown. She stopped. Through the closed door, she bellowed invective at the eavesdropper, threatening to report him to the management. The Seminole janitor bounded

55

away like a panic-stricken deer, leaving his broom behind. The long, ebony locks of his hair floated behind him as he ran.

"You have to be firm with Indians," Violet May instructed. "You treat them like children."

Kirk returned hours later. He stood in the doorway in drenched clothes and stared at the sleeping women in his room. One, two, three, four, five, six, seven. There were seven of them. Nine counting Sheila and Skeezix. They were scattered about the room in disarray, in every imaginable sleeping position, wrapped up in bedspreads, sheets, or no covers at all. He could see the mandolin cases in the shadows and a box of cough drops on the chest of drawers. Violet May was snoring and he could hear it above the wind. It suddenly struck him that Sheila and Skeezix might one day—1970?—grow to be hefty North Dakota women like Violet May, fierce, eagle-beaked matriarchs with big hams, antique thoughts, and the slightest remnant of a pretty face.

Kirk undressed in the bathroom. Naked, he made a bed for himself out of the bathtub, arranging towels about the cold enamel as the women slept in the next room. He wrote a note and pinned it to the front door of the bathroom. It read:

I AM IN HERE.
SLEEPING.
K. Q.

Then he put the hook in the latch and retired.

The dike was hopeless. As soon as they had stacked ten sandbags, the water was lapping over them. They couldn't keep up with it. Eugene's teeth chattered the whole time they were outside and he started to turn blue at the end. Kirk feared for his health. The townspeople didn't like the orchestra's attitude about manual labor. They had to take a boat back to the hotel. Wind-whipped raindrops stung their stubbled faces and made a terrible racket on everyone's clothes. The water was up to the door handles of the stranded Model T's. When Kirk got to the hotel, the water was coming in the front door and into the lobby, carrying a host of uninvited fish, reptiles, and amphibians. Kirk was not frightened of the hurricane. He was only angry at it. In his mind, he could barely distinguish the hurricane from all the other obstacles, all the other enemies who kept him in obscurity. The hurricane was simply a new enemy, an enemy he felt compelled to battle. If this hurricane kept up, he would not make it to Palm Beach tonight and he would lose one of the most important battles he had ever fought against obscurity. To leave the world known only to a small circle of family and friends was far worse a blow than the strike of a hurricane.

And no hurricane could deliver the pain that Skeezix had delivered tonight when she asked for Thomas Edison. It was not that he was envious of the man: Kirk granted that his fame was deserved. It was only that he felt, as an innovator, he was of equal stature and that he had as much power to impress himself on the American mind as Edison did. That he could not even convince his own family of this was much more of a disaster than the dike of Lake Okeechobee giving away.

6

Kirk awoke to find the Riverside Lodge drifting off its foundation. The giant wood structure launched into an extended Lake Okeechobee and floated there like some catacombic iceberg, moving slowly with the wind. He could no longer ignore the possibility that they would never reach Palm Beach tonight, that the hurricane would thwart his first chance for national recognition. On the east coast of Florida, luminaries and newspapermen gathering at the Breakers Hotel might return to their hometowns without ever hearing Indian jazz on the mandolins. They might return to their hometowns without ever hearing the real voice of America.

Kirk called for his clothes. He got dressed and stepped out of the bathroom. The bedroom was steamy from the body heat of seven women. Sheila was hiding under the covers of her bed. He could hear the mandolins humming in their cases. They hummed in sympathetic vibration to the howling wind. They were out of tune. Kirk had several red nicks on his face, still wet, from trying to shave in a floating building.

"Ladies," he said, "I think you should go back to your rooms and get dressed. This is no way for a mandolin orchestra to meet its public."

The women filed out of the room in their nightgowns and

58

union suits, Emily Jackson bringing up the rear. Kirk had never seen the women in his orchestra in their pajamas before and he could not help raising an eyebrow as they left. Emily Jackson, slender in her concert attire, looked sickly in her union suit, with meager, caved-in haunches that reminded him of a swaybacked horse.

When they were all gone, he closed the door and looked at Sheila's form underneath the twisted sheets. A rush of adrenaline gave him such a moment of weakness he thought he would fall down. Lily saw the collapse of his face in agony. She knew the look all too well. It came before every concert.

"Sheila," Kirk said, "this is Daddy. Get out of the covers now. You can't breathe in there."

"Daddy, this building is *floating*," she whimpered.

"I know it is, sweetie."

"Well, it's not supposed to float!"

"Daddy's not going to let anything happen to you," Kirk said. "Now get out of the covers."

Sheila flung off the sheets and stared at her father through a glaze of tears. "We're going to drown, Daddy, and nobody can help us!"

Skeezix sat in the bed across from Sheila. Her back rested on the headboard and her legs were straight out over the covers. Her toes pointed straight to the ceiling. The toenails, from the largest one to the smallest one, were clipped in a perfectly even arc, like crescent moons. She rubbed her knee and thought: This is like the *Titanic*, only we are in warm water instead of cold, and we will be saved. She looked at Sheila and said, "I hope you know everyone can see your underwear."

Lily got their raincoats out of the trunk. She remembered the day she bought them. It was a Saturday in late March. They cost $2.50 apiece at Barnwell's Department Store downtown. The girls were shopping with her and she made them try the raincoats on, incuding the oversized yellow hats. The twins huddled in front of the three-way store mirror and stared at their reflections with wide-eyed wonder. Lily thought they

59

looked better suited for a whaling expedition off Nantucket than for April showers in the heart of the great plains. Kirk was not with them. He was at home composing at the Steinway, often hopping downstairs to see how some part would sound on the xylophone. Lily remembered that she was relieved to be away. Now Lily fastened Sheila's snaps. She went to Sheila naturally, without glancing at Kirk. It was an unwritten rule that Lily would deal with the more difficult one. Kirk put on Skeezix's raincoat. His fingers were tense and impatient. He once broke a tiny bone in Skeezix's finger when they were younger, trying to force her hand through a tight sleeve.

When they were snug in their raincoats, Kirk went searching for inner tubes. He found an old wheel from a Model T in a storage closet downstairs. He couldn't pry the tire from the rim.

"Help me with this, would you?"

There was an Indian slouched over in the corner of the hallway amid shards of broken glass from a fallen mirror. He was of no use to anybody. He was green with fright and babbling to his God in the Hitchiti tongue. Kirk finally got the tire loose himself. Then he found another one in another storage closet and some bicycle tires as well. He raced up the stairs with them, knocking into the swaying bannister.

Lily and he tied the tubes to the girls with mandolin strings. They tied the automobile tubes around their waists and the bicycle tubes at the crooks of their elbows.

"You couldn't drown now if you tried to," Kirk said.

"Yes, but," Skeezix said, "what happens if we have to use the lavatory facilities? Did you ever think of that?"

H. Russell Truitt, first chair second mandolinist, knocked at the door and informed Kirk that Eugene had been hurt. A lamp had rolled off the table and struck him on the head. He had a bump above his right eye like a goose egg and he was deathly pale. Kirk thought that he didn't have much of an orchestra without Eugene. Eugene was not only a virtuoso mandocellist, he actually listened to the other parts when he played and blended intuitively. He'd have cockeyed balance with only H. H. Pickering and Ella Griffith Bedard holding forth in the mandocello section.

"I'll be down in a minute, Russ," Kirk told him. H. Russell Truitt was an elegant man with silver hair who preferred Vivaldi over Indian jazz. He went out of his way to be thoughtful to the girls and often surprised them with a daisy or a peppermint when they were unhappy. He looked at them now in their rain attire with the crudely-tied floats. He began to giggle helplessly. He leaned towards Kirk and talked so the girls couldn't hear him. "They look like mutant toads," he said and left.

Lily made two little bundles of snacks and snapped them in the bottom front pockets of their raincoats. The snacks were cubes of gray Swiss cheese and greasy buttermints she had saved from supper. When she placed the bundle in Sheila's pocket, Lily could feel her heart pounding against her ribs.

"You have to calm down, sweetheart."

"I can't help it, Mommy," Sheila said. "I'm so very, very frightened."

"I know you're frightened, honey."

"God is very angry at us, isn't he?"

"Don't be silly. It's just a bad storm and it will pass."

"But, I'm afraid I'll never see you again!"

"Well, it's times like this that we have to pray. Right?" Lily said. "The Lord's Prayer, the twenty-third Psalm—those are good."

"His rod and his staff will comfort me," Sheila said.

"Yes. Now if we become separated, you try to find a high place. You eat your food a little bit at a time. And don't you worry. Mommy and Daddy will find you . . . ."

Lily was sobbing now and Kirk yanked her away. He dug his fret hand into her upper arm, leaving five, separate grapelike bruises on her white skin—four on one side of her arm, one on the other. "Don't you dare fall apart on them now!" Kirk muttered ferociously into her ear. His head swelled with blood. "They need your strength, not your whining!"

The hotel slowly drifted east, towards the Atlantic. The

61

vermin that lived in the walls—termites, lizards, skinks, and cockroaches—were out scrambling in the open, alarmed at the metamorphosis of their home. The skinks scared the girls the most with their shiny, snakelike skin and their desperate, hell-bent wriggle. The curtains were covered with roaches, from the hems at the bottom to the valances at the top. They clung to the stiff linen fabric with their hairy legs, antennae undulating slowly, testing the air. The roaches were black in the dim morning light. Lizards sought refuge in the shadows of the mandolin cases around the room. They hid quietly out of human sight with their tiny black eyes alert and moving, ever-cautious of predators.

When Kirk was searching for tires, he had heard an odd sound coming from the kitchen. He heard it again now. The sound came from one of the hotel's cooks, a black woman in a hairnet. She wore a white cotton uniform blemished across the front with gravy stains and under the arms with yellow perspiration marks. She sat on the floor in the middle of the kitchen amid sliding cans of Oregon blackberries and California tomatoes, amid clattering frying pans and colanders, amid rolling lemons, grapefruit, and tangerines, loose eggs, fallen cakes, and rat-gnawed lettuce heads. The storm had rattled loose the icebox latch and milk bottles were crashing out onto the floor. With each pitch of the hotel, cold milk rolled across the floor of the kitchen and chilled the cook's private parts. She clutched a leg of the carving table with both hands and moaned with each new surge of wind.

"Listen to that," Kirk complained. "Can't someone go sing her a spiritual?"

"What is it, Daddy?" Skeezix asked. "It sounds like a ghost."

"It's just a crazy lady in the kitchen," Kirk said. He turned to Lily. "As if Sheila is not frightened enough already . . . . Adults should be models of composure in times of danger."

"We can't all be models of composure," Lily said. The tone of her voice revealed a disdain for Kirk that she had concealed before at all costs. Though she did not blame him entirely for their predicament, she could not separate her husband from the hurricane. The tyranny, the arrogance, the intimidation, the coercion, the granite artistic stance, the reckless lunge at fame—the hurricane was a grotesque extension of her husband, carried out in a nightmare.

At seven A.M., the eye of the hurricane passed and Kirk could nearly hear the blood drain from the tense muscles of his orchestra. Gantt, the high school teacher, rowed up to the hotel in a small boat and knocked at their window.

"It's Gantt."

"I came to rescue your daughters," he said. "The amazing mandolin twins."

He had no hat and his hair was soaked to the scalp. His teeth were chattering. The wind had died down so they could hear it. Skeezix peered at him from underneath the brim of her rain hat. He looked determined and crazy. Kirk noted his banjo case at the bottom of the boat. It was wrapped in canvas and tied tightly with frayed hemp rope in bowline knots. All around the boat, Lake Okeechobee swirled. The chocolate-brown water was in every direction as far as they could see. Islands of foam and debris dotted the expanse of water like hammocks.

"You came to what, Mr. Gantt?"

"This hotel can't last much longer," he said. "Let me take them. I have room for two small ones. I'll try to get back to the courthouse before the eye passes again. The courthouse is the only safe place."

Lily sat on her bed with her blue-veined hands pressed into the chenille bedspread and shook her head. "No."

"You have to let me take them, Mrs. Quintaine."

Lily's head swayed like a pendulum, precise and rhythmic.

"Let them go, Lily," Kirk said.

"Daddy?" Sheila whimpered.

"Go with Mr. Gantt now."

Lily put her arms around her daughters. She dug her nose into the rubber-coated cotton of Sheila's raincoat at the shoulder. Lily could feel the cartilage in her nose shift. She thought of the summer of '21, when the twins were five. Or was it '22? It was sometime before the Charleston. That summer, the girls would pretend their sandbox was a boat. Skeezix would be the captain and stand at the helm wearing a pirate hat and holding a sword made of newspaper. On my boat, she would say, we have three rules. Number one: There will be no talking on my boat. Number two: There will be no screaming on my boat. Number three: We will raise our hand if we need to speak to the captain. Is that clear? Sheila and the neighborhood children would sit obediently on the hard boards with their bare toes buried in the sand. Skeezix would eventually kick sand in someone's face and they would flee, red-faced and in tears, to return that night holding their mother's hand. As the injured party and guardian walked solemnly up their porch steps, Sheila would dance around the inside of the house in delight. "You're in trouble now, Skeezix." Lily recalled that it was as excited as Sheila ever got. And how many times did she apologize for Skeezix that summer? It must have been a hundred times.

The women members of the orchestra began to congregate in the Quintaine's room again. They were dressed and in better color now that the storm had subsided. When they entered, they looked first at the collage of inner tubes, mandolin strings, and yellow rubber that contained Sheila and Skeezix. Then they looked out the window to see the high school teacher in a rowboat. Kirk explained Gantt's presence to the women members of his orchestra. He gesticulated with his hands and kept a calm tone. The women nodded in sympathy. Violet May stepped up and put her hand on Lily's shoulder. Skeezix looked up at her.

"You have to let them go," Violet May said. "It's the right thing to do."

"Get your hand off me, old lady!"

The girls leaped with their mother's scream. Lily turned towards Kirk. She glared at him through a film of tears. "AND QUIT LOOKING AT ME BECAUSE I'M NOT A MODEL OF

COMPOSURE!"

Kirk closed his eyes and shook his head in disapprobation. He was furious she had broken down in front of everyone.

Over the past few years, he had become more aware that he was at the source of her instability. He made halfhearted attempts to assuage his guilt by remembering Valentine's Day, her birthday, their anniversaries. He would buy her chocolate in heart-shaped boxes, long-stemmed roses, and published greeting cards—all things he knew were in dire contrast to the imagination in his work. Kirk was aware of the feeble nature of these acts of good will, and, often, poring over manuscript paper in the wee hours of the morning, his eyes hollowed out from a double day of work, his face scratchy from the next day's growth of beard, his very bones aching in weariness, he would honestly concede that he put his music before his family. He would experience genuine contempt for himself. But regardless, there was no excuse, no justification for Lily's demonstration now, this outrage of behavior, this emotional diarrhea. He took a deep breath and poked his head out the window.

"Mr. Gantt," he said. "I'm entrusting you with the lives of my daughters."

"I realize that, sir."

"Just so you do. How deep is this water?"

"It's very deep."

Kirk nodded. "How far has the hotel drifted? Do you know that?"

"Five, maybe six city blocks."

The girls got in the boat and Gantt rowed off. Skeezix sat in the bow. She waved at the congregated heads in the window of their hotel room, smiling pleasantly. Sheila sat in the stern with her hands clutched around the sides of the boat. She looked at the churning water all around her with a sick expression. She whispered the twenty-third Psalm to herself. When the boat was nearly out of sight from the hotel, Lily, who had not been able to watch them go, dashed to the window and screamed at Gantt.

"You let anything happen to them, Gantt, and I will kill you!" She turned to her husband and said quietly, "You let them go with a stranger, Kirk."

Gantt rowed steadily in the eye of the hurricane, his jaw tight with exertion. His bow tie was still tight around his neck from the evening's social function. He wore a canvas coat that came down to his ankles. It matched the color of the canvas that covered his Egyptian banjo.

"I can't stop rowing," he said. "But I have a pack of chewing gum in my inside coat pocket. If you'd like a stick, help yourself. It's in the inside breast pocket of my suit coat."

Skeezix got the gum, careful not to rock the boat. It was Adams' California fruit gum, her favorite. She took the wrapper off a stick and flicked it into Lake Okeechobee. The gum tasted funny because of the fishy smell of the lake. She chewed and looked at her sister.

"Gum's good, Sheila. Won't you have a piece?"

Sheila's hands were white from clutching the sides of the boat. Skeezix ached inside for her. Gantt rowed the boat and looked at Sheila. He breathed heavily as he rowed. Skeezix thought that Gantt was a kind man and an educated man, but he didn't have sympathy for Sheila. No one had sympathy for Sheila like Skeezix.

Sheila just didn't fit. No matter where she was, she didn't seem right there. On Sunday afternoon automobile excursions on the gravel roads through the wheatfields, Sheila would sit in the back seat of the Model T with her knees turned in and her feet twisted. She never fit in their games either. When they played Red Rover at Thomas Jefferson Elementary in Bismarck, Sheila would trot across the playground and lunge feebly at the interlocked arms of her playmates. She had no intention of breaking through the line. In skip-a-rope, she had to be forced to go "in." She only liked to turn the rope. And she never got mean during Hot Peppers. When they played marbles, she didn't protest when Skeezix hunched. It took all the fun out of cheating. Sheila didn't like to get dizzy. She would somersault two or three turns down a hill, then stand up and watch Skeezix go all the way down. She wouldn't chew the paraffin from the jars of strawberry preserves. She said it wasn't food. Skeezix loved to chew the wax. It absorbed the slightest flavor from the fruit inside and recorded her toothmarks. The one thing Sheila did like was her paper dolls. And her mandolin. In truth, if there was one place she did fit in, it was behind the music stand in her father's mandolin orchestra.

Gantt started talking. He wanted to know what kind of truant officer in North Dakota would allow them to be out of school for three months of the year. He asked them questions and more questions. Sheila wouldn't answer, so he asked Skeezix. He tested her for fifteen minutes, until the Glades County Courthouse was in sight. Had she heard of Romulus and Remus? Where was the Magellan Strait? Who invented celestial navigation? Where did the Aztecs live? What were the four elements of music? What was six times seven? What was the capitol of Maine? Who shot Abraham Lincoln? Where was her esophagus? Where did bananas come from? Who wrote *Evangeline*? Spell Louisiana. Conjugate *venir*.

"Your parents have not neglected your education," Gantt said finally. "I will say that for them."

"Thank you."

"In fact," he continued, "you're impressive young ladies. You have good teeth, good skin. Your mother keeps you clean. You read music better than any fifth-graders *I've* ever seen."

"That's from practice."

"Can I ask a question?"

"It depends."

"Does your mother give that awful speech before *every* concert?"

"What's so awful about it?"

"She's some kind of saint to tolerate that father of yours."

"You watch what you say about my father, mister."

"Let me tell you something about your father, little girl. He's a first-rate oddball whose misplaced conviction has startled enough people into following what he'll do next. Indian jazz on the mandolins . . . . That has to be the most ridiculous thing I have ever heard of!"

"I will slap your face, Mr. Gantt!"

It was Sheila. Her voice trembled with emotion. "I don't care *who* you are."

"He's just mad Daddy wouldn't let him sit in," Skeezix said. "That's all it is."

The muddy water flowed south. There was a definite current and they were going against it. Gantt began to cough and wheeze as he rowed to the courthouse. Skeezix's rump was sore from sitting on the hard wooden board. She shifted her weight and pinched her underdrawers. The sun came out and she took off her rain cap. There was a thin red line under her chin from the elastic strap. She felt it with the calloused third finger of her fret hand. The gum had lost its flavor. She tossed it into the water. Things were floating by them: Coca-Cola bottles, milk cans, mahogany branches, coconuts, ducks and their ducklings, duck decoys, a lady's bicycle, a breadbox, a vapor bath cabinet, an ice vat, a bowl-back mandolin. The larger things were encapsulated in bubbly whitish-brown foam. Gantt heaved. Skeezix began to doubt that he would make it to the courthouse.

A flock of water birds passed overhead. From their position in the sky, the boat was like the other debris in the water, distinguishing itself only by two yellow dots that were Sheila and Skeezix sitting in the boat, this and moving sticks that were Gantt's frantic oars. There were thousands of birds: ibis, egrets, herons, limpkins, and storks. The Seminoles would shoot them down with arrows and pluck them as chickens. The birds finally lighted in the upper branches of a strand of custard apples not yet submerged by the rising water. The birds were shoulder to shoulder on the tops of the trees. From the girls' distance in the boat, it looked like a mound of snow.

A cow floated by with several turkey vultures perched on

its bloated carcass. The buzzards glanced at Sheila and Skeezix with little interest and resumed eating. Then came a puppy springer spaniel balancing on a two-by-four. Sheila reached for it and fell in. She quickly floated away.

7

In 1926, Thomas Edison was one year away from a wheel chair. He couldn't walk without a cane. He hobbled along slowly, hunched over, his eyes focused on the ground in front of him. Now he stopped and peered at a man standing at the edge of his swimming pool. The man was fishing coconuts from the water with a minnow net.

"We was lucky, Henry," Edison said to his next-door neighbor. "An uprooted ficus, a few smashed windows, a little debris here and there . . . Minimal damage."

Henry nodded. "It's too bad we couldn't say the same for the little town of Moore Haven."

"What's that, Henry?"

"MOORE HAVEN!" Henry repeated, shouting into Edison's ear. Edison wore an Acousticon, the most advanced hearing aid of its day. The beneficial results of the device, however, varied from day to day.

"Oh yes, Moore Haven," Edison said. He shook his head in sympathy. "That was a sad case, wasn't it?"

"Certainly was."

" 'Course now," Edison said, "That area up there is one of the most dangerous places on earth. Why a catastrophe like that was bound to happen sooner or later."

"I guess you're right."

"The problem was, Henry," Edison said, tweezing the white hair of an eyebrow between his thumb and first finger, "nobody ever bothered building a decent dike around Lake Okeechobee."

Henry was Henry Ford, the billionaire automobile manufacturer. Ford had purchased the Fort Myers property adjacent to Edison's in 1915. He bought it to be near his idol. He revered the great inventor and had since boyhood. He treated him like a king. In the past decade, he had lent Edison over a million dollars but never asked for a cent in repayment of the loans. He gave him a brand-new, custom-made Model T every year. He looked after his personal health, at every opportunity discouraging Edison from his self-prescribed all-milk diet. Ford constantly fed Edison's ego. In the daily Parcheesi games on the south verandah of the Edison house, Ford always made certain that the great inventor won.

They continued along the property, inspecting the hurricane damage. They walked onto the pier and greeted the Pinkerton guard stationed there. Edison was the world's most famous living man and had been for the past thirty-five years. To protect his privacy, he had hired four armed Pinkerton security guards to patrol his fourteen-acre estate. Three of them were stationed along the fence on MacGregor Boulevard while the other one stood guard at the pier on the Caloosahatchee River. Still, people got through. Aspiring inventors, creditors, autograph hounds, teenagers-on-a-dare, and newspaper and magazine reporters all managed to get in. They posed as gardeners, painters, deliverymen, mail carriers, and old friends to get a glimpse of and perhaps a word with the great man.

They walked to the end of the pier. Ford helped Edison sit. Edison took off his shoes and socks and rolled up his pant legs to the knees. He put his feet into the cold water of the Caloosahatchee River, grinning when his toes first touched.

71

Edison wore a great, wide-brimmed straw hat whenever he was in Fort Myers. Ford thought it gave him the ruthless air of a sugar plantation baron. The hat was old and deformed with different colored straws, ranging from yellow to dark brown. Many of the straws had broken from the weave and their frayed and curled ends jutted out all over the hat like ideas.

Mrs. Edison soon brought a tray with lunch and the daily mail. Lunch was a large glass of iced milk and a bowl of bananas and cream. Bananas and cream was one of the few things Edison would ingest besides milk. The bananas, however, had to be the perfect ripeness, they had to be cut in one-half-inch wedges, and the sugar had to be thoroughly mixed with the cream or the crystals would irritate his dentures. Ford got crab salad on pumpernickel toast and a bottle of Coca-Cola. Ford ate standing up and, as he chewed, he kept his eyes on a lone heron perched on a piling post close to shore.

The mail was mostly from creditors whom Edison recognized from their return addresses. He flipped through these pieces without opening them. He got two more honorary degrees today, one from Milliken University in Decatur, Illinois, and one from an all-girls college in Bismarck, North Dakota. His October issue of *Scientific American* came. There was a letter from a Mr. Lloyd Loar, acoustician at the Gibson Mandolin-Guitar Company in Kalamazoo, Michigan, requesting Edison's input on the Virzi Tone Amplifier. A letter farther down the pile caught his attention because of the extreme care of the penmanship. Edison squinted at the return address.

Miss Skeezix Quintaine
Glades County Courthouse
Moore Haven, Florida

Edison said, "Hand me my milk there, would you, Henry?"
"Something interesting there?" Ford asked.
"Look at this handwriting."
Edison opened the letter and read.

Dear Mr. Edison,

Please allow me to introduce myself. My name is Skeezix Quintaine and I am ten years of age. I had the pleasure of making your acquaintance when my father's mandolin orchestra played at your home on September the sixteenth. I trust you recall my sister and I. We are twins and we play in the second mandolin section of my father's orchestra. We are sometimes billed as the Amazing Mandolin Twins.

Something very terrible has happened here. Perhaps you have read in your newspaper, Mr. Edison, how the town of Moore Haven was washed away by Lake Okeechobee during the hurricane. Unfortunately for us, we were present for this catastrophe. The hotel in which we were staying was swept off its foundation and drifted into the raging waters. THE ENTIRE HOTEL! I am sad to report that the storm claimed one of our orchestra members, Mr. Eugene Gaylord Smith. He was crushed by falling furniture when the hotel tipped on its side. Eugene played mandocello and sat in the front row. Perhaps you remember him.

Mr. Edison, we can't find my sister. She's lost. We were rescued by a man named Broadus Gantt and she fell out of his boat. Her face turned white when she hit the water. She was too frightened to cry. If I live to be a hundred, I shall never forget the look on her face as she drifted away.

I know the terrible thing has not happened to her. I know this in my bones. My mother and father tied us both up very well in floats so we could not drown. But I know that my sister is frightened out there in the Everglades. Sheila does not like the outdoors. She quit Girl Scouts after our first campout because she did not like the bugs and not having a toilet.

We have been looking for Sheila every moment of daylight for the past five days. So far, we have had no luck. We have found many people, but they are mostly dead. My mother covers my eyes when we pass their bodies, but I can still smell them. The smell almost makes you throw up. The Red Cross workers from Miami come by and dump bags of lime over the bodies. We see the workers all the time drinking whiskey in the rescue boats and my mother says they're a bunch of drunks. My father says he'd drink whiskey too if he had to do their job.

Mr. Edison, would you help us? On behalf of my poor sister, I beseech you. I know that a great man such as yourself could invent some sort of an electronic contraption that could find a lost child in the wilderness. I know that if you really set your mind to it, Mr. Edison, you could do it!

Please forgive me for being so very bold. I assure you I was not raised this way. But we are in the throes of a terrible dilemma and the flame of our hope is flickering away. My mother has been crying every night even though she tries to hide it from me. She won't look at me I guess because I remind her of Sheila. My father has not slept or changed his clothes for a week. He paces around with muddy shoes and his jaw is tight and his eyes are all popped out like a fish. But maybe the worst thing of all is that there is no music anymore. For the first time in my life, there is no music. Nobody plays. Mr. Du-Quesne got his harp guitar out once but he only tuned it and put it away.

There's nothing so awful as losing one of your family. Nothing so awful in all the world.

Please come to Moore Haven. We are at the Glades County Courthouse.

Very humbly yours,
Skeezix Quintaine

Edison held the letter in his hand for a moment and gazed out over the Caloosahatchee River. A white mist hung over the water so that he could not see the opposite shore. He shook his head in wonder.

"This girl," he said out loud. "She's remarkable."

But there was an ache in his heart. Edison had read the letter with a sense of wonder, but with melancholy and regret too. He had six children of his own, three by his first wife and three by his second. None had ever shown a spark like this Skeezix Quintaine.

Edison had never participated in his children's upbringing. He felt it was the woman's responsibility. He was busy in his New Jersey invention factory, poring over inanimate objects. The children turned out how they turned out. And he never had much luck with them. Edison was not interested in the dilemma of a child growing up under a famous father. He had no sympathy for it.

Now Edison handed the letter to Ford.

"'The flame of our hope is flickering away,'" Ford read incredulously. "Surely the girl's mother wrote this letter!"

"Don't be so sure, Henry. They were very bright children. You could tell that."

Edison thought of the night the mandolin orchestra played on the verandah. He thought of the two little girls playing their mandolins with their feet barely touching the floor. How he had admired their discipline!

Do you remember when they played here, Henry?"

"Certainly do," Ford said. "The father was a Grade A crackpot. Don't you remember? He kept playing this . . . uh . . . Indian music."

"What's that?"

"INDIAN MUSIC," Ford repeated, louder.

"Indian music? You mean like American Indian music?"

"Yes, with jazz."

"You say they played American Indian music with jazz, eh?" Edison asked. "I don't really remember that. Could you hand me my bananas?"

Mrs. Edison had placed the bowl of bananas on a pedestal whose base rested in a pan of water. The pan of water prevented the ants from reaching the bananas. She had no such device however for the flies and Ford had to brush them away from the fruit. Ford served the bananas and cream to Edison and tucked a cloth napkin in his shirt collar for the dribbles.

"What chance do you think that this little girl is still alive?" asked Ford.

Edison shook his head. "Slim to none."

"What I want to know is what could possibly be invented to pinpoint a child in three hundred or so square miles of swamp?"

Ford grimaced. He could tell that the question annoyed Edison. The billionaire automobile manufacturer felt his ears turning hot. When would he learn that the great inventor would not tolerate a question presented in the negative?

Edison was thinking deeply. He took a bite of his bananas and said, "Even a low-flying airplane would most likely miss her."

Suddenly a boat appeared out of the mist. It was a double decker steamer with the words S.S. JUNGLE-RAMA, FT. MYERS, FLORIDA painted in black letters on the hull.

"There he is!" a man shouted into a bull horn. "The legend himself. Mr. Thomas Alva Edison, ladies and gentlemen."

The Pinkerton guard on the pier produced a silver whistle on a chain and blew it with all his might. The noise sent the water bird Ford had been watching to the sky in a scramble of gray-blue feathers. On the boat, Northern tourists clamored to the railing. They murmured, "That's Edison?" and "That's really him?" The man behind the bull horn was a nationally-known orator. He wore a tuxedo with a white bow tie and patent leather shoes that reflected the sun like a mirror.

The other three Pinkerton guards were on the pier within seconds, their service revolvers raised. One of the guards informed the orator that if they did not leave the premises at once he and the captain would be imprisoned and the boat would be confiscated. The orator nodded graciously, unshaken. He continued speaking into his bull horn.

"So the next time you turn on a light," he said, "or press that toaster button down, or listen to your phonograph, I want you to thank the man who made it all possible. Mr. Thomas A. Edison."

There was a smattering of applause. Many of the tourists though, seeing Edison in a battered straw hat and bare feet, were uncomfortable intruding on the old man's private life.

Ford waved meekly at the crowd. He was glad they didn't recognize him. Edison gawked right back at the crowd. He had his eye on a little girl in the upper deck of the boat. She was in her grandmother's arms, her little legs straddling the woman's torso, a bottle of Coca-Cola tipped to her lips. Edison winked at her. A grin broke out over the girl's face as a stream of brown liquid trickled down her chin. The grandmother stared and stared at Edison. She had seen a photograph of him in a science textbook a half century ago.

The orator continued: "Mr. Thomas Edison is a man of great wealth and fame. He can live anywhere he wants in the world. But where does he choose to live? He chooses to live in the garden paradise of the world, Fort Myers, Florida. And you can too for as little as thirty-five dollars down and five dollars a month."

When the boat left, Edison picked up his cane and his shoes and walked to the house. Mrs. Edison was at the piano.

"Mina, do you remember that mandolin orchestra that was here about a week ago?"

"How could I forget?" she said. "I couldn't get that Indian jazz out of my head for two days!" She put her fingers on the keys of the piano and recalled fragments of "Heap Big Injun" and "Red Wing." Ford nodded and smiled. Edison couldn't hear it.

"Do you remember the two little girls in the group?" he asked.

"Lovely children," Mrs. Edison said.

"They were at Moore Haven when the hurricane struck.

77

Here read this."

Edison handed the letter from Skeezix to his wife. She read it and said, "Their poor mother."

The next morning, Edison was at the pier in a white linen suit, a Panama hat, and new shoes from Lord and Taylor. He had rented a steamer called the *Suwannee* to take up the Caloosahatchee River to Moore Haven. He had the letter from Skeezix in his inside coat pocket. It was seven A.M. and already his face was flushed with the heat.

He had two suitcases. One contained the tools of his trade: a microscope, a Bunsen burner, glass test tubes wrapped in towels, litmus paper, and several jars of various chemical compounds. He had packed this suitcase himself. The other suitcase contained his personal belongings: a razor and strap, a mahogany box for his dentures, an extra battery for his Acousticon, and seven days worth of clean underwear. Mina had packed this one.

Ford was going too, along with Al, the Pinkerton guard, Silas "Buster" Nobles, the captain, and a mother goat named Priscilla for Edison's supply of fresh milk.

Edison kissed his wife goodbye. In the distance, he saw mockingbirds flitting about the tops of the royal palms that lined MacGregor Boulevard.

"You find that little girl, Thomas," she said.

"Don't you worry," he said. "As long as there's *me*, there's hope."

"Henry, you take good care of him now."

"You know I will, Mina. You know I will."

That night, the voyagers slept under the stars as the steamer plodded up the Caloosahatchee River. Edison slept with his clothes on under two layers of mosquito netting. He was curled on his side, in a fetal position, and dreamt happily of children playing little mandolins. The moonlight painted his hair silver.

No one else slept well. The crickets and frogs were deafening. Ford fidgeted in a chair by the captain's wheel. Al, the

Pinkerton guard, paced back and forth from bow to stern with bloodshot eyes. Even Priscilla was unnerved. She sat huddled near Edison, chewing her cud.

The river was so narrow in spots that the spiders could weave their webs between tree branches on opposite sides of the shore. The boat glided under the spider's taut canopies. The voyagers could look to the sky and see giant golden silk spiders framed against the stars.

Below them, great manatees rose from the black depths of the river to view the curiosity invading their territory. Their whiskered faces popped above the surface of the moonlit water. They snorted air and disappeared again.

"They got damn walruses in this river!" Al, the Pinkerton guard, said. "Did you know that, Mr. Ford?"

"Those are manatees."

"Manatees? Never heard of 'em. I guess they couldn't really be walruses, could they? Walruses live in Alaska and . . . up there." The guard glanced at Edison. "How does he sleep through all this shit?"

Edison had made the expedition into the Florida jungle several times. He journeyed into the Everglades as the head of the Edison Botanical Research Corporation, an organization dedicated to the domestic production of rubber and funded entirely by Ford. During World War I, it became apparent that the United States' dependency on overseas rubber was unsuitable. So, Ford or Harvey Firestone, the tire manufacturer, or John Burroughs, the naturalist, would travel with him into the Everglades to tap exotic trees for possible rubber sap. They took the same steamer, the *Suwanee*, with Silas "Buster" Nobles at the helm. Buster was an Okeelanta catfisherman with a keen understanding of the internal combustion engine and a way with the dirty joke. Edison was fond of the lavender orchids that grew wild on the cypress trees in the Everglades and often brought some home to Mina. She would put them in a glass vase and set them on the nightstand.

Edison had been to Moore Haven one time in 1924. Harvey

Firestone and he had stayed at the Riverside Lodge on the third floor. In the evening, Firestone and he went to the theater on Main Street where he snoozed through a Gloria Swanson film incognito.

Edison could not recall the Glades County Courthouse Skeezix Quintaine spoke of.

8

D uke Ellington and the Washingtonians took a bus to Savannah, Georgia. There they picked up Henry Flagler's East Coast Railroad to Palm Beach. They arrived two days before the gala reopening of the Breakers Hotel and played for tea time under the coconut palms.

Duke wore a tiny moustache. It was trimmed a quarter of an inch above the top of his upper lip and it extended east and west only as far as each nostril. He had a tuxedo with a satin lapel and tails that hung over the piano bench. He beamed out at the audience from behind a six-foot Steinway grand whose cabinet hosted racing lizards. The lizards were the color of clay and paused often to inflate scarlet pouches under their throats. Duke brushed them off when they landed on his music. His music was ten pages of staff paper taped edge to edge and draped in a clutter cross the top of the piano. "Creole Love Call" was written in bold letters on the first page.

Wealthy Northern vacationers milled about the courtyard gaping at the Negroes in their tuxedos. They found the music exotic and wonderful. It was a curious mixture of New Orleans, Trinidad, and Harlem. The tourists sensed the innovation and the importance of the music. Here was a man who could write jazz down without losing it. The tourists stood among deep purple bougainvillea blossoms, sipping illegal gin, and listening to "Black and Tan Fantasy," "East St. Louis Toodle-oo," selections from "Chocolate Kiddies," and "Yam Brown." The tourists watched the orchestra while, above them, mockingbirds flitted between the fronds of the coconut palms.

Besides Ellington, the most striking member of the orchestra to the tourists was Sonny Greer, the drummer. He had a gigantic bass drum with a scarlet macaw painted directly on the calfskin head. A large cymbal hung from a leather thong attached to an iron dowel that retracted into the drum. A snare drum rested on a tilted metal stand that put the playing surface at a forty-five degree angle to the floor. Two cymbals clashed together with the aid of a spring-operated hi-hat stand whose pedal conformed to the sole of Sonny Greer's patent leather shoe. The drummer's outfit was augmented by an array of novelty effects: temple blocks whose sound holes were the mouths of Oriental dragons, Balinese gongs, hand-tuned kettle drums, Indian tom-toms, Cuban tumbadores, bird whistles, ratchets, sandpaper blocks, triangles, and castanets. Behind the drummer, framing him on his throne, was a gold set of tubular chimes. He struck these with a rawhide hammer. Sonny Greer also sang. He used a megaphone to project his voice. During the intermissions, he posed for photographs with the megaphone.

Along with Greer, the tourists were fascinated by the trumpet and trombone men, Bubber Miley and Joe "Tricky Sam" Nanton. These musicians placed rubber toilet plungers into the bells of their instruments to produce grunts, growls, swoops, and splats. Many of the tourists' previous association with the trumpet and trombone was with the military and particularly with the marches of John Philip Sousa. Still, they did not find the Negro musicians blasphemous. They found them fresh and exciting. Partly because of European endorsement, starting with Antonin Dvorak, many Americans embraced their new art form with patriotic fervor.

There were ten members in Duke's Washingtonians. Sidney Bechet was on clarinet. Toby Hardwick was on C melody and baritone saxophone. Freddy Guy played the banjeurine. His banjeurine had a scroll and was a remnant from the 1890s banjo orchestra craze. During this period S. S. Stewart and other musical instrument manufacturers tried to elevate the status of the lowly folk instrument by making it look as much like a violin as possible.

The wealthy Palm Beach audience perspired under the coconut palms. Among the listeners was Kermit Roosevelt, son of Teddy. He leaned against a trunk of one of the palm trees and held a gin rickey. He looked dapper in wool knickers, argyle knee stockings, and two-tone shoes. Irving Berlin, the Tin Pan Alley songwriter, was also in the crowd. He stood with his arms folded in front of the brass section. Bula Croker, a genuine Cherokee princess, sat in an Afromobile near the stage and nodded her head in time to the Negro jazz band. The Indian princess peered intently at Sonny Greer when he put the megaphone to his lips.

Duke's success with the crowd was due to his ingratiating manner, the unique arrangements, and the new popularity of jazz. When the band finished "Creole Love Call," the tourists applauded wildly. They tossed their hats into the air and shouted "Bravo!" A syndicated columnist from the *Chicago Tribune* in attendance hailed Duke as an American genius. Later, in an article dispatched to newspapers in the major cities of the United States, the columnist wrote, "Ellington has performed the miracle of composing jazz without losing the spontaneity of its improvised origins."

Another listener in the crowd was a Fort Lauderdale handyman named E. A. "Buck" Tillman. Tillman was employed by the Breakers Hotel and was weeding the bougainvillea patch when Ellington played. Tillman also had the distinction of being an officer in the American Red Cross, South Florida division. During the first intermission, he overheard a conversation between Bechet and Ellington.

"Dig this," Bechet said. "A little birdie told me some cats are coming tomorrow that'll cut us all."

"What cats?"

"A mandolin band from North Dakota," Bechet said.

"A mandolin band from North Dakota?" Duke repeated. "Don't jive me, Jackson."

"It ain't no shit. I hear they're solid."

"They play jazz?"

"They play it *all*."

Bechet produced a bottle of corn liquor from his clarinet case and took a sip. He offered some to Ellington. "Juice?"

Ellington declined.

"And get this: They got two little kiddies in the band. Twins, I was told. They're little Mozarts. I guess they sit back and just fly on those little mandolins."

"Two little kiddies, huh?" Duke said. "I could dig it. I could dig that."

"And you know where they're playing tonight?"

"Lay it on me."

"Thomas Edison's."

"You mean *the* Thomas Edison's?"

"Damn straight. The dude who did the light bulb and shit. Man's got a pad in Florida."

"I'm hip."

Bechet said, "That mandolin band don't play nuthin' but class gigs, baby."

Duke nodded. "A mandolin band from North Dakota, huh? I wanna hear these cats."

"You bet."

Sidney Bechet tugged on the starched collar of his tuxedo shirt. It was stained yellow with perspiration. "This place is like an oven, man!"

E. A. "Buck" Tillman relayed the Ellington/Bechet conversation verbatim to Kirk one week later. It was on the fifth unsuccessful day of locating Sheila. Tillman was at the helm of his boat, an old decrepit pile of lumber named the *Corona* that had been leased by the Red Cross. Kirk sat near the stern and listened to the story of Ellington with little interest. His eyes furiously searched the sawgrass for any trace of his daughter. With every ticking second of his Elgin wristwatch, he battled the rising despair in his heart. He interrupted Tillman's story several times to scream into the swamp. "SHEILA! SHEILA!"

He was wearing the same suit he had worn to the Friday night concert, six days ago. It hadn't been changed. There was a sliver of mud under each fingernail. There was a layer of scum over his teeth. He had two fever blisters from overexposure to the sun. One was under his nose and the other was by his lip. Lily dabbed the sores with a greasy ointment designed for horses. She also made him wear a bandanna to protect his head from sunburn. To Lily, Kirk's appearance became less and less that of a master musician and more and more that of some deranged sea pirate.

"SHEEEEEEEE-LAAAAA! SHEEEEEEE-LAAAAAAA!"

Before the hurricane, Kirk would have listened with passionate interest to Tillman's first-hand account of Ellington. He had a clear position on the man then. He admired Ellington. He respected him. He considered him a formidable talent. His music was unique and distinctively American. Kirk was intrigued by his compositions and his writing for the baritone saxophone independent of the bass line.

Kirk, however, could not discount the weaknesses in his music. The first was Ellington's reliance on the standard band instruments: the cornet, the trombone,the clarinet, and the drums. Great music could never be produced on timeworn military instruments. Ellington's second weakness was the music itself. It was jazz and jazz only. He flatly ignored the music of the Shoshone, the Algonquin, the Navajo, and the Seminole. The music of the native American must be incorporated into the new composed jazz to produce a music that truly reflected the American culture.

Before the hurricane, Kirk would have had a different reaction to a story of an Ellington triumph. He would have had a different reaction to the Negro band leader wowing Palm Beach celebrities. He would have had a different reaction to the jazz composer being hailed as a genius by a syndicted newspaper columnist.

The stories would have caused him pain, resentment, and jealousy, but mostly pain. When would people realize that he was the American genius and not Ellington? When would they see the profundity of Indian jazz on flat-backed mandolins? Couldn't anyone see that this music was the ultimate and final cultural break with Europe, that it was the last leather thong stretching across the Atlantic Ocean severed?

The only stories Kirk would have liked to hear from E. A. "Buck" Tillman were that Ellington's band was flat, that Greer's drumheads collapsed in the heat, that the band's blend was miserable, and that they ignored dynamic markings. Better yet, he would have liked to hear about European intellectuals rightfully concluding that Ellington's music was provincial, narrow in scope, and the reflection of a very small segment of society, namely certain Negroes in Louisiana.

But this was before the hurricane. This was before the town of Moore Haven was moved down the map along with his daughter Sheila.

"I thought you might be interested in hearing that," Tillman said after the story.

"SHEEEEE-LAAAAA! SHEEEEE-LAAAAA!"

Kirk did not want to hear about Duke Ellington. He was not interested in him. But it was more than that. Ellington reminded him of his ambition. He despised his ambition. His ambition was as destructive and as merciless as the hurricane itself. One of his last official acts as father, besides preparing her life-saving device, was fining Sheila 25 cents after last Friday's concert. He fined his own daughter—a *child*! If Sheila was lost for good in the Everglades, he would never be able to forgive himself for that.

When Sheila and Skeezix were four years old, Lily took a train trip to Montana to help her ailing mother. It was August and Kirk agreed to take care of the children. The first few days were bearable for him. He poured their Post Toasties in the morning and played Parcheesi with them in the afternoon. He walked down to the lagoon with one on each side of him, carrying bags of stale white bread to feed the swans. And at night, he kneeled with them to say their prayers. "If I should die before I wake, I pray the Lord my soul to take . . . ."

But no matter how hard he tried, he could only view baby-sitting as mindless tedium, especially when it excluded him completely from his work. At the time he was under pressure to produce a new number for a gala ball for the D.A.R. in Minot. He was writing a piece called "The Sacajawea Strut" and, inspired by Ellington, was busily at work creating a mandocello part independent of the bass line.

Prolonged and unrelieved bouts of baby-sitting produced in him a spiritual helplessness, a profound and unreasonable exhaustion, and a vague rage. He could not hide his irritation with the constant attention the twins required and their constant demands. Sheila spilled her grape juice for the third time one morning several days after Lily left.

"Here!" he screamed. "Here's the rag! Clean it up yourself! I am not your royal servant!"

His daughters twitched from the vibration of his voice.

He resigned as nanny. They would have to fend for themselves. The first few days passed without incident. They played in the sandbox and around the yard. When they needed a drink, they came inside and shoved their high chairs across the kitchen floor to the faucet. They put their lips to Mason jars of icy well water as their father wrote music in his room. On the third day, they wandered away. They went to McKellum's Creek, several blocks down the road. When they returned they walked to their father's room. Sheila knocked gingerly on the door.

"What?"

"Daddy, could you come and look at Skeezix?"

Kirk flung the door open to find Skeezix red-faced with tears streaming down her face. She collapsed on him, murmuring "Daddy." She was covered with leeches. They were on her thighs, her buttocks, her knees, her heels, and her toes. There were probably twenty leeches, each the color of mud and the size of an elm leaf. Kirk felt he was being punished and he lashed back.

"I THOUGHT I TOLD YOU NOT TO LEAVE THE YARD!"

"Daddy." Sheila had sighed. "Don't yell at her now."

Kirk squinted into the sunlight and recalled that day six years ago. It was where he had established his pattern of tyranny and neglect with his children. The tyranny and neglect was always followed by guilt. Still, the guilt had no effect on future patterns of tyranny and neglect. He hated himself.

The sun bore down on the Red Cross boat inching its way through the sawgrass. A gray cloud drifted near the sun. The rescue team gazed into the sky with longing. The cloud promised relief from the heat. The rescue team was Kirk, Lily, Skeezix, the remaining nine male orchestra members, Broadus C. Gantt, Tillman, and ten additional Red Cross workers.

"You never seen such well-dressed niggers in your life!" Tillman said about Ellington's band. "I thought you would be interested in the story." Tillman wiped his brow with a handkerchief. "He obviously thinks very highly of your musical ensemble."

"Oh, ensemble, huh?" Kirk growled with utmost contempt. How he hated hicks trying to sound sophisticated! "Listen, Tillman. You and those stupid dogs' job is to find my daughter. If you have to entertain someone, why don't you entertain the frogs!"

"Please don't be offended, Mr. Tillman," Lily said. "We are all under great strain right now. Please forgive my husband. I thought your story of Duke Ellington was very interesting. It sounds like he regards Kirk as some sort of Wienerschnitzel polkamaster."

"What do you mean, Mommy?" Skeezix asked.

"Well, honey, some people don't believe North Dakotans can play jazz."

E. A. "Buck" Tillman was forty-five years old and wore a white uniform with embroidered shoulder tabs befitting his rank in the American Red Cross. But he was a drunk. He signed his name with an X, and had a dental condition Lily deemed deplorable. His neck was tomato-red from long days in the sun. He knew where every hidden still was in the south Florida swamp and he smelled like booze. Booze and dogs. He had three dogs, an English setter named Rex and two half-breed coonhounds that yelped like coyotes. The dogs had done some first-rate hunting in their day, according to Tillman.

On the first day, they gave the dogs Sheila's mandolin case to get her scent. Everybody decided it was the thing that smelled the most like her and they kept it in the boat to refresh the dogs' memories. Day in and day out, the dogs would bound into the water to later joyfully return with bobwhites, snakes, tin cans, boots and sticks—items that did not resemble Sheila in the slightest. Worse, Tillman rewarded the dogs for whatever they brought in. He had a big burlap bag of rock candy. The dogs chewed the candy with their heads down, dripping onto the bottom of the boat, while the rescue team watched in fascination.

"No wonder they don't care what they bring in," Kirk complained one day. "They know you're going to reward them if they bring in a cowpie. What kind of moron are you, Tillman? . . . SHEEEEE-LAAAAA! SHEEEEEE-LAAAAA!"

In the late afternoon, they came upon a gang of large buzzards standing awkwardly by a rotten cypress log covered with resurrection fern. Their coal-black feathers were scrambled across their backs, jutting up in every which direction. Their feathers gleamed under the sunlight. They were feasting on something that could not be seen from the boat. The dogs stood up with their paws on the edge of the boat. They barked and yelped at the buzzards but they wouldn't go after them. Rex, the English setter, slavered into the rainwater of the

Everglades. When the boat got close enough, the buzzards glanced at the rescue party casually and calmly took to the sky. They seemed to sense that there was no competition for the things that they ate. No one else wanted it.

"It seems to be a female youth of some sort," Tillman said from the helm.

Kirk looked at Lily and said, "I'll go."

He stepped out of the boat and trudged through the swamp. An alligator spied him from a spot near the log, his dragon paws dangling limply just below the surface of the water. Above, a flock of egrets dashed across the sky, their feathers achieving a silver luminance in the haze of the Everglades. The rescue squad watched him go. They could see that his head was trembling from twenty yards. Valentine T. Peck guzzled a half-pint of gin and looked away. Xavier Tesch and H. H. Pickering bit their lips and looked down. The Red Cross workers despised the mandolin orchestra. They considered them weak and effeminate. They especially despised Broadus C. Gantt, who they thought was part of the mandolin orchestra, and that gold Egyptian banjo he had to take everywhere with him. Skeezix buried her head in her mother's bosom. She could feel her heart racing. "I know it's not Sheila, I know it's not Sheila, I know it's not Sheila," chanted Skeezix.

Kirk bounded back, tripping over his feet, and thrashing in the water. "LILY, I CAN'T BREATHE!" The alligator crashed away in a panic, slapping its tail in the water.

What Kirk had seen was bloated organs: the kidneys, the pancreas, the liver, the intestines with hundreds of geometric beak marks in them. It wasn't Sheila.

"Go cover that with lime, Tillman." The color had drained from Kirk's face.

When Lily's heart had slowed down, Skeezix said, "I wrote Thomas Edison a letter last night. Maybe he can help us. I hope you don't mind."

9

The women in the mandolin orchestra took the first relief train out of Moore Haven. It arrived two days after the hurricane struck. The train came from Sebring, a small town one hundred miles north that had been undamaged by the hurricane. The passengers on the train were doctors and nurses from Sebring with chlorine water treatment units. Also on board was a vast array of Florida idlers along for the ride. These included Haines City cowboys, Okeelanta catfishermen, Chicago tourists with bow ties and ukuleles, and Seminole Indians from the Brighton reservation. The Indians sat on the train in their damp strip shirts and gazed with stone faces out the open windows.

They saw the ladies on the platform. The women musicians, in their formal attire and skillet-shaped mandolin cases, looked foreign and exotic to the Indians. They thought they might be Gypsies.

Emily Jackson sat on her mandobass case with her knees together and her hands clasped around her knees. She wore a lavender flapper hat with an ebony ribbon. She wore patent leather shoes with four straps that fastened with pearls. She gazed at the surrounding scenery, aware that hooligans, low-lifes, and Indians were gawking at her from the windows of the train.

"Would you look at that?" one of the cowboys said. "She's jest a sittin' there on that coffin. Ain't she got no respect for the dead?"

"Mebbe not," another answered. "But she is a pretty little morsel."

"A young thing."

The cowboys on the train thought the coffin contained the mortal remains of one of the flood victims. In that coffin was someone's poor flesh souring in the ninety-degree heat. They did not guess that the coffin contained a giant mandolin.

Lily walked among the lady musicians on the platform in a black silk dress and kissed each one of them good-bye. She held Skeezix tightly by the hand. Skeezix wore a cranberry-colored taffeta dress that matched the one Sheila had. But she did not wear the charm bracelet because the jangling it made was too much to bear. In the west, sabal palms rose out of the sawgrass prairie, their spiked fronds like hands against the sky. From the train, the body odor of the passengers drifted out the open windows to the ladies' nostrils in sickening drafts. Out of the corner of her eye, Lily could see changing patterns of light caused by a conductor walking up and down the aisle of the train. He wore a blue pressed uniform and had a gold watch chain. Lily swatted a mosquito on Skeezix's neck.

"Ouch, Mommy!"

Violet May Cooper set her mandola case on the platform and threw her arms around Lily. "Oh honey, you'll find her. You'll find her."

"I do hope so, Violet May."

"You will. You will. I saw that life preserver you and Kirk made for her. No one could drown in that. We must put our faith in the Lord."

Skeezix saw Violet May's old hands against her mother's black dress. Her hands were pink and wrinkled and looked like claws. Her father said that Violet May Cooper had failing eyesight. Her music had to be in universal notation; she could no longer read the alto clef.

"You pray for your sister now."

"I will, Mrs. Cooper," Skeezix said. "You got lipstick on Mommy."

Lily kissed Mrs. Evelyn Thompson Witt, Ella Griffith Bedard, Beatrice Templeton, Adeline DeVekey, and, lastly, Emily Jackson. Then the ladies got on the train. They withstood the six-hour trip to Sebring with the ogling Floridians, none of whom had the courage to ask what was in their cases.

They arrived in Sebring at six P.M. They were taken to the 138-room Kenilworth Lodge and accomodated there at federal expense. Each room had a paddle fan with a chain and an army of cockroaches an inch long and better. On occasion, the ladies would take their instruments out of their cases and run arpeggios. They pressed their effeminate fingers against the white copper frets of their mandolins and gazed out the windows at orange groves. They awaited word on Sheila. The ladies in the mandolin orchestra loved the twins as if they were their own children, but they believed Sheila was dead.

The same night the ladies arrived in Sebring, Lily had the wherewithal to cancel their next engagement. It was at the Governor's Inn in Tallahassee for the 26th of September.

Dear Sirs,

Kirk Quintaine's Progressive Mandolin Orchestra will be unable to honor its obligation to perform at the Governor's Tea on September the 26th. We were in Moore Haven the night the hurricane struck and have suffered damage to our personnel and our property. We will be detained here for an indeterminate amount of time. Please accept our deepest regrets. We are certain a local orchestra of suitable quality can be obtained to take our place. This notice constitutes the disavowal of all obligations under the current contract.

Musically yours,
Lily Quintaine, Manager
Kirk Quintaine's Progressive
Mandolin Orchestra

93

Lily broke down after she wrote the letter. In the Glades County Courthouse, Kirk and Skeezix and the relief workers looked on as she began to sob in cavernous gasps. Oh Sheila, I may never see you again, she cried. My daughter. My daughter. The little girl who is more myself than I. Lily envisioned Sheila. She saw her face in her mind's eye. The thought that that visage was all that remained of her was too horrible to sustain. Lily could not look at Skeezix because Skeezix was proof that Sheila was gone. I am weak in the face of tragedy, Lily thought. Tragedy should be visited upon stronger people. It should be visited upon farmers, plumbers, soldiers, ministers, thieves, and laborers, not upon young ladies with delicate hands and hearts who practice music and sing. It hurt to breathe.

But sometimes Sheila's death was preferable to the idea that she was still alive out there in the swamp. A quick and merciful drowning was better than the slow death of fright. She saw her daughter perched on the roots of a cypress tree with the eyes of insensate alligators above the surface of the water as the night closed in.

Sheila was not a brave child. She was not an independent child. She counted on the care and guidance of those who loved her. And she was afraid of everything. She was afraid of spiders, of snakes, of dogs, of thunder, of the darkness, of infection, of automobile accidents, of foul balls and meteorites and eclipses of the sun.

She would only sleep on clean sheets with her own pillow. Her own pillow was a battered lump of comfort that leaked goose feathers and smelled like hair. Lily had packed it in the trunk from North Dakota with the rest of their belongings. Sheila could not sleep without her pillow.

Then there was the matter of her bodily functions. She would only eliminate in a toilet. And that was final. She would hold it until her kidneys burst before she would go behind a tree. She wouldn't even go to an outhouse in the wooded public parks of Bismarck. Skeezix would. Skeezix would sit on a carved hole and drop chocolate pebbles into a foaming pit beneath her but not Sheila. To Sheila, it was barbaric and she would not talk about it.

How could Sheila survive in the Everglades?

Lily was angry and she had someone to blame. If she had trusted her instincts, the twins would never have gotten on the boat with Broadus C. Gantt. But she did not blame Gantt because he was a man of conviction and courage who had believed that night the hotel would shatter in the storm. Gantt had believed he was saving her daughters' lives. She blamed Kirk. She blamed Kirk because he was a coldhearted man who could reason in the face of disaster when the only truth was love. He had let them go. He was her husband of fifteen years and she loved him, but he could not suffer enough for that. She wanted the guilt to press into his shoulders as he walked and drive him into the ground.

The night Lily cried, Skeezix wanted to pray. They knelt down on the hard floor of the Glades County Courthouse and put their elbows on the Red Cross cot. The cot rested on a bedspring with blistered silver paint.

Their bare feet extended from their nightclothes as they prayed. The pink bottoms of their feet faced the relief workers in the shadows of the courthouse. Most of them smelled like frog eggs and signed their names with an X. Lily had her drawers, her corset, and her corset cover on under her flannel gown because of the men in the room. The thought of their impure longings was too horrible to sustain. They were watching her as she prayed.

"Mommy, you have to close your eyes."

"Okay, sweetie."

Lily thought on the child's world of fantasy. As an adult, nothing was more crucial than nourishing it. How important it was the children believe in Santa Claus and the Tooth Fairy and the Easter Bunny and the dead man whose spirit soared to an enchanted kingdom where all was sparkles and gaiety. How important it was they believe that by bowing their heads, lacing their fingers together and closing their eyes, they could talk to God, the giant in the sky who listened to millions of people at once. Skeezix mumbled next to her and Lily thought: Why are we so intent on setting them up to be destroyed by reality? Why is that so important to us? Why, if we endeavor nothing else in our lives, do we make certain we shield our children from the world?

Beads of perspiration broke on her forehead and rolled into her eyes. Forgive me God, Lily prayed. Forgive me my blasphemous thoughts.

Skeezix prayed for her sister. She prayed that His rod and staff would comfort her in the swamp. She prayed the bears and tigers would stay away from her. She prayed an Indian would come along and take her out of the rain. Lily listened and nodded. She waited for the prayer to be over.

"Are your eyes closed, Mom?"

"They're closed, Skeezix. They're closed."

When Skeezix had exhausted her requests for Sheila, she began to bless people in North Dakota. They were people Lily had since forgotten. Skeezix blessed cousins, deceased aunts, pets, schoolmates from Thomas Jefferson Elementary, and Sunday school teachers. She blessed Eugene Gaylord Smith, the first chair mandocellist who had lost his life in the hurricane.

"He's with You now in heaven," Skeezix said.

Lily heard Kirk's footsteps as he paced in front of the courthouse door. Out the windows, she heard the crickets in the saw palmetto. Aside from that, it was silent in the courthouse. The relief workers huddled in the shadows listening to Skeezix's prayer. Lily could feel their eyes on her. She knew they saw the outline of her hips against her gown.

"Skeezix . . ."

"What, Mommy?"

"Honey . . ." She brushed a mosquito from her heel.

"What is it?"

"I want you to . . ."

96

"To what?"

"Skeezix you have to at least consider the possibility that your sister is not coming back."

Lily looked behind her. The relief workers looked away as if they were not listening. She looked at Kirk and saw the fever blisters about his mouth. He wasn't listening. Her knees were sore from kneeling and they wouldn't have been ten years ago. "You have to think of that, honey. I pray that it's not true. I pray with all my might. I pray that she is still alive out there. But she might be gone. We have to start at least thinking about that."

"Mommy, Sheila is out there. I know it."

"I know you *wish* that," Lily said. "I wish it too. But sometimes our wishes don't always come true."

"Mommy, I don't wish that. I know that."

"How do you know that?"

"Something happened. I received a sign tonight. Sheila's out there."

"A sign? Oh Skeezix, stop."

That night there was a commotion in the courthouse. An Indian put a frog in Broadus Gantt's banjo case. The Indian's name was Raymond Osceola and he was one of the relief workers. He had a face as big and round as a pumpkin and wore cowboy boots he called "shitkickers." He had befriended Skeezix from the start and told her Indian legends on the rescue boat. They were stories about giant frogs and stone canoes and fairies four inches tall and people created in ovens. He could pick up cockroaches with his fingers and flick them alive. He had been decorated in the war and could drive a Model T. He had a common law wife in Fort Lauderdale with an Irish name.

Osceola was nothing but a two-bit Indian to Lily though and she was afraid of him. His hair was unclean, his teeth were rotten, he drank whiskey, and he resolved his health problems with the medicine man on the Brighton reservation. He had once lectured them on mosquitoes. Only the female of the species hunts for blood. He said "of the species" as if he were a summa cum laude Northwestern graduate and not a third grade dropout from the government school in Clewiston. Lily watched with deep suspicion his interest in Skeezix. He ingratiated himself with Skeezix to get to her. He would love to put his filthy Indian hands on me, Lily thought.

When Gantt opened his banjo case in the morning, a six-inch frog leaped out. Its feces were on the calfskin head, the Egyptian motif fretboard, the rhinestone-studded headstock, and the engraved tuning pegs.

"All right! Who did it?" demanded Gantt. "You, Osceola?"

"Get your finger out of my face, Banjo Man, before I break it off."

The laughter rose and resonated the sound chamber of the courthouse. The relief workers stood with tin cups of steaming coffee, their skin pale and their eyes still dull from sleep.

"Neanderthals!" Gantt screamed in outrage. "Every one of them!"

A tear rolled down his face as he inspected the damage to his instrument. Then he looked up from his gold banjo and spoke to the relief workers. His voice quivered but his conviction did not. "I still believe civility, decency, and literacy will triumph over depravity, villainy, and ignorance."

"No shit," Osceola said.

Skeezix asked Lily if she thought Mr. Osceola put the frog in Mr. Gantt's banjo case. Lily replied that she was certain the Indian did it. "What's more," she said, "I think its inhumane to imprison us with these drunken degenerates twenty-four hours a day. Especially me being the only female."

"I'm a female, Mommy."

"The only adult female."

Early morning sunlight flooded the courthouse windows and slipped through the Venetian blinds to make yellow stripes on the muddy floor. The Red Cross leader, E. A. "Buck" Tillman, approached Osceola and demanded the truth.

"He fondles that banjo like it's his goddam lover!" Osceola said.

"Watch your language, mister," Tillman said. "There's a child in this room."

"My mother gets less respect than that banjo."

"That would not give you the right to deface someone's personal property," Tillman answered.

"How was I supposed to know the frog would shit in it?"

The remark brought hearty chuckles from the relief workers.

Kirk stood next to Tillman. Lily saw the blood rush to his lined and sleepless face. She prayed that Osceola would back off. Perhaps he could offer an apology. Even a lame one would help. It could avert a fight. She knew Kirk was at the point now where he had no regard for his personal health. He would risk injury to his mandolin fingers without a second thought. If a confrontation occurred, objects would go flying around the room and Skeezix would again see that side of her father Lily had always tried to hide from her.

"Never touch another person's instrument without their permission," Kirk growled. "Never." He turned to a bearded man by the window who was fanning himself with an ibis wing. "What are you snickering at, Turtle Breath?"

He was not challenged. The Red Cross workers and the National Guardsmen had a certain respect for Kirk, a certain fear of him. Over their Chesterfield cigarettes and homemade gin, they rumored among themselves that he was some sort of a genius. He was a composer of music, like Ludwig Beethoven, and put black marks on lined paper that they were not supposed to understand. When he stood at the podium with a baton, he made a room full of mandolins sound as one. Kirk Quintaine had some kind of magic they did not understand and thus he could not be disposed of with a simple fist to the jaw or a broken bottle to the skull. Every day the relief workers listened to Kirk scream into the swamp for his daughter and every night. they watched him pace, back and forth, back and forth, in front of the courthouse door.

The relief workers, however, did not have the same fear or

respect for Gantt. Nor did they for Fink, Lichtenfels, Schwartzendruber, Clancy, Pickering, Tesch, Truitt, or DuQuesne. As a whole, they despised the men in the mandolin orchestra who stayed back to search for Sheila Quintaine. They despised their clean fingernails, their soft buttocks, their ribbed black hose, their embroidered handkerchieves, their sunburn creams, their pile cures, and the tiny bottles of nerve and liver pills they kept in the inside pockets of their coats. The relief workers thought the mandolin orchestra had a condescending attitude towards them. They did not like the way the musicians fawned over their instruments, especially Gantt, and the way they treated them as if they were not worthy of getting near these wonderful mandolins, banjos, and guitars.

On the first day out, a woman's corpse fell apart at the shoulder socket as the relief workers were lifting her onto the boat. One of the men, a toothless illiterate with hollow eyes, stood holding an arm. There was a diamond ring on one of the corpse's fingers. Except for Tillman, the relief workers roared with laughter at the macabre scene. In the meantime, F. W. Clancy and Winthrop Ethridge DuQuesne vomited hopelessly over the side of the boat, further contaminating the death waters around Moore Haven. Their knees buckled with each heave.

Osceola looked at them with what Lily saw as a depraved satisfaction. Finally Osceola spoke. "They should have taken the train to Sebring with the rest of the women."

The only person in the mandolin orchestra the relief workers liked was Valentine T. Peck, the concertmaster. This was because, after the hurricane, he was in a drunken stupor most of the time. He sat in the boat with his head back and his Adam's apple to the sun and grinned. He said silly things and shared his booze with them. When he had to pee, he peed over the side of the boat without scrupulously hiding from Lily as did the other mandolin orchestra members. The relief workers, however, could see by Kirk's reaction to Peck's behavior, the concertmaster's mandolin-playing days were numbered. At

100

least with Kirk Quintaine's Progressive Mandolin Orchestra.

The rescue workers felt it was unfair that their job be exacerbated by the presence of a genius, a lady, a kid, and a host of homosexuals in their very boat. Especially since this Sheila they were looking for was as dead as a doornail. They were certain of that. When was this group of crazy royalty from North Dakota going to figure that out, they wanted to know?

10

One night Skeezix woke at three A.M. ready for the toilet. She looked around the dark interior of the courthouse and saw her father sleeping on the floor. His mouth was twisted from the pressure of the floorboards against his jaw. There was a rat crawling on the windowsill above him. The rat paused often to sniff the air. Skeezix could see the tension in the rat's body.

She looked away from the windowsill to the cot next to hers. Her mother was sleeping peacefully. Skeezix could tell that, in her sleep, her mother had forgotten about Sheila. Skeezix could tell her mother was having sweet dreams. Skeezix imagined her mother was dreaming of the things she loved: Dakota wheatfields, sunflowers in August, "Schubert's Serenade," grand pianos, butterscotch sundaes, Ingram's Milkweed Cream, the poetry of Cicero, and red roses. Skeezix looked at her mother's face in the night. She thought she was lucky to have so beautiful a mother. Her mother was as pretty as Gloria Swanson. She had a face like a china doll. Her lips looked like they were painted on.

There was a rustle in the shadows. Skeezix looked away from her mother and saw Raymond Osceola. Skeezix got out of bed and walked barefoot across the muddy courthouse floor.

Crawling cockroaches suddenly stopped dead in their tracks. Their antennae undulated slowly. The cockroaches were alert to the new motion in the room.

"Mr. Osceola, why aren't you asleep?"

The Indian was baffled by the question.

"Skeezix. Uh . . . Uh . . ." He shrugged. "I guess I couldn't sleep."

"My mother would not appreciate you staring at her while she's sleeping. She's very afraid of Indians."

"I wasn't staring at your mother!"

"Don't lie to me, Mr. Osceola. I saw you."

"Shhhh. No reason to wake anybody else up."

"And why do you have to have the bottle all the time? The stuff smells so awful."

She went outside. It smelled like kerosene. The relief workers had been pouring it over the stagnant water to kill the mosquito larvae. There was a pile of mud-encrusted shovels on the courthouse steps. The muddy imprints of the gravedigger's hands were on the shovel handles. Skeezix relieved herself, looking at the moon.

She brushed a horsefly from her forehead and thought about Mr. Osceola. How could she explain the man? On the one hand, he was the only one who smiled at her and, along with Mr. Tillman, gave them hope they would find Sheila in the swamp. On the other hand, he was a drunk, he played a mean trick on Mr. Gantt, and she had caught him looking at her mother while she slept. Right now he might be looking at her in that steady, attentive way like a cat ready to pounce. She watched the clouds in their silent drift across the night sky, thinking about Raymond Osceola inside the courthouse, when suddenly she was startled by a noise coming from . . . where? She looked all around her. The noise was a loud "Kee! Kee! Kee!" and it was coming closer. Then she fixed her eyes on the mahogany tree across the street. The hurricane had torn the tree down the middle like a wishbone. Half of the tree lay in the stagnant water of the street with its leaves wilting on its dying branches. The other half stood erect, tottering, like some amputated giant. A massive area of its pink flesh was exposed at the break. The owl flew through the standing half of the tree, yelling "Kee! Kee! Kee!"

The bird had seen Sheila.

The owl flew to the courthouse and then turned south. Skeezix looked at the window to see if the bird had waked anyone else. She watched the owl disappear under the blueberry dome of sky. Skeezix had never had any doubt that Sheila was still alive out in the Everglades, but the owl's message was the reassurance she needed.

"Bye, owl," she said.

One of the owl's talons was injured. It hung down like a snake. It was the owl that had crashed through the window of the Riverside Lodge.

Skeezix kept the incident to herself. She did not so much as consider telling her father. She knew he had no patience with what he called "the child's fantasy world." He would put the incident in that category and immediately discount it. She wanted to tell her mother and at times came very close. But her mother had changed since Sheila disappeared and Skeezix sensed that her own confidence in the owl's message could alter the last real hope her mother had. Skeezix sensed the tenuous line keeping her mother sane and she knew enough not to disturb it.

Perhaps the most difficult of all was keeping the incident out of her letter to Thomas Edison. As she wrote the letter, the temptation to burst forth with the news was at times unbearable. As an inventor, she knew he understood magic and hope and the possibility of all things. Maybe she could include it. But on second thought, she considered that he was a scientist first and foremost. She had arrived at her conclusion that Sheila was still alive by unscientific means. There was more than a chance he would consider the owl incident childish. It was safer not to jeopardize the high esteem she knew the great inventor had for her sister and her. She had to give herself every advantage in coaxing him to Moore Haven.

Day after day went by with no luck, no sign of Sheila. One afternoon, E. A. "Buck" Tillman asked Skeezix what she would do if she were in Sheila's shoes. It was towards the end of the day and Skeezix could see the wiry black hairs on his chest and his legs where his uniform clung to his skin with perspiration.

"Now say you was in your life preserver," the Red Cross captain said.

"Were," Skeezix corrected. "Were in your life preserver."

"Skeezix," Lily said. "It's impolite to correct strangers."

Lily looked around the boat at the relief workers. They were all glaring at Skeezix. It was clear that they had had their fill of the genius little kid. Lily assumed they longed to be home in Fort Lauderdale where they could resume their lives as gas station attendants, tile-layers, ditch-diggers, bounty hunters, and hoboes.

Towards the end, only Tillman and Osceola had any tolerance left for the mandolin orchestra. The musicians all sensed it and Skeezix did too. Skeezix looked at the faces of the relief workers and could not judge whether or not they believed Sheila was still alive. She *could* tell, though they did not care.

Tillman started in again on Skeezix. "Say you *were* in your life preserver," he said. "And you floated into a pine tree like this one over here. Now here is the parenthetical situation I'd like to present to you: Would you, if you were Sheila, stay up in that tree and wait for help to arrive? Or would you get down and search for yourself?"

"It's been five days," Skeezix said. "No one's going to stay up in a tree for five days. That's the dumbest 'parenthetical' situation I've ever heard."

"Yeah, well . . ." Tillman said, cowering, "I think it would behoove her to stay up in that tree. You got some dangerous elements in this swamp. You got water moccasins, you got 'gators, you got razorback hogs."

Skeezix sighed. She could not resist saying the last line of his worn-out sermon with him: "The sawgrass itself'll cut you like a knife if you rub it the wrong way."

As Tillman spoke to Skeezix, his eyes shifted between Lily and Kirk. He tried to judge by the expressions on their faces if he, by his elevated diction, had bamboozled them into thinking he had a Bachelor of Arts degree from a fancy New England school.

"Is your sister built about like you?" Tillman asked.

"She's skinnier. Why?"

"Because if she was built like you, she could live a couple of weeks on her extra baggage there."

"Ha-ha," Skeezix said. "Very funny. I'm roaring with laughter. The tears are streaming down my face. I'm splitting my side. That was so funny, I'm going to die. Look at this. I'm falling down, I'm laughing so hard . . . ."

Tillman turned grim. "You know what your problem is, Skeezix? You can't take a joke. Everyone's so dad-blamed serious on this boat. Can't you see? You gotta have a little levity in a situation like this."

"A little levity is one thing," Broadus Gantt said. "A quart of gin a day is another."

For this remark, Raymond Osceola belched in Gantt's face. It was a languorous, loving, and booze-rich belch with Osceola's cider-colored face only inches from Gantt's.

H. Russell Truitt, first chair second mandolinist, sat near the bow of the boat with his hands folded across his lap. He watched the scene in horror. His jaw tightened and he shook his head in disdain. He said, "How much longer will we be forced to endure this barbaric behavior?"

"You wanna know how much longer, Professor?" one of the relief workers said. He was standing in the boat now with a clenched fist. "For as long as we goddam say!"

"SIT DOWN!" Kirk yelled. "And you watch your mouth in front of my daughter, mister. What is your name?"

"I don't have to tell him nothin'."

"What's your name, tough man?"

"Lenny."

106

"Lenny. Don't you ever threaten one of my musicians in front of me. Do you understand that?"

Lenny was a small man, not yet in his twenties, with a blond crewcut that shone like gold under the sun. He smoked Chesterfield cigarettes and flung the butts as far as he could into the Everglades. He had become chummy with Valentine T. Peck and they often shared their bottles. But Peck was the only one he liked; he thought the rest had a haughty attitude. Lenny didn't think the musicians had the right to look down on the relief workers just because they kept their music in black concert folders and their instruments in nickel-plated cases. Lenny happened to be a musician of some standing himself. He was a self-taught harmonica player. He felt he could do an imitation of a train pulling into the station and then pulling out again as well as anybody in the state of Florida. He had a wife and baby in Fort Lauderdale where he was employed as a custodian for one of the grammar schools. Lenny finally sat down on Kirk's insistence and took a sip from his bottle of gin. He grumbled, "She's dead, anyway."

"What?" Kirk demanded.

"Your daughter. She's dead. There, I said it."

"What do you mean?"

"Wake up, mister! We've been out here a *week*. There's nothin' left in this swamp but buzzards and snakes."

That afternoon wore on with the relief workers and the mandolin orchestra nearly coming to blows on several more occasions. For long, silent stretches of time, they did nothing but stare at solitary clouds in the sky, praying they would move in front of the sun and give them relief from the heat. In the meantime, Tillman's dogs brought junk out of the swamp and he rewarded them with candy.

Skeezix watched her father scowl at the dogs whenever they came dripping into the boat. He'd kick them if they got near.

Rex, the English setter, returned once with a black ibis. The bird hung limply from the dog's jaws and Skeezix looked at its dead eyes.

"Now look at that bird," Tillman said. "Not a toothmark on it. That is the sign of a master retriever. These birds are good roasted, did you know that?"

Her father interrupted him. All afternoon, he interrupted him in as rude a way as she had ever seen. When the Red Cross captain started talking about his dogs or the Florida frontier, her father started screaming into the swamp for Sheila. Or he would say, "Haven't we already covered this area, Tillman?"

How many times had she heard that?

After a while, the Everglades started looking the same. One cypress root, one palmetto tree, one wild orchid, one resurrection fern, one osprey nest began to look like any other. Skeezix imagined the sawgrass of the Everglades as one endless coat of fur, dotted here and there with tufts of greenery. It was like burrs on a cat's hide. And each time the dogs would go into one of those tufts of greenery, they would come out with anything but Sheila.

It was Saturday, September 24, one week after Sheila had disappeared. At seven P.M. Tillman guided the boat into the courthouse after another fruitless day. The dogs bounded out before the boat stopped. They raced up the courthouse steps, their wet paws slipping on the smooth marble. Gantt followed, clutching his Egyptian banjo. Skeezix was next. She paused on the second step to pinch her drawers from her bottom. The rest of the passengers disembarked while mockingbirds flitted above them. The mockingbirds were in royal palm trees whose broad, cementlike trunks were bent by the hurricane.

Kirk walked over and put his arm around his wife. Winthrop Ethridge DeQuesne was behind them. He stopped and gawked. It was the first display of affection he had seen in the three months they had been on tour. DuQuesne was on his way to check on his harp guitar. It was in its special case in a closet in the courthouse with the rest of the mandolins. The stern, bearded musician had a premonition that his instrument was next in line for one of the relief worker's pranks.

108

"Lily," Kirk said in a low voice that Skeezix couldn't hear. "our only hope, I think, is that she drifted in with some Seminoles. Osceola says there's a lot of them out there. They go out in their canoes and hunt frogs and turtles. They might run into her."

"Kirk, we can't give up on her."

"I know we can't."

The relief workers stopped and looked at Kirk and Lily too. They had never seen them embrace before either. One of the relief workers said that Kirk shouldn't kiss her with that sore on his lip and another one said he hoped he didn't have a sore where it counted. The relief workers made their sexual comments without laughter. They swigged their gin. When Kirk and Lily got to the top of the stairs, Rex, the English setter, was leaping at the door.

"These are the most worthless dogs I've ever seen," he said. Then he turned around because Skeezix was yelling at him.

"He's here! He's here!"

Silas "Buster" Nobles edged a rowboat next to Tillman's *Corona* and Ford helped Edison out. The great inventor's white linen suit was wrinkled from sleeping in it and his shirt was stained with milk. He had a big smile for Skeezix that exposed all of his dentures.

"No luck, sweetie?" he asked.

"No, Mr. Edison."

"Don't worry, we'll find her."

Lily led the mandolin orchestra down the steps to welcome Mr. Edison. She wore a pale blue cotton dress stained on the back and under the arms with perspiration and all around the hem with swamp water. The dress was marked on the lap and on the bosom with muddy paw prints from Tillman's dogs. Her face was red and dried out from the sun and her nose was flaking. Her hair flopped about in greasy strands from days without washing.

"We must look like a terrible mess to you," Lily smiled, taking the inventor's hand.

"The last time I saw you, young lady, you were dressed up like an Indian," Edison said. "This is quite an improvement!"

Al the Pinkerton guard scanned the faces of the relief workers. He felt the weight of his service revolver in the holster beneath his armpit. His eyes stopped on Raymond Osceola. He looked at the Indian's strip shirt and the pointed cowboy boots. Al had seen a Seminole like him put his head between the jaws of an alligator at a tourist show in Fort Myers. So this is our National Guard, he thought.

The relief workers stuffed their gin bottles into their front trouser pockets, making a conspicuous bulge. They feared Al might be a federal agent. They edged down the steps of the courthouse to get a closer look at the great inventor.

"Is that really him?"

"What the hell is he doing here?"

Lenny took a drag on his Chesterfield. "God, he is an *old* fart."

That Edison seemed to know the genius little kid and had spoken to her first when he got off the boat did not escape the relief workers' attention. They also noted the live goat on Edison's boat and wanted to know what that was doing there.

Ford and Edison went through and shook each mandolinist's hand. Ford had something to say to Lily. He had enjoyed her singing and xylophone playing very much that night at Edison's. He had been following the progress of the J.C. Deagan Musical Instrument Manufacturing Company in Chicago and believed they were elevating the status of the lowly xylophone to an instrument of concert distinction. He also said that Edison had some interesting ideas in locating Sheila and that she should be encouraged. When Ford got to Kirk, he simply shook his hand and said, "How do you do." The automobile manufacturer was unnerved by the orchestra leader. Ford knew of Kirk's unusual and dogmatic musical principles. Ford thought he might be some sort of genius. The real McCoy.

Edison, however, was unnerved by no one. He had little interest in Kirk's work. He was interested in Kirk as a father,

110

as the man who had raised these remarkable children. He treated Kirk openly and genially. He put his arm around Kirk as they walked up the courthouse steps, pressing his ancient fingernails into Kirk's shoulder with affection. "That daughter of yours," Edison said, "she is some sort of a brain."

"Did she write you a letter or something?" asked Kirk.

They dined that night on chlorinated water and canned Vienna sausages. The meal was compliments of the relief train from Sebring. The sausages were flesh-colored tubes one inch in length and packed six to a can in salty water. Edison wouldn't eat them. He drank his goat's milk and let Skeezix have some too. A child should have her extra calcium, he said. The goat was tied out front to a palmetto trunk. Flies buzzed around its swollen udder. Skeezix had learned the goat's name, Priscilla. High in the twilit sky, several buzzards circled above the goat, looking for a meal before retiring for the evening.

They ate supper at one long table at the south end of the courthouse. There were twenty-five people at the table: thirteen musicians including Gantt, eight relief workers, and four guests. Skeezix sat on the same side of the table as Edison, two down from him. She sat silent throughout the meal, chewing her sausage and staring at him. She drank the goat's milk. It was warm. But it was rich and delicious. She had had nothing to drink for the past week but chlorinated water and Coca-Cola. She heard Priscilla bleating outside the door.

Moths buzzed around the kerosene lamps. Cockroaches crawled around their shoes. Flies gathered around the rims of the sausage cans. A man she didn't know, Mr. Ford, kept brushing the flies away. He seemed to be the only one uncomfortable in the filth. Skeezix felt a tap on her shoulder. Her mother whispered that it was impolite to stare.

E.A. "Buck" Tillman, as Red Cross captain, filled Edison in on the rescue effort to date, counting on Ford to tell him when Edison had not heard. Tillman used his most professional tone when speaking to Edison and it made her father cringe. Her father added things that Tillman left out as did Broadus Gantt.

111

Edison wanted to know from Gantt the exact direction Sheila floated when she fell out of his boat. Edison produced a battered Rand McNally map of the state of Florida to get his bearings.

"So you've been using hunting dogs," chuckled the inventor. Edison looked at Skeezix and winked. He had her neatly written letter folded up in the inside pocket of his coat.

When they finished supper, Edison requested music. Since his instrument was closest to him, Broadus Gantt took out his Egyptian banjo and performed "Humoresque" by Dvorak. Skeezix could tell he was nervous in front of Edison. She did not know that Edison could barely hear it anyway.

Next came a hastily assembled quintet with Clancy on mandobass, DuQuesne on harp guitar, Pickering on mandocello, Xavier Tesch on second mandolin and Lichtenfels on first. Valentine T. Peck, though not drinking in front of Edison, was still too drunk from the afternoon to play. The quintet played "Under the Double Eagle" because they knew Edison loved marches followed by "The Minstrel Man" by William C. Stahl. The latter featured a mandola countermelody of familiar tunes, "Listen to the Mockingbird" in the B section and "Dixie" in the Trio. Since there was no lady to play the mandola part, H. H. Pickering played it on his mandocello. Mandolin music written in universal notation made transposition unnecessary. Edison tapped his toe to the music.

H. H. Pickering popped an A string in tuning so that he was playing half-sound at the top. Eugene Gaylord Smith would roll over in his grave, Skeezix thought. The sub-bass strings of the harp guitar were wretchedly out of tune with the mandobass, Lichtenfels couldn't find his high frets, the tremelos were uneven, the unison passages were not together, and there was not one shade of a dynamic. The men's fingers were clumsy from over a week without practice.

Skeezix watched her father for his reaction. She expected to see him wincing, cringing, and shaking his head in disgust. She expected to see him stop the horrible performance, make

112

them tune up and play right. And then at the end, to make them play an Indian jazz number to keep that in the forefront of the public's mind.

But her father wasn't even listening. He was chewing sausages and looking at Edison's map of Florida. That Sheila's disappearance could change her father so drastically was strange to Skeezix. It was not right or wrong. It was strange. Tomorrow would be different though and things would be back to normal because Edison was here and they would find Sheila.

After the mandolins were finished, Ford begged Lily to sing one number. She obliged and stood behind the chair in which she had been eating. With her fingers clenched tightly around the top edge, she sang "Summer's Idyle" by Rothleder with Broadus Gantt doing the accompaniment honors on his Egyptian banjo. Outside, Tillman's dogs howled.

The relief workers drank the chlorinated water throughout the evening. Intimidated by the famous inventor and his crew, they did not get out their gin. They were quiet and controlled their belching. They sat erect in their chairs and acted as if they were members of a well-drilled and disciplined rescue team. When Broadus Gantt got out his gold banjo, they were forced by the circumstances to listen. They begrudgingly admitted that he was a fine classical banjo player and were perhaps contrite for vandalizing his instrument. When Lily sang, the relief workers acted as though they preferred a trained soprano's rendition of "Summer's Idyle" to Lenny doing his train impression on the harmonica.

"Let's everyone get a good night's sleep," Edison said. "And we'll get a fresh start in the morning."

Edison slept on a Red Cross cot like everyone else. He woke up in the middle of the night to find Skeezix watching him. The next morning he confided to Ford that he could no longer look at those big, hopeful eyes.

"People have made a Jesus Christ out of me, Henry," he said. "They think I don't go to the bathroom. They think my mouth doesn't smell in the morning. If that girl is dead out there, I can't bring her back to life. Shit, Henry, there's just as good a chance we find her buzzard-pecked bones as we find her alive. Then who's going to tell Skeezix? Will you?"

11

On Sunday mornings before church, her mother placed them next to the dining room table.

"Stand still!" she ordered.

Then, in a flour-coated apron, she prowled around them as if they were the enemy, studying their faces from every angle of light. When she detected a flaw, she wetted a finger with her tongue and began the erasure, carefully dabbing at a trace of milk on the corner of a lip or a donut crumb on a chin. Sheila remembered the smell of her mother's saliva. It was a strong smell and not a good smell from a beautiful lady. Then her mother used her little finger to extract the last specks of sleep from their fluttering eyelashes.

When their faces were spotless, she did the final inspection on their hair. She used the same saliva-coated finger to tame unruly strands. If this did not work, her mother clenched her teeth and yanked the obstinate hair from its scalp with her hand, showing the same frightful indelicacy she used to pluck a chicken feather. When they howled, she said "Sorry," preoccupied. From their hair, she moved to their ears, checking for wax. She pulled up on their earlobes to check, not for dirt, but for soap residue. Next, she checked their necks, particularly the hollow right below their Adam's apples where the scapula and sternum met. That spot was an insidious hiding place for dirt, her mother said.

She checked their hands on both sides and their fingernails for uneven clippings. She checked their dresses for hanging threads and wrinkles and lint. She checked the bows on their dresses and on their shoes and in their hair for imperfect loops. She checked their charm bracelets for gaps, and their stockings for runs and equal lengths on each leg. It was not unusual for her mother, if she was not satisfied, to yank their dresses off and retire to the ironing board, leaving them shivering in their underdrawers to gaze at swirling clouds of dust in shafts of sunlight coming through the dining room window.

Perhaps her mother was most meticulous about their shoes. She would not tolerate smudges, uneven polishing, tilted bows, uneven shoestring lengths, or "shoddy buckling" as she called it. If Skeezix buckled on the third hole of the strap, then *she* must also. Sometimes her mother bent over her shoes to correct the buckling and Sheila would see the top of her head. She admonished them in muttered snaps, "Why didn't you check this earlier?" Her mother's face was red like a tomato from leaning over.

Even old shoes had to be maintained properly. They spent many a Saturday night with crumpled rags in their hands, listening to the radio and applying an even coat of polish to the edges of the soles of their old misses' strap sandals from Sears. Her mother, by God, would get her $2.95's worth out of any pair of shoes and Sheila thought of this, first thing, when she fell out of Broadus Gantt's boat. Another time Skeezix and she had fallen into the creek by their house and she came home holding the shoes in her hands, waving them in the summer wind to dry them. Her mother said the shoes were ruined. No amount of washing and drying would take the crick-water smell out of them. Her mother threw both pairs of shoes on the trash pile in front of their house along with the egg shells, the evergreen trimmings, and the oil cans.

These shoes are ruined, Sheila thought, feeling her toes in

the warm water. She reached again for the puppy. He kept drifting farther away. When she turned around, Skeezix and Mr. Gantt were standing up in the boat. They shouldn't be standing, she thought. They could tip the boat over and that would be the end of his banjo. Dim light covered the spilled waters of Lake Okeechobee. It was a fraudulent sunrise. Sheila saw that Skeezix's face was red. Her mouth was open too and she saw the crinkled surfaces of her back molars. Skeezix looked like she was doing her silly imitation of a lion. She was screaming at her. What was she screaming?

"SHEEEEE-LAAAAA!"

Sheila frowned at her sister and concentrated on her lips. Sheila silently moved her lips to Skeezix's speech. She's saying my name, she thought. Then the nightmare rushed in. Her heart began to pound up in her ears. The nightmare was so cruel and so utterly hopeless that, even as she drifted away from the boat, she knew it was a nightmare and she would soon wake in a warm bed in North Dakota with her head on a good feather pillow and a Teddy Bear named Fluffer by her side and her mandolin snapped safely in its case under the springs. She paddled to the boat, her arms and legs making white foam in the water, but it was too late. A song went through her head.

The song was "Joy Boy" by A. J. Weidt. The part that kept going through her head was the A section. The mandocellos had a grace note passage in the A section that she had always loved. Sometimes she would steal a glance at Eugene Gaylord Smith and watch his eyebrows leap with the grace note. His eyebrows gave the note a joyful push. Mr. Edison had loved "Joy Boy." She remembered him bobbing his head to the music in Fort Myers.

She floated away. The eye of the hurricane passed and the wind started to blow again. At first, she imagined the wind as an enraged bull whose magnificent face towered over the Everglades. All of the bull's fury, power, and hard muscle came funneling through two huge nostrils in the sky. The snorts from the bull rippled the water and knocked over the trees. She drifted farther from Moore Haven. The hurricane stopped being a bull. The hurricane became so completely odd and startling that she could no longer associate it with anything in life. It was a whistle and her head might be coming off. She grabbed her life raft and said, "Yea though I . . . Yea though I . . . Dickens! No God is ever going to hear *this*!"

The rain drilled into her hat. It resonated her whole skull like a drum and made her dizzy. The rain assaulted the exposed parts of her cheeks, leaving them numb. Several times she tried to protect her cheeks with her hands but she felt herself slipping from the inner tube when she did this so she had to grab back on again. "Joy Boy" bounced along in the back of her brain. It was a happy little fox-trot.

She was getting hit by things besides rain. The wind brought in sticks, boards, books, utensils, rodents, and birds. The debris thumped off her inner tube and her hat and went back into the water. She tried to change directions by pedaling the water beneath her inner tube. She kept getting hit no matter what direction she turned. Then with a sudden ineffable blast, the wind drove a piece of metal clean through her cheek. The piece of metal stuck in her tongue then dropped into the hollow below her bottom teeth. The hollow began to fill with blood.

Now she screamed but the whistle of the hurricane was louder still. "Joy Boy" wasn't in her head anymore. Her neck started to tingle. She put her hand on her cheek and felt the hole. With the tip of her tongue, she tried to feel what the metal was in her mouth. It was a dull piece of metal but mostly she tasted blood.

Uh-oh. I think I have wet my pants.

The piece of metal was a coin. It was a buffalo nickel, 1918D. She fished it out of her mouth with her finger the next morning and held it under the sun. The coin was streaked with clotted blood. Her tongue was swollen up like a baseball. Also, there was a hanging piece of flesh from the entrance wound in her cheek. It was like a piece of gristle in a steak and she could not resist touching it and pulling on it to see how far it would stretch.

Sheila ended up in an osprey's nest at the top of a cypress tree. Through the hurricane, she had been blown from one tree to the next. Each time, she climbed up the branches as the flood waters rose. Finally, though she was hugging the trunk, the wind pried her loose and deposited her back in the water. For hours, she kept up the routine until finally she reached a pile of broken branches. In her confusion, she thought at first it was a beaver dam. It was not until the storm was finally over that she realized she was up high in a bird's nest. She woke to find herself lying on eggs.

After she retrieved the coin from her mouth, she untied the inner tube. She took off her rain coat and hat. Her pajamas were soaked. She didn't have anything to change into, so these would have to be dried. She looked all around her. There was not a trace of civilization for as far as she could see. Still, a girl could not be too careful in exposing her naked posterior. She peeled off her pajamas and hung them over the osprey nest.

She didn't have any clothes on and she was embarrassed. Even though no one could see her, she was still embarrassed. Some of the most real dreams she had in the night were about this.

She looked below her. The flood waters had receded and there were alligators on the high ground. They looked like punctuation marks from up here. In the nest, one of the eggs rolled over on its own accord. The egg was smaller and a different color from the other ones. Where's your mommy and daddy? She looked to the sky and saw buzzards everywhere. Your mommy and daddy were probably killed in the hurricane you poor little fellas.

She stood on the broken branches in the nest and reveled in the gentle wind. It blew her hair dry and took the prune wrinkles from her hands and feet. It felt so wonderful to be dry! She wished she had a mirror to look at her wound though. Her mouth felt so funny. The nearest it had ever felt like this was the time she, on a dare, put fifteen sticks of Wrigley's Double Mint chewing gum in her mouth. She remembered the advertisement from her mother's *Better Homes and Gardens:*

There was a crooked man
And he went a crooked mile —
He found a crooked dollar
Against a crooked stile;
He straightway bought a package
Of Double Mint gum —
And lo and behold
It straightened him some!

Sheila hoped the swelling in her tongue would go down. If it didn't, she might require hospitalization. The hole in her cheek might need stitches also. The problem was there was no hospital in Moore Haven she didn't think. Where could they take her?

She had been in the hospital two years ago during Christmas vacation. She had had pleurisy and had to be in an oxygen tent.

Everybody in her family thought she was weak, especially Grandmother Howser. She came over for dinner one Sunday wearing a blue silk dress with little pears on it. She always had a wad of tissue stuffed down into her bosom, this great bosom that had nurtured legendary people. Her grandmother also had a beard that Sheila hoped she would never inherit. Grandmother Howser had her plate stacked up with pot roast, applesauce, string beans, dinner rolls, and a square of strawberry jello with baby marshmallows arranged neatly across the surface. She reached her blue-veined hand into a giant serving bowl in the center of the dining room table and withdrew a steaming ear of sweet corn.

Sheila had a problem. She strained when she ate; she breathed loudly through her nostrils when she chewed. On that day, Grandmother Howser peppered her corn and the dinner table grew silent. Sheila knew they were listening to her breathe. It was a sign of her weakness; Skeezix didn't do it. Her father said it didn't seem right that it should be that much work to eat. Grandmother Howser said Sheila was simply not a born masticator. It was something she was going to have to learn.

"I masticate fine!" Sheila had said in a rare moment of rebellion. "Leave me alone."

Later that night, she overheard her mother and grandmother whispering about her future in childbearing. Unless she gets stronger, they agreed, she'll never be able to endure it.

Skeezix was on their side too. She didn't like the way her sister breathed when she ate either. *Why do these people sit there and worry about me all the time?* During the 11:30 recess at Thomas Jefferson Elementary, Skeezix would stand at home plate with her arms folded and watch her run the bases. When she came in to score, Skeezix would study her like she was her own name in the newspaper. If she was a little bit flushed or breathing too hard, Skeezix would make her sit down in front of everybody with her back on the fence that separated the playground from the wheatfield. And remember Camp Tu-Ende-Wei? If she caught a crayfish in the creek, Skeezix would not let her take it off the line. The big ones pinched hard enough to draw blood and she feared for her sister fainting. But there was nothing like the hospital. How could she forget the solemn look on Skeezix's face through the plastic shield of her oxygen tent? Skeezix had looked up *pleurisy* in the encyclopedia and found out it could be fatal, which meant she could die. Skeezix became this religious person for a while with this zany air of blessed assurance. When Sheila came home from the hospital, she found her mandolin restrung, tuned, and polished. Skeezix waited on her hand and foot for a week afterwards, doing her chores for her, making her feel like a queen. Skeezix even set her second mandolin parts out on the bedspread so she wouldn't have to get out of bed to practice.

I am not an invalid, Sheila thought. I am all right. Not

everyone could have made it through this hurricane. She put her hand on her cheek. She pulled the little tendon coming out of the hole. It was drying up and felt like a piece of leather. She needed Mercurochrome and possibly stitches she thought. If she was in North Dakota, Dr. McIntosh would treat her wound and give her a lollipop wrapped in cellophane afterwards for being a brave little girl. But what would Dr. McIntosh do about her tongue? How could he treat that big thing in her mouth? Her tongue was so swelled up she could hardly talk to herself anymore.

Sheila looked at the buzzards in the sky. They were everywhere. She feared nodding off in the daytime because of them. They might think she was dead and descend on her. She wondered if they could, as they made circles in the sky, see her chest rising and falling as she slept. She began to name the buzzards after people in the mandolin orchestra. Each bird had a characteristic that distinguished it from the others. One was big, one was small, one was medium, one had a black head, one had a red head, one had ruffled tail feathers, one had a certain feather missing, one landed smoothly, one landed roughly—she could tell them all. They were cannibals though. That was one thing. They would eat each other. She watched from the osprey nest as they floated down to perch on their own dead. The buzzards pecked away through the black feathers of their own kind in the same methodical manner they used on any dead thing. Sheila had one good thing to say about the buzzards: They waited until something was completely dead before they converged on it. If there was the slightest flutter in a living body, the buzzards waited patiently in the sky until the twitching stopped.

She found a drinking hole. It was a bubbling, underground spring that flushed out the muddy and contaminated flood water. The drinking hole was marked off by two fallen cypress logs whose rotting crevices were loaded with resurrection fern. She drank the water and also used the area as a lavatory facility. She would not tolerate the odor of urine in her nest.

Animals found the drinking hole too. She met raccoons, otters, deer, bobcats, and even a black bear once. The animals were injured and weary from the hurricane and she did not fear them. She usually waited until they left before she used the lavatory facilities. It didn't seem right that they watch her as she eliminated even though they were animals and she knew it didn't mean anything to them.

On the second day, she tripped over a muddy shoe on her way back to the nest. She found human debris in the swamp all the time, washed out by the hurricane from the homes of the Moore Haven residents. So the shoe was not an unusual find. But this shoe was unnaturally heavy and seemed to be connected to something else. She nudged it with her foot.

"What is this? A leg?"

She followed the leg with her eyes up to a torso and a chest and a neck and finally a head partially hidden by a clump of saw palmetto. The head was moving. It was moving with tiny, gray worms. "Joy Boy," with full mandolin orchestra, began to pound in her head. She vomited helplessly on her already-stained pajamas. She started to fall over and caught herself on a cypress branch.

"Oh my God. A body!"

She knew who it was. She knew by the dress. It was the woman dancer, the one who made up the two-step to "Big Chief Battle-Ax." Skeezix and she had seen her leave the courthouse on Friday night in a Packard. The thin man in the tuxedo was at the wheel. Now she was dead. She guessed the buzzards hadn't found her yet because of the saw palmetto.

What to do? The body was fifty feet from the tree with the osprey nest. If the idea of that woman being eaten by worms down there didn't drive her out, the odor surely would. But could she afford to leave the osprey nest? It was unlikely she would find another location with such a perfect view to spot the rescue boat. It was unlikely she would find another location with a fresh drinking supply.

She had one alternative. She peeled off her pajamas once

123

again and hung them over a bottom branch of the cypress tree. Naked, she gathered up armloads of mud and began to pile them over the woman's body. Sheila's bare stomach was as hard as a kettle and she fought with all her might to stifle the heaves. She put the mud first on the woman's head because that was the most nauseating. Maybe the rest of the body would be easier after the head was covered up. Sheila had never buried anything before with the exception of two baby rabbits in North Dakota. Skeezix and she, in dresses with sashes, had fashioned tiny coffins out of tin foil. They dug the rabbits up a week later to see what they looked like.

It took the entire afternoon to cover the woman with mud. When she thought she was finished, she saw a finger or a toe protruding from the mound. She piled on more mud.

Flies buzzed around the woman's body in a frenzy. Sheila could not fool them. They knew there was a body under the mud. Their iridescent shells gleamed in the sunlight.

Animals came to the drinking hole and watched her. An otter came. Two raccoons came. A bobcat came and watched her from behind ferns moving with dragonflies. She paused and watched them back. She wondered if these animals had ever seen a human being before. She wiped her brow with a tiny segment of her right wrist that was not covered with mud. It was hard work.

The next day she put her raincoat on a cypress pole and stuck it into the nest. It was for the rescue boat that hadn't come yet.

One of the eggs hatched the next day. It was the egg that was slightly smaller and a different color than the other ones. The baby bird's mouth was open so wide. It made her laugh. How could anything open its mouth that wide? It was all throat. She named the bird Cuckoo because it reminded her of the bird that came out of her Grandmother Howser's cuckoo clock, the one across from her china cabinet in the dining room.

Sheila tried to eat. The buttermints her mother packed had dissolved in the hurricane but the cheese was still good. She found that by rubbing the cheese between her thumb and fingers and making it into little grains she could get it down her throat past her swollen tongue.

By the fourth day the tendon hanging out of her cheek had dried up and turned brown. It finally fell off with a little help from her thumb. Cuckoo's mother returned. At least she thought. It was a bird she had never seen before and it flew right to the nest. Before it landed, however, Sheila saw that it couldn't be the bird's mother. It was a barn owl. It was making a lot of noise. It turned around and flew away.

"Why haven't they found us yet?"

Sheila took her raincoat off the pole and put it on over her pajamas.

"We're dying up here, Cuckoo."

She put the bird in the right pocket of her raincoat and climbed down the tree. She looked up to the buzzards one final time, said, "I'm not your food!" and started walking back to Moore Haven. She felt in her left pocket for the coin that had gone through her mouth. She wanted to make sure she had it to show Skeezix when she got back. Skeezix wouldn't believe it!

12

heila was Lewis and her baby bird was Clark. They were on their way to the Pacific Northwest with their Indian guide, Sacajawea. The towering cloud formations above the sawgrass were the Rocky Mountains. The tiny deer splashing through the swamp water were bighorn sheep. The sabal palm trees were the totem poles of the dangerous Blackfoot Indians. The roots of the cypress tree were beaver traps. The giant webs of the golden silk spiders were fishing nets for coho salmon. The alligators were lurking Sioux braves.

Sheila had a cypress stick that was six feet high. It was her rifle. She aimed it at the alligators and fired. Pow! Pow! Pow! If she stamped her foot in the water at the same time she fired the gun, the alligators would splash away and disappear. Pow! Pow! Pow!

"Good shot, Lewis," Sacajawea said.

"Thank you, Sacajawea," Lewis said. "The only good Sioux is a dead Sioux."

"Watch out! A grizzly!"

"Where?"

"Over there!"

Pow! Pow! Pow!

"Thank you, Lewis," Sacajawea said. "You saved my life."

"That's one grizzly bear that's not going to bother anybody again," Lewis said.

"Look at Clark," Sacajawea said. "He's heap hungry."

"Clark is *always* hungry," Lewis sighed.

Sacajawea bent down and caught a tadpole with her fingers. She gave it to Lewis who in turn fed it to Clark. Lewis looked down into the pocket of his buckskin coat and talked to his companion. "Are those cohos good, Mr. Clark? They are, are they? Then why, no matter how many times we feed you, you never seem to be full?"

The great explorer and his band trudged through the Marias Pass of the Rocky Mountains, pausing to take potshots at scalp-hunting savages, crazed grizzly bears, bloodthirsty mountain lions, and an occasional deranged moose. After a particularly close call, Lewis took the rifle off his shoulder and blew across the tip of the hot barrel.

"How much farther do you think it is to Oregon, Sacajawea?"

"When the great eagle in the sky flies to the end of the double rainbow over the teepee of the great Sitting Bull we will be in the fertile land of our dreams."

"Why don't you just shut up, Sacajawea!" Lewis said finally. "You don't know where we are anymore than I do!"

Sheila grew tired of the game. It was hard to imagine the little bird in the pocket of her raincoat as a major American explorer. And there wasn't really a Sacajawea. She made her up. She was really all by herself.

Sheila put her hand under her pajamas. She touched the flat space at the base of her spine above her posterior. It was wet with perspiration. She had never perspired there before. She didn't think a person was capable of perspiring there.

And her pajamas! This was the *fifth day in a row* they had been next to her skin—and not just at night. All day long. P.U. Was this really Sheila Quintaine, impeccably dressed member of the amazing mandolin twins? It did not seem possible that she could stink like this. The only time she had come close to smelling like this was when she wore a tree costume in the third grade play. If she did not make it to Moore Haven soon, she would have to find a way to wash these pajamas. Perhaps she would run across a box of Ivory flakes washed up by the hurricane.

She wore her raincoat and rainhat, even in the heat. She kept the collar of her raincoat turned up over the back of her neck. She had to cover every bit of exposed skin because of the mosquitoes and the horseflies. She hated the horseflies especially. They were coarse and hideous and dim-witted like the trolls in the *Three Billy Goats Gruff*. Plus when they bit, it really hurt! Horseflies also had an irritating lack of fear for her, the superior human being. Sometimes, when she saw one coming, she took her Lewis and Clark musket and swung at it. She never once struck one. The swinging made her tired. It made her perspire more too.

Her tongue was a little better. It was very sore and stiff, but the swelling had gone down. She could now push it outside her mouth and taste her salty moustache. She resisted the temptation to put her finger on the place where the coin had imbedded itself in her tongue. That would be putting more germs in an already-unclean place.

In the late afternoon, they came upon a still pool of water. Sheila took Cuckoo out of her pocket.

"Look at that, Cuckoo," she said. "It's a perfect reflection of the sky. I know. You're hungry."

Sheila bent down and snatched a tadpole out of the water on the first try. It was a trick she learned from Sacajawea, Indian guide. She popped the tadpole down the bird's gullet.

"You hear my stomach growling, Cuckoo? I'm hungry too. You know what? I don't think you're an eagle or a hawk. I think you really are a cuckoo."

A mockingbird flew across the water, chirruping as it went. Sheila saw four white stripes against its gray back. The long tail bobbed as it flew. It was like a lever controlling the singing. The mockingbird landed in a scrub pine on the other side of the pond. The tree had tiny pinecones, miniatures of the ones she knew in North Dakota.

Closer, a turtle basked in the sun on a cypress log. The top of its shell was dry and gray. It was like a helmet. The turtle's neck was black with bright yellow stripes. Sheila poked her Lewis and Clark musket in its vicinity and the turtle fell into the water like a dropped plate. She walked over to the log and found five eggs in a crevice. She remembered breakfast at Thomas Edison's home in Fort Myers less than a week ago. When she had found out the little eggs on her plate were turtle eggs, she had looked across the dining room table at Skeezix and made a face. Edison's chef had prepared them well. They were attractive on the plate. They were cooked sunny-side up, sprinkled with pepper and topped with a parsley sprig. The turtle eggs looked delicious next to the bacon and grits and toast. Still, neither Skeezix nor she touched them. They did not so much as poke the whites of the eggs with their forks. They would contaminate the tines with turtle juice and they would not be able to eat the rest of the breakfast.

Now Sheila looked at the turtle eggs in the crevice of the log. Except for a few grains of cheese, she had not eaten for five days. She needed nourishment. She knew that. How badly she needed nourishment was the question. She knew from her mother that raw eggs wouldn't hurt you. A person just didn't eat raw eggs was all, her mother said. That was the reason you didn't eat cookie dough. The eggs in there hadn't been cooked.

Sheila bent down and picked up one of the eggs. She held it between her thumb and first finger and looked at it.

"I need to pretend this is my favorite food," she said.

She broke the shell in her fingers and poured the warm egg down her throat. But she was not eating raw turtle eggs. She was not lost and alone in the Everglades. She was not wearing pajamas in the daytime. She did not smell. She did not have a hole in her cheek and a fat tongue. She had not recently buried a woman whose head was crawling with worms.

These turtle eggs were really coconut macaroons fresh out

129

of the oven. She was in her mother's kitchen in North Dakota. She was standing on a rag rug by the sink and staring out the window. Oh, look! There's King chasing a rabbit in the garden. And listen! Daddy's composing another Indian rag in the living room. She bit down on her macaroon and the odor of toasted coconut and sugar filled her nostrils.

"How about a nice glass of cold milk with that macaroon?" her mother asked.

"Thank you, Mommy."

There was a tin can on the kitchen counter with its lid off. It was Dromedary coconut flakes. There was a little camel painted on the can. She looked and looked and looked at the camel until every one of the turtle eggs was in her stomach.

"OH DADDY, WHERE ARE YOU?"

The swamp was noisy at night and she could not hear herself crying. Amid the uproar there was a loud croaking that she thought must be some giant frog. It was a bass sound and it made her think of F. W. Clancy on his Gibson Style J. There were also some frightening sounds that punctuated the racket: growls, hisses, and hoots. She could not have made a worse mistake than leaving the nest. She did not know how to get back to it now. Her heart started to pound. It was her father's heart pounding in her. She needed his strength and it was there.

There was one sound that was close. It was a hissing sound. It was like a machine. It was like the sound the giant presses made at the Chinese laundry. She moved away from the sound. Her feet stirred the warm waters of the Everglades. She was under the stars.

Her father. He was stronger on this tour than he had ever been. She loved him for that. She loved him the most when he stood firm. That was her father at his best. When he stood firm. She loved to think of him challenging the local musicians, the town wonderboys of fretted instruments. She thought of her father with Mr. Gantt. She thought of her father with the ukulele wizard in Georgia.

There was another one too. It was at the beginning of the tour, in July, and it was one of the best. They were in Cedar Rapids, Iowa. They were playing for an American Legion dance. It was for World War I veterans. It was mostly farmers. Some of them wore doughboy helmets with their overalls. The dance took place in a barn at the edge of town. The lighting was poor and they could hardly see their music. Her mother brushed straw from the bars of her xylophone. They could hear pigs squealing outside. They had to share the stage with the Linn County Farm Bureau's Chorus. The chorus was sixty members strong and directed by the wife of the local mortician. The members of the chorus were mostly farmers in overalls with scrubbed beet-red faces. They sang light classics like "The Happy Wanderer" and popular music like "Oh How I Hate to Get Up in the Morning." They also sang "De Ole Ark Am A-Moverin," a Negro spiritual that her mother said was the rage of amateur glee clubs.

One of the tenors in the chorus approached her father during the first intermission. He had a mandola case under his arm.

"What do you have there, friend?" her father asked.

"A Gibson H-4," the man answered slowly.

Sheila assumed he was a farmer by the overalls. He was a short man and he squinted at her father through gold-rimmed spectacles. He was flanked on his left side by a stern-looking woman in a black dress with a print apron and a cameo at her collar. On his right was a thin man who had a black suitcoat over his overalls.

"Would you like to see it?" the man asked.

"Why not?" her father answered.

When the man opened the mandola case, Violet May Cooper gasped. It was the *new* H-4 with elevated pickguard, sunburst finish, engraved tuning pegs, and inlaid-pearl fretboard. It made Violet May Cooper's mandola appear second-rate. Winthrop Ethridge DuQuesne later said he would have been no less shocked had the chicken farmer produced a five-hundred-dollar Style U harp guitar.

"I can read alto clef and universal notation," the man continued. "I know Lloyd Loar. I painted his ten-string mando-viola for the patent office."

"You *painted* it?"

"Yes, I did."

Sheila stared at the man in the dim light of the barn. The man had a queer habit. He rocked as he spoke, shifting his weight from one foot to the next. His companions, the man and the woman, stared at her father. They didn't let up. They stared at him with suspicion. Sheila thought they did not show him the proper respect. They never said a word. Their lips were grim lines on their faces.

"Mr. Quintaine?"

"Yes?"

"You'll agree it's a quality instrument then."

"Yes."

"Would you mind if I join the mandola section for a couple of numbers?"

"Sorry fella," her father said. "No sit-ins."

The man's thin companion finally spoke. "Sir. You don't seem to understand. This here is Grant Wood, the artist."

"I don't care if he's Pablo Picasso," her father said. "I have a policy. That policy is: no sit-ins."

Grant Wood did not close up his mandola case. He and his companions did not quietly walk away to disappear into the dark recesses of the Iowa barn. They did not move. They stood there. They stood there firm as if they might influence her father. Her mother later said it was North Dakota granite up against Iowa slate.

Grant Wood rocked back and forth on his feet and began to talk in earnest. He told her father that he liked Indian jazz on the mandolins. He told her father it was an interesting thing he had done: combining Negro music with Indian music on American mandolins. Grant Wood was even willing to concede that her father's Indian jazz might be an important American

132

expression. However, there was one flaw. Her father's attitude made his listeners outsiders looking in. Until he involved the American people, allowed them to become a part of the music, they would never accept it as theirs. He alone would term his music "The Voice of America" as long as he insisted on his stance. Finally, Grant Wood told her father he had become the kind of European he so publicly despised; arrogant, elitist, and condescending.

"Look, Mr. Grant," her father said patiently.

"It's Wood. My name is Grant Wood."

"Look, Mr. Wood." Sheila walked over to her father and stood next to him. Skeezix had gone out of the barn to investigate the livestock. "You're a painter, right? I'll try to explain it to you in terms that you can understand. Suppose you spent a long time on a painting that was very dear to you. Say a portrait of your mother. Would you allow a stranger to come up with a paintbrush and alter the flesh tones of her face? Fix the part in her hair? Take the wrinkle out of the collar on her dress? Change the background on her cameo from brown to black?"

"That's not a valid comparison, Mr. Quintaine, and you know it!"

"Oh, it's a very valid comparison, Mr. Wood. Suppose I let you bring your mandola up on stage. You've never played these arrangements. You might be out of tune with us. Your idea of allegro may be ten metronome markings off of ours. You may build a crescendo at a different rate than we do. What happens is that you alter the sound of my orchestra. You mar my painting. And, let me tell you something, Mr. Wood, I've spent a long time getting this painting exactly the way I want it." Her father put his arm around her. "Did I explain that pretty well, Sheila?"

She was looking at Grant Wood's woman companion. The woman's eyebrows sank lower and lower on her face. By the time Sheila's father had finished his speech, the woman looked like a tiger ready to spring.

"In all my born days," she finally said, "I have never heard anybody talk like that to my brother."

Her voice was a constricted whine, unpleasant to the ear. Sheila thought that's what any woman would sound like after thirty years among chicken coops and musty cellars.

The man in the black suitcoat folded his arms and sighed. "Come on, Grant," he said. "This fella here's like talkin' to a stone wall."

Grant Wood closed his mandola case and fastened the snaps. "I'd like to say one more thing to him, Dr. McKeeby."

"Well, all right then."

Grant Wood turned and squinted up at her father. "I don't think the amazing mandolin twins are charming. I don't think children oughta be playing the mandolin. The high-tension double strings would give their little fingers blisters. Children should play the ukulele. Or the xylophone."

"The mandolin has never hurt my fingers, Mr. Wood," Sheila said. "I love the mandolin. I always have."

"Of course she would say that," Grant Wood said to her father. "You have them *trained*."

Her father slowly leaned forward until his face was not more than an inch from Grant Wood's. Then he raised his right index finger and thumped it on Grant Wood's chest, between the two brass buttons of his overalls.

"Say whatever you want about me, cornflake," her father growled. "But don't you dare ever insult my children."

In the scuffle that followed, Grant Wood's eyeglasses tumbled to the floor and broke. His sister snatched them up and put them in her apron pocket before somebody stomped on them. Grant Wood got some pretty good swings in for a painter, Sheila thought. Fortunately, none of his blows connected with her father's face.

H. H. Pickering, Xavier Tesch, D. E. Lichtenfels and Valentine T. Peck all rushed to the front of the stage to restrain her father. Her mother came too, throwing her xylophone mallets down into the straw. The World War I veterans in their doughboy helmets rushed up to the stage next. They were followed by the Linn County Farm Bureau's Chorus, including their stern director, Mrs. Iva B. Witt.

Skeezix came in from the outside when she heard the commotion. She could not see anything because of the tightly knit crowd that had gathered around the feuding artists. She tried to squeeze through the overalls and aprons to get to the front but everyone was packed too tight. It was easy to guess what had happened. Her father had insulted the local virtuoso again.

The police were called, but before the flivver arrived Grant Wood's companion, Dr. McKeeby, restored order when he produced a pitchfork. He held the sharp tines of the pitchfork within three inches of her father's cummerbund. The barn became dead silent. Very quietly, he said, "I think you and your progressive mandolin orchestra best move on."

Her father had managed to offend nearly everyone in Cedar Rapids. The American Legion was reluctant to release their paycheck, one hundred and thirty-four and 00/100 dollars made out to "Quintaine's Mandolin Orchestra." They did so only after her mother, wearing a Plains Indian warbonnet, pleaded with them for over an hour. Sheila had never seen her mother so angry. She threatened to stop giving the "Voice of America" speech at the beginning of each concert. She threatened to stop wearing the Indian costumes. At the end of the evening, as the farmer's wives collected their pie tins and cake pans, all carefully labeled with their names on a strip of adhesive tape, her mother told her father she was tired of Indian jazz. She told him that, if this was what it cost, she didn't want to have anything to do with it anymore.

Grant Wood, she had learned, was on the verge of national recognition for his regional paintings. He had studied extensively in Europe and had three one-man exhibits in Paris. His recent paintings of workers at a dairy equipment manufacturing plant were raising eyebrows from California to New York. He's the hometown hero, Kirk, her mother had said on a dark bus bound for Moline. These farmers, they adore him. You know what they think of you? You're the crackpot orchestra leader who broke Grant Wood's glasses. That's all you are to them. That you invented Indian jazz doesn't mean a thing to these people.

"Oh, so he's on the verge of national recognition, is he?" her father had said. "If you haven't learned anything in fifteen years of marriage, Lily, you should have learned that doesn't mean a thing to me. The world is full of rich and famous people who don't deserve it. They're made rich and famous by all these low-thinking individuals, people with brains the size of a pea. I would rather have the respect of flies! Be reasonable, Lily. Is this Grant Wood a painter with a great vision? A man who paints the people who work in a dairy equipment plant?"

That was her father. He never faltered. He stood firm. Yes, he stood firm. When there was no reason for it, he stood firm. When all logic was against him, he stood firm. When every sign was in the opposition's favor, he stood firm. After he had lost every last ally, he stood firm. When only an idiot would stand firm, he stood firm. In the Everglades, she remembered his words. "Say what you want about me, but never insult my children." That's what her father said.

Sheila took Cuckoo out of her raincoat pocket. She stroked the fine down at the top of the bird's head. She lay down on a cypress log in the swamp and looked up at the stars. I would defend him again and again and again. Skeezix might not. If she had been there when Grant Wood said a mandolin was not a good instrument for children, Skeezix might have agreed with him. She often complained how the mandolin strings hurt her fingers.

Sheila fell asleep. In the morning, she awoke to find a Seminole Indian staring at her. He was in a dugout canoe and his Indian skin was the color of apple cider.

13

The Indian's hair was black as coal. It gleamed in the morning sun. The bangs of his hair stopped an inch above his eyebrows. The rest of it was cut in even length all the way around. It was a bowl cut.

The Indian's teeth were yellow with brown streaks. They looked soft and leathery. His teeth looked like they would fold up if he chewed.

He wore a strip shirt with a black background. She counted fifteen different colors of cloth sewn on.

His feet were bare and he had the creeping eruption. The parasite's travels were recorded across his feet in inflamed curlicues. The skin around his toes was yellow and jaundiced. His toenails looked soft and pliant as if they might be lifted as easily as toadstools.

The Indian grinned at her pet bird.

Sheila said, "I've been injured."

She showed the Indian her tongue. When he leaned in to inspect the wound, she saw that his vision did not come to a point. He had ebony eyes and one of them was wrong. She couldn't tell which eye was wrong, but one of them was.

"Oh my God, you're cross-eyed!" she said under her breath.

She named her rescuer Big Chief Cross-in-the-Eyes. He

poled her across the Everglades in his dugout canoe. He stood in the back with his diseased feet on the etched-out bottom of the canoe. She sat in the front with her back towards him. She folded her legs, Indian-style. Between them was the turtle he had caught. It was a black soft-shell turtle with a queer, angled snout. The snout was hideous. It was like a little straw. The turtle had a smooth neck that strained to the sky. Sheila thought it wore a look of anguish on its queer face. The anguish had no connection with the human universe and that disturbed her. It flopped around in the bottom of the canoe with no regard for them. She named the turtle Tom Potts after the bulging-eyed character in *The Hole Book* by Peter Newell.

Big Chief Cross-in-the-Eyes had a bottle too. It was half full with a clear liquid. There was a cork in the top. Sometimes he took the cork out and pressed the bottle to his lips. The liquid filtered through his brown teeth. It was gin. She knew by the smell. He offered her some.

"No thank you."

The canoe made tiny ripples in the water. She felt the hot wind on her face. The Everglades were silent. There were creatures out there, thousands of them, but they were silent. They were ferociously silent. Frogs, alligators, birds, and insects hid in the sawgrass and the dwarf cypress. They were building their strength for the eruption at night. It was silent now in the day, but she felt the life of the swamp even more.

In the distance, she followed a flock of ibis. They were flying above the spiked crowns of cabbage palms. The cabbage palms were tightly packed in the hammock and their trunks were black as if they had been burned. There were white ibis and black ibis and their beaks were curved like eyebrows. When the birds cleared the hammock, they were flying above an eternity of sawgrass.

After a time, they reached the Indian village. Big Chief threw his pole down on the bank. He pulled the turtle out of the bottom of the canoe and held it upside down by the tail. The turtle's feet flapped in the air.

The inhabitants of the village gathered around them. There were sixteen Indians. In their strip clothing, they were a dazzling sea of color. The children peeked into her raincoat pocket to see the little bird.

There was a baby in its mother's arms. The baby had fat brown cheeks and it was sleeping. Horseflies buzzed around a line of drool running off the baby's lips.

Most of the men had bottles of gin. They had their brown hands around the necks of the bottles. The bottles were at different levels of consumption. Sheila thought: drunken Indians.

Dogs raced around the huddled villagers. There were black, tan, and yellow ones. Their barking pierced the silence. One of them was a sand-colored dog with half of his coat gone to the mange. He had sick and dry eyes and he came up close to her and growled. His old gums trembled and she could see his teeth. Dog feces were all over the bank. She was the only one with shoes.

There was a putrid odor. It was garbage she thought. She imagined a fly-covered pit somewhere with egg shells, cantelope rinds, and meat scraps spoiling in the sun.

No one spoke English. Big Chief Cross-in-the-Eyes talked to the villagers in Indian language. She did not know what he said to them until he pointed to his tongue. He is describing my injury now, she thought.

The village consisted of seven huts arranged in a V. Each hut had six vertical posts. The posts were the trunks of sabal palms. Attached to the posts at the top was a gabled roof of thatched palmetto fronds. The floors were made of cypress logs cut in half and nailed to the vertical posts. The floors were two and a half feet off the ground. Only one of the huts did not have a floor. It was the kitchen hut at the point of the V. She was taken there.

An old woman sat on a log, presiding over a fire. The fire was where the ends of four logs met. She controlled the intensity of the blaze by moving the logs in and out. The woman had dry, wrinkled skin and piles of necklaces.

The woman prepared a liquid provision in a whittled cypress bowl that Sheila began to understand was for the wound in her mouth. The old woman stirred the concoction with the stem of a water lily.

"Now this is going to help my tongue, right?"

The old woman smiled at her, revealing a dental horror.

Sheila took the bowl. She wondered who had had their lips on it. When she tipped it to drink, the eyes of the villagers were on her.

"OOOOWWWWWW!"

The potion felt like a lighted match to the wound on her tongue. The villagers laughed.

"My God, this must be about ninety percent fire water!" she said. "Do you all have to stare at me like that? Don't you know that it's cruel to stare?"

Afterwards, the old woman dipped a wooden spoon into a kettle off to her side.

"Sofki," she said.

Sofki was a white soup. It was like the grits she had at Edison's house only sofki was thinner and less flavorful. It was lukewarm. It was not awful. It was better than raw turtle eggs. She drank the entire spoonful. The woman gave her a bright orange biscuit next.

Over in the corner on a crude wooden table sat a white hand basin. It was alive with flies and the rim of the basin was black with them. Coating the bottom was a golden syrup. The syrup was studded with drowned flies like raisins. She knew it was honey. There was nothing else that looked like that. Honey was something she could eat. Honey was something the Indians couldn't ruin or change.

Sheila chewed on the dry orange biscuit and eyed the honey. After the potion, the wound on her tongue was numb and it didn't hurt to chew. She eyed the honey. She was aware of herself breathing loud through her nostrils as she chewed. She wondered if this bothered the Indians as it bothered her

140

family. The Indians watched her eat, though some of the children were bored now and went to play with the dogs. She eyed the honey.

The old woman sat on the log and looked at Sheila, then looked at the basin, then looked at Sheila, then looked at the basin. The old woman finally hobbled over to the basin and brought it to her. The weight of her necklaces pulled her head toward the ground. Sheila broke off a chunk of biscuit and dipped it into the honey.

It was heavenly. Dipped in the honey, the biscuits tasted like pumpkin pie. She had five of them. The Indians watched her eat, grinning.

Her stomach bulged. For the first time in a week she felt like a human being again. She wanted to play the mandolin. She wanted to run her fingers along the scroll of her Lyon and Healy Style B. She wanted to polish the pickguard. She wanted to tune up. She wanted to hear eight strings vibrate in a G major chord. She thought the G chord, in all its inversions up and down the neck, was the prettiest sound on the mandolin.

"I would like to thank all of you for the food."

The Indians gave her a strip skirt. They cut up her shoes for bracelets for the children. They put Cuckoo in a reed cage by the sewing hut.

At night they had a feast. The old woman took Big Chief Cross-in-the-Eyes' turtle and plunged it into the fire headfirst. The turtle was perfectly alive when she put it in the fire. Its queer, dragonlike paws beat the air wildly before it died in the flames. They passed the carcass around and tore off bits of the charred flesh.

This is where I draw the line, Sheila thought. She passed the smoldering turtle to the Indian on her left.

The gin bottles went around. Even the children drank from them.

"I see why you are all sick," Sheila said. "There is no sanitation here whatsoever. You don't cover your food. You let the dogs go wherever they want. You drink *this stuff* instead of

141

milk. It's no wonder your teeth look like that. You see my teeth? White. That's the way they're supposed to look. White. Have you ever heard of dairy products? It's what comes from cows. Dairy products have a mineral in them called calcium. Calcium gives you healthy teeth and bones. If you don't have calcium, you won't have healthy teeth and bones. It's as simple as that. Having the children drink gin with their meals instead of milk . . . . It's an abomination! Where's Cuckoo? The dumb bird makes a better audience."

Later there was music and dance. It was log drumming and nasal chants. Big Chief Cross-in-the-Eyes motioned for her to get up. She wondered if she was a double image in his eyes. She pranced around the fire with him and some other Indians for a while then ran out into the darkness crying.

"I WANNA BE HOME!"

For as long as she could remember, her life had never been in tune. There were always dissonances: dissonances among her sister, her mother, her father, the orchestra members, her classmates, her teachers. Still, the dissonances occurred on an instrument of harmony and, by careful adjustment, could always be brought back into tune. But now, after a desperate week in the Everglades culminating at a camp of primitive Indians, the dissonances reigned. And she had exhausted every last resource in trying to repair the disharmony. She had popped every last string. She might never see Skeezix and her mother and father again.

She cried that night, loud, deep gasps that she was very ashamed of. She knew that her crying was loud enough to keep people awake. It was not like her to be so inconsiderate of others. Salt tears ran off her cheeks and spotted her strip skirt. Her sore tongue swelled. Saliva filled the hollow beneath her bottom front teeth.

In the night, she could feel the Indians' eyes on her as she cried. She knew that they, not speaking English, didn't know what to say to her.

The night was framed by the pointed ends of palmetto

fronds hanging off the roof of the hut. Sudden lightning in the distance made her eyeballs jump. Did any other white people see that lightning? Were there white people in that suddenly illuminated distance?

She heard the dogs. They raced in the distant palmetto underbrush in their frantic dog life, chasing a rabbit or a rat or a bobcat, to return to the Indian camp so that she could hear their panting, then racing back to the bushes again.

A mosquito lighted on her wrist. Instead of slapping it she decided to watch and see what it would do without her interference. The mosquito filled itself so full of her blood that it could not move from the spot. The mosquito dropped over dead on her wrist with its insect gut inflated like a balloon with her blood.

The Indians did not have a lavatory facility. They, the men and the women both, relieved themselves through the cracks in the platforms of their huts. Through the night, she heard the Indians' urine pound the marl earth beneath the platforms. The Indian women did not wear underdrawers and they lifted their long strip skirts in one remarkably quick and easy movement. Oh, it was such a repulsive act! She vowed she would never stoop to their primitive level. She would not make that mess underneath her bed. If she felt the need to visit the lavatory during the night, she would walk into the woods to find a suitable shelter, even if it meant risking a snakebite.

She was filled with regret. She should never have left the osprey nest. It was the worst thing she could have done. The regret was deep and merciless. She thought it was the cause of her crying. Over and over again, she thought the same thought: If she had stayed a while longer in the nest, she might have met the rescue boat. Tonight, instead of sleeping on a split log in a foul-smelling Indian camp, she might be sleeping next to her sister on a soft mattress with a tightly covered sheet smelling of Ivory soap. Why had she left the osprey nest? Why had she done it? Why? Why? Why?

She had a vision of her rescue. From high in the tree, she looked down and saw her father at the helm of a tugboat. The tugboat glided through the dwarf cypress trees. It was formed in her imagination from a drawing in her *McGuffey's Fourth Eclectic Reader*. In her vision, her father had his hands cupped over his mouth and was yelling into the wilderness. "Sheila! Sheila! Sheila!"

"I'M UP HERE, DADDY! I'M UP HERE!"

Her father would pursue her to the ends of the earth. In the dreariness of the Seminole camp, she had that one consolation. Her father's mulish diligence, normally reserved for his Indian jazz, would be applied to her rescue. He would look behind every blade of sawgrass in the Everglades. He would not give up. He would not give up when all others had.

But she could not ignore one dreadful possibility. They might find her corpse. Or what they thought was her corpse. After a few days in the heat with the buzzards and the snakes and the worms, she imagined that one corpse was fairly indistinguishable from another. She had learned that lesson from the body she had found under the osprey nest. She had only been able to identify it by the shoes. They were the shoes of the woman dancer from Moore Haven. The rest of the woman dancer was mostly gone.

So they could find a girl's bones about her size and conclude that it was her bones. They could gather up the skeleton and place it in a coffin for burial in the buffalo grounds of North Dakota. It was a gruesome thing to consider—her skull under the closed lid of a coffin—but consider it she must. Her father would give up on her if he thought he had found her. In which case she would be obliged to live at this Indian camp until her old age.

Here she was crying again: Please find me daddy please find me daddy please find me daddy please find me daddy please find me daddy . . . . She said it close to a million times before she finally nodded off to sleep on the split log of the platform.

Later in the night, the thunder woke her. It was raining. The rain poured off the palmetto frond roof of her hut and drummed the ground below. The air was suddenly cool. The

144

Everglades themselves seemed to sigh in relief. She reached her hand out and let the cool rain drum her palm. She heard the dogs finding shelter beneath the platforms of the huts.

"Oh Lordy," she said out loud. "I have to use the lavatory facility."

It was not simple. The pumpkin biscuits were at the lower end of her intestine. They seemed to plead for escape.

She walked into the night. She cringed with every step. They had taken her shoes. The rain cooled her hot shoulders.

On the return trip, she saw a struggle in the pantry hut. She hid behind some saw palmetto and watched in the rain.

Two women were wrestling with a man. The man had been a dance partner earlier, but it was not Big Chief Cross-in-the-Eyes. The women grappled with the man in silence. The man, however, ranted and raved. He spewed rivers of indecipherable Indian language into the rainy night. The indecipherable quality of the Indian's language was disturbing enough, but the delirium-edged foundation of his words was a challenge to her sanity. It was a mean challenge to her sanity.

What they were doing was tying him up. They tied him up like a calf in a rodeo. First his hands, then his feet. Then they lashed him to a post of the pantry hut.

Raindrops collected on her eyelashes and clouded her vision. She wiped her eyes with her fingers and saw the man try to bite the women! He nipped at them like a mad dog. In the night, she saw his exposed gums at the base of his teeth.

An object went hurtling through the air. It made a perfect rainbow arch. She did not know what the object was until it landed with a crash on a rock in the distant swamp. It was the Indian's bottle of gin.

She later found out it was the Seminole custom for the women to tie up their drunken men. They untied them only after they were sober.

Crash! The glass bottle broke on the rock and suddenly she was awake to something important. *Where did the Indians get their gin?* Even if they had their own still, a crude still hidden in some moss-shrouded mahogany hammock, and, even if they were sophisticated enough to distill their own liquor, what was the likelihood that it would be so similar to Valentine T. Peck's gin that she could identify it instantly by its smell? The Indian's gin smelled like Valentine T. Peck's. Almost exactly.

And what about the bottles? The glass bottles? There were no glass blowers in this camp, and, even if there were, the bottles would be erratic in shape and color. The Indian bottles were all the same. They were clear glass with a long neck. They were manufactured bottles.

The Indians at this camp had a connection with a white populace. They were being supplied. At the heart of the drunken Indian tied to the post were speakers of the English language. Who were they?

14

On the second day, there were visitors from a neighboring camp. The visitors pulled up in seven dugout canoes. The canoes were loaded down with alligator tails, turtle, green coconuts, and gin bottles. The dogs on shore were in a frenzy.

The new Indians walked up the bank and gathered around her. They stood silently and gazed at her face. Mosquitoes lighted on the ebony hair on their heads and flew away again. The new Indians looked at her with wonder and curiosity. They wore bright and beautiful clothing like Big Chief Cross-in-the-Eyes' tribe. Their regal impression, however, was destroyed when they smiled and exposed their brown teeth.

She was not afraid of them. They did not touch her. They had gentle smiles.

The new Indians' arrival was a comfort in that now she knew Big Chief Cross-in-the-Eyes' camp did not exist in isolation. Sheila thought Big Chief Cross-in-the-Eyes' camp might be one in a whole network of Indian villages that spanned the Everglades and, like stepping stones, eventually led to the coast where the white man dwelled.

Big Chief Cross-in-the-Eyes himself told the visitors the story of her rescue. Though she did not undertand the Indian words, she sensed that he embellished the story for dramatic effect, injecting fictional elements of heroism and hardship to dazzle his listeners. He told them about her pet bird. He made her show them her wound. Dutifully, she stuck out her tongue for the visitors. The Indians examined it with great concentration. She had the feeling they were not looking at her wound as much as everything else around it. They studied her incisors, her taste buds, her gum line. She imagined they were searching for clues that made her different from their race.

"Can I put my tongue back in my mouth now, Chief?"

She counted seventeen Indians in the visiting tribe. This did not include a baby in its mother's arms. There were ten men, four women, and three children.

One of the men did not wear a shirt. He was a thin and homely Indian with a Roman nose and buck teeth. He had a hairless chest. The skin of his chest and midriff was smooth and unblemished, the color of cider. He wore black trousers made of a lightweight material held up around the waist by a rope. He was barefoot with creeping eruption. And he was pigeon-toed. He had a half-full bottle of gin in one hand. He grinned at her with affection.

"Don't get too near me, Tarzan," Sheila said.

Thereafter, she referred to the visitors as Tarzan's tribe.

It was soon after their arrival that her hope faded. Though their presence dispelled her fear of total isolation, and the gin bottles promised a further encroaching civilization, Tarzan's tribe showed no more interest in returning her to her people than Big Chief Cross-in-the-Eyes'. They did not speak a word of English. They seemed perfectly content to let her sit here and rot. They seemed perfectly content to let her rot for an eternity under a scorching sky with primitive people who did not speak English and had gruesome sanitary habits.

In the afternoon, they had a baseball game. It took place in an open field of white marl behind the camp. The marl blinded like snow under the sun.

The Indians used pumpkins for bases. They used a pumpkin for the pitcher's rubber too. The pumpkins were

148

medium-sized ones with dry brown stems that provided good handles for moving them around.

That was the infield. Natural barriers marked off the outfield. A cornfield was the right-center stands. A canal was the left-center. They intersected in center field. The canal was thick with water lilies, so thick that it only revealed itself as a body of water under close inspection. Then she saw, in the tiny patches of water between the lilies, the eyes of alligators rising and falling.

A natural backstop for the game was provided by a clump of banana trees behind the kitchen hut of the camp. There were scores of different-sized banana trees growing in the single clump, all with giant green leaves shredded by the hurricane. Off some of the larger trees, mule-ear-shaped bananas protruded from the top of long curved stems that ended near the ground in waxy red flowers.

The Indians used baby coconuts for baseballs. They made a pile of them at the pitcher's mound, like a squirrel's stash. Whenever one got lost in the banana trees or the canal or the cornfield, the pitcher simply took another one off the pile. For a bat, the Indians used a cypress branch. It was about three feet long, crooked, and worn smooth from use.

The game was for men only. Children were not allowed to play. The children, however, managed other diversions during the game. Some of them hid giggling in the cornfield, awaiting home run balls. Some of them flung sticks into the canal for the dogs to fetch. Still others made nuisances of themselves around the kitchen hut where the Indian women squatted in their strip skirts and pounded corn with rocks.

Sheila sat in the shade of a cypress tree and watched the game. She was on the third base side. She decided to keep score. She made a scoreboard in the marl earth with a stone. The scoreboard was a rectangle divided at midpoint. Perpendicular lines through the rectangle denoted innings. She put a V in the top box for Visitors. That was Tarzan's tribe. She put an H in the bottom box for Home team. That was Big Chief

Cross-in-the-Eyes' tribe. V and H.

She expected a crude and primitive version of the game she knew. How wrong her expectations were! She was astonished to see a sophisticated athletic performance. The Indians knew how to play baseball and well! Every elaborate nuance of the game was contained in their playing. There were sacrifice flies, stolen bases, spitball curves, and called third strikes. The Indians even trotted around the bases after a home run. They trotted around in that slow, cocky, and triumphant way she knew so well. Once Tarzan hit a home run into the cornfield and as he languished around the bases afterwards she said, "*Surely* he has seen Babe Ruth to know to do that."

The umpire in the game was an elder from Tarzan's tribe. Everyone called him connymack. She assumed connymack was Indian for umpire as sofki was Indian for grits.

Connymack sat on a stool behind home plate and panted like a dog in the heat. He gave the impression that he was too fat to get up. He had silver-white hair cut uniformly short. The clipped silver bristles gleamed in the sun. He wore a strip shirt with a turquoise background and his belly pushed against the bottom of the shirt like a boulder about to tumble. Around his massive neck, he wore what looked to her to be a silk scarf, green, fastened at the side with a gold neckerchief ring.

The Indians had a certain respect for him. They never openly defied his judgment. The Indians grumbled about some of his calls but they never challenged him. During the game, several children took turns fanning him with a palm frond and bringing him water.

Connymack had a problem with his feet and ankles. He constantly scratched them during the game. He seemed to have some terrible and evil itch that would give him no peace. She wondered if it was sand fleas, mosquitoes, creeping eruption, gnats, wood ticks, or hook worms. He raked his old fingernails across his crusty feet, sometimes drawing blood.

One time she stared at him scratching and he looked over in the direction of the cypress tree and saw her. He winked at her before she had a chance to avert her eyes.

"He saw me, he saw me . . ." she muttered.

After a safe interval of time, she glanced back at him to see if he was still looking at her. He wasn't. He was taking a swig of gin from a bottle he kept behind his stool.

And then, all of a sudden, it struck her. Connymack. Connie Mack. It was an American name and she had heard it before. But where? Where? And then she remembered. F.W. Clancy had said his name out loud. It was at Edison's house, on his porch after breakfast. Clancy was reading the sports section of the Fort Myers paper and commented on the standing of the Philadelphia Athletics in the American League. Clancy was an avid Athletics fan and blamed their woes on the manager, Connie Mack. Connie Mack was the manager of the Philadelphia Athletics!.

But there was more. Hope began to blaze in her. She felt her heart pounding underneath her strip skirt. Connie Mack. Skeezix and she knew the name too.

During the last intermission on that long night at Edison's, Skeezix and she wandered through his house. No one seemed to mind. No one seemed to care. In a dark hallway off the living room, they found newspaper clippings tacked to the wall. In shadows filled with mosquitoes, they squinted at photographs of Edison in the news. There was a picture of him with John Burroughs, the naturalist. There was a picture of him with Harvey Firestone, the rubber tire manufacturer. Him with Henry Ford. Him with Coolidge himself. But there was one photograph with a baseball bat. Edison with a baseball bat? What an unlikely pairing! Imagine the dedicated genius, the work fiend, holding the very symbol of frivolity and leisure. Also in the photograph was a kindly-looking man wearing a fedora. He stood behind Edison, guiding his swing. Skeezix had edged up close to the newspaper clipping in the dark hallway and read the caption underneath the photograph.

" 'Thomas Edison, Fort Myers resident, receives some time-ly batting pointers from Philadelphia Athletics manager Connie

Mack. The Athletics arrived in Fort Myers on Tuesday to begin spring training. The world-famous inventor took time from his busy schedule to greet the team. UPI photo.' "

"Let's get out of here, Skeezix. I don't think we should be here."

"Why not.?"

"I don't know. I feel like we're being . . . peeping Thomases!"

"Look," Skeezix had said, "if he didn't want people looking at these pictures, he wouldn't have them tacked up on the wall."

"I know, but we weren't really invited here."

Now Sheila recalled the conversation and concentrated on the key words. Spring training. Skeezix had said "spring training." The Athletics had been in Fort Myers. But, most importantly, these Seminole Indians had been there too. They had been there to watch the Athletics play. And not just once or twice, but many, many times. It was the only possible explanation for their thorough knowledge of baseball. It was the only possible explanation for their uncanny duplication of professional athlete mannerisms. And it was the only possible explanation for their faith in Connie Mack as the ultimate authority on the game.

Yes. These Indians had been to Fort Myers. Enough times to learn the game of baseball well. They could easily go again, and this time, take her with them.

All day, she pleaded with them. She pleaded with anyone who would turn his head her way.

"Take me to where the baseball is. That's my home. Can you understand that? Surely you can see I don't belong with you. I belong with my own mother and father. White people. They live where the baseball is. Where you saw the baseball."

She knew the Indians did not understand her words. Still she spoke to them with the hope they would respond to the urgency and the unhappiness in her voice. The Indians seemed to want, more than anything, that she be happy. Perhaps if she kept up a nagging whine, they might come to realize that they had failed.

152

"I know I'm fortunate that you're good Indians and that you've taken good care of me. But I belong with my own people. *My own people.* All you'd have to do is put me in the boat and *go* there! Go to where the baseball is. What more can I do to make you understand?"

She accompanied her words to the Indians with sign language. The sign language was so explicit and simple she felt only an idiot could fail to understand its meaning. When she spoke of white people, she touched her own face. When she spoke of baseball, she swung an imaginary bat. When she spoke of Fort Myers, she pointed to where she thought it was. She pointed with such emphasis that, several times, she nearly wrenched her shoulder from its socket.

"Take me to Connie Mack town. How about that? Connie Mack."

Generally the Indians stopped what they were doing to listen to her. As she spoke, they nodded deferentially and smiled, exposing their ruined teeth. On several occasions, however, their expressions faltered and frowns replaced the smiles. At these times, they seemed to have doubts about having credited her with sanity.

Once she went so far as to wade out into the water and mock-launch one of the canoes into the Everglades. The Indians seemed really baffled by this move. And when she came out of the water she had a bloodsucker on her foot. The bloodsucker was in the crevice between her big toe and her second toe.

She pleaded with Tarzan, the tribe leader. He smiled throughout her speech. The smile never faltered. His eyebrows moved and jumped as she talked. They recorded every gradation of her pleading. He gave an air of wholeheartedly agreeing with everything she said. She could not be certain, however, what it was he was constantly agreeing to. She finally walked away from him, shaking her head in despair.

How she wished the Indians would give her some sign of comprehension! She would be happy with the tiniest, the

153

slightest sign. Anything to confirm that an act of communication had been committed. For instance, why couldn't one of the Indians move his lips with hers when she said "Fort Myers" or "Connie Mack"? That would be a sign. There was no reason they could not move their lips to Connie Mack. They knew that word. She had heard them say it many, many times.

Hour after hour on the day of the baseball game, Sheila pleaded with the Indians. She pleaded with them to take her to Fort Myers. And hour after hour, she searched their Indian faces for any inkling of understanding. There was none.

"I think this sun has fried your brains," she finally told them. It was an unkind remark and she knew it. She had never said such a thing.

She retired to the bedroom hut. She lay down on a platform under the thatched palmetto fronds, alone with her thoughts.

The next morning she saw her reflection in a pool of water. She could not believe what she saw. She frowned and frowned and frowned into the water. She leaned down and put her face close to the surface of the reflection. Then, slowly, she pulled it back. She inspected the left side of her face. Then the right.

"You are a liar!" she said to the mirror.

A dragonfly buzzed over the water. The pool recorded its iridescent wings with total accuracy. The mirror was not lying.

Her face had turned the color of cider. She looked like them now.

She noted too the collar of her Seminole costume in the reflection. It further defined the image of the stranger in front of her. Maybe stranger was the wrong term. Maybe the term was a person she had once known.

It was like a nightmare she had once, long ago. In the nightmare, an evil force dispersed and scattered her identity throughout the house in Bismarck. Her identity was everywhere except in her. It was in little fragments in the chairs, in the lamps, in the counters, in the sink, in the windows, even in the air outside of her body. She did not know who she was. In that nightmare long ago, she stood desperate in the

154

bathroom of their house with nothing holding her together. It was a nightmare of incomparable terror.

Now she looked into the reflecting pool and said, "This is me. Sheila Quintaine. I'm one of the amazing mandolin twins."

She checked her eyes. Thank God they were still blue. She bared her teeth. Still white. So far, anyway. She had noticed in the last several days that there was a coat of slime over her teeth from not brushing. She felt the slime with her healed tongue. It wouldn't be long before her teeth were brown like theirs.

Something else. There was a thin white streak on her brown face. It was on her left cheek. She leaned in close to inspect it.

It was the scar. It was the place where the coin had entered during the hurricane. The scar was white like milk. The scar was the color of her skin during the winters in North Dakota.

That tiny mark was the extent of her paleface. She had to laugh when she thought of her desperate pleas to the Indians, trying to make them understand the concept of the white race by pointing to her own face. It was no wonder they did not understand her.

15

The next day, her prayers were answered. The Indians took her to Fort Myers.

They left early in the morning. It was a purple dawn. Smoky clouds in the distance hailed the sun's approach. Dew sparkled like diamonds on the sawgrass. The sawgrass extended far into the eastern horizon. It finally disappeared in a haze. The haze was the last, loitering residue of the night.

Birds erupted in song high in the cypress trees. They hopped from twig to twig as they sang, making the leaves tremble. She could hear their wings and their tails. She could hear their airy feathers. She could feel all of their little hearts beating. The birds' lively little hearts beat into the morning.

They took three canoes for the journey. Two of the canoes were for the men and her. The other one was for coconuts.

She was astonished at how many coconuts the Indians managed to pile into one canoe. It was so loaded down that the side railings were only a half inch from the surface of the water. The coconuts were fat and smooth, pale green. She likened their shape to monkey skulls. She stared at the load of coconuts in the canoe. Lizards appeared from out of the dark crevices of the piled coconuts. They looked at her with their tiny, ink-black eyes before disappearing back into the crevices.

She assumed the boatload of coconuts was for tourists in Fort Myers. She thought the tourists would gladly pay a nickel apiece for a coconut from an authentic American exotic in brilliant costume.

The Indian's dogs went berserk on their departure. They barked and barked and barked. They leapt high into the air. They raced in a mindless crisscross of the Indian huts. They urinated. They kicked up clumps of sandy marl onto the hems of the women's strip skirts.

The yellow dog dove into the water and followed the canoes for fifty yards or more. It swam with great efficiency, its neck arched, its jaws shut, its eyes intent. Two lines of rippled water followed the dog. Finally, it seemed to sense the futility of its ambition and turned around and paddled for shore. Then on the bank, the dog kept its head low to the ground. She thought the dog looked embarrassed, aware of the foolishness of its deed. The dog braced its four paws into the marl and shook the water from its coat. Indian children leapt away with delight as they were sprayed.

Sheila waved good-bye to the Indians on shore. She had a tender spot in her heart for them, especially the old woman who had made the potion for her wound. The old woman stood on the bank now and waved. She squinted at Sheila through cataracts that veiled her ebony eyes. She smiled at her and exposed the brown remains of her teeth. Her teeth had a queer connection with her head. Her teeth looked like extraneous flakes of bone from her skull.

"Good-bye, old woman," Sheila called. "I'll never see you again."

Before Sheila left, the old woman fixed her hair. She put it on top of her head to keep her neck cool for the journey. The old woman used a bone hairpin. Sheila felt her ancient brown fingers tugging, pulling, straightening, and caressing the hair on top of her head. The old woman touched her intimately as her mother did. While the old woman fiddled with her hair, Sheila sat patiently in the early morning, quiet, sighing from time to time. Afterwards, the old woman said, "Sofki."

Sofki. Sheila had not only begun to tolerate the thin white gruel, but in the week she had been in the Indian camp, she truly began to crave it. With a little honey and banana, sofki was better than Cream of Wheat.

The Indians poled the canoes out into the Everglades. One of the canoes had the coconut boat in tow. She was not in that one. She was with Big Chief Cross-in-the-Eyes again. They turned a corner past a clump of fireflags moving with dragonflies. The Indian camp was out of sight.

With the tip of her tongue, she felt the inside surfaces of her bottom teeth. Determined not to let her teeth deteriorate, she had brushed them last night. She made a toothbrush by wrapping layers of coconut matting around a mahogany stick. She made toothpaste by mixing the ash from the kitchen fire with water. She brushed and brushed and brushed last night. She brushed hard. She brushed until she spit blood. The effort eradicated the coat of slime on her teeth. That was for certain. But now she feared she might have rubbed off some of her tooth enamel as well. It was a worrisome idea because she knew that once her tooth enamel was gone, it was gone forever. It couldn't be replaced. It didn't grow back. Tooth enamel was an issue of mortality that her fourth grade teacher, Mrs. Hazel B. Froelich, used to perk up the eyes and ears of her pupils in afternoon health class.

The Indians poled her through the sawgrass. Sheila began to fantasize about the culmination of the journey, the imminent reunion with her family. As the vision of the reunion became clearer, she saw less and less of the Everglades around her. The music in her head, as constant as her pulse during the waking hours, became more prominent. It became slower and more insistent. Oh, it was grand and glorious music! It was the andante section from "Manitou," an Indian novelty two-step, one of her father's favorite pieces. Her rib cage was the body of a mandolin. The tremelo of the orchestra was the fluttering of her heart.

Her mother was strangely unimportant in her vision. The person who made her sister and her presentable in the public eye, the person who knew every sprout of hair on their bodies was only a dim figure in the background.

But she saw her father clearly. She saw him on the dock at Thomas Edison's home as the Indians paddled her to shore. He was not a handsome man. He was unappealing to the public, even revolting to some. She had never known this as she knew it now. Her father, the man who was everything in her life, was a person most people preferred to be no part of theirs. They preferred to have no part of this man who broke out into a sweat when the mandolins were playing in perfect ensemble, when they were playing the Indian jazz that was his passion. Most people preferred to have no part of this man who would stay up all night with a mandolin, fiddling with the bridge until the twelfth fret harmonic was mathematically in tune. Most people preferred to have no part of her father, this wizard, this oddball, this fanatic. And now, as she glided through the Everglades in the dugout canoe, it occurred to her that she had been changed because she loved him. She had been changed from most people. She was odd too. She would always be like her father.

Kirk Quintaine. He never kissed them. He never hugged them. He never touched them unless it was to correct their hand position.

He *did* touch them, though, in her vision of the reunion. As the music in her head became stronger, the picture became clearer. Yes, there he was standing on the dock, and, as the Indian canoe glided in, he reached down with his pink and refined hands and pulled her up, hugging her. Her strip skirt billowed in the sultry October air as her father's strength drew her from the canoe.

Edison was in the vision. He walked among the Indians on the dock, giving each one of them a shiny new quarter. When he leaned down to place it in their hands, a shock of white hair fell down into his eye. The Indians did not know him. The

Indians did not know that the grinning old man in the vested suit and fancy shoes was the most famous person in America. Had they known who he was, they would not have cared. His inventions, the ones that altered civilization, were of no interest to them. They sat on the dock inspecting their quarters as flies buzzed around their square Indian foreheads.

Skeezix was in the vision. She appeared from her father's right side.

"You look like an Indian, Sheila," she said. "And you smell like one too."

"Is it that bad?"

The marvelous music of her vision was becoming overwhelming and unbearable. The ability of the mandolins to hold her, to clench her very insides, was remarkable. The music was made by adults she knew. She saw their big, strong-knuckled hands perched over their pan-shaped instruments like the talons of eagles.

Her father put his around them. "My children," he said. "My children. You . . ." It was now in her vision that her father's eyes changed. The piercing glare disappeared. The glint of granite determination vanished. His eyes became soft with love. " . . . You are the most important thing in my life."

Contemplating her vision, Sheila's eyes welled with tears. Throughout the journey, the Indians had kept a close watch over her, but now they were gawking. They were staring at her with their eyebrows low and their square Indian foreheads furrowed. They made ferocious attempts to decipher the meaning of her actions—the misty, blinking eyes, the quivering lips, the balking tongue.

"I wish you would all quit looking at me like that." When she spoke, it was as if a shoehorn were pressing out against her throat. "If I thought you could understand it," she said, "I would try to explain it to you."

One of the Indians offered her a coconut. With a wide knife, he cut a wedge in the chin of the monkey skull. She drank the coconut milk. The coconut milk was almost clear, but not quite

160

clear. The coconut milk was warm and salty. She dug the snow-white flesh out of the coconut with her fingernails. The raw meat gave sufficient hint of her mother's macaroons to make her ache for home cooking, hot ovens, sinks with flowing faucets, the flour-caked aprons. When she was through with the coconut, she tossed it out of the canoe where it landed and bobbed on black water teeming with garfish and turtles.

These Indians were considerate Indians, she thought. That much she could say for them. In terms of their elimination procedures, she could not ask for more consideration. Primitive people that they were, they could easily have urinated over the side of the canoe, forcing her to cover her eyes from their Indian nudity. But they did not. They did not dispose of their bodily waste over the side of the canoe. They always stopped the canoes and waited patiently for the person in need to wander out into the swamp and find a temporary lavatory facility that was safely and totally out of her view. She thought this procedure was in deference to her and not a result of their natural modesty.

It was such an elimination stop that found them in front of a tangle of vines at high noon. Beyond the vines, she looked upward and saw a flock of ibis in the bleached sky. The birds floated over the crowns of wild royal palm trees. The Indians began to unload the coconuts from the canoe and put them into fishnets. This was more than an elimination stop. The Indians had business in this hammock.

When the coconuts were loaded, the Indians carried them, twenty or thirty each, over their backs in the fishnets. It was like Santa Claus and his sack of toys. They went into the hammock with the coconuts. She followed them.

It was cool under the trees. Black mud squirted up between her toes. Above her, furry spiders lay still in the center of their webs. Black butterflies with yellow bars on their wings fluttered beneath her nose. And unknown wildlife, made frantic by the human intrusion, shook the underbrush in every direction.

Destruction from the hurricane was everywhere in the

jungle. Uprooted cypress trees lay in fallen angles to the sky. Ripped-out palm fronds rested in the crooks of still-standing trees. The fronds were in various stages of descension. Broken twigs, Spanish moss, air plants, and wild orchids lay strewn over the jungle floor. They passed the severed arm of a gumbo limbo tree. Its white and splintered flesh was fresh and brilliant in the dark shadows of the jungle.

Sheila walked behind Big Chief Cross-in-the-Eyes, following close. She watched the coconuts bounce and settle against his back with the movement of his walking.

"Where are we going, Chief?" she asked. "Where are we taking these coconuts? Can you tell me that?"

Her question was answered when farther into the jungle they came upon a picket fence. The fence was unpainted and the slats were smooth with moss. In the middle of the fence was a gate where a guard stood. The guard was a thin man with necktie and suspenders. He had a gun in his hands that was so big and heavy he couldn't hold it up. Sheila stared at his face. His skin was rosy pink. It deepened into scarlet at the white collar of his shirt. The last time she had seen skin that was this color was in North Dakota on the face of Clyde Rillard, a bass in the Methodist chancel choir.

The guard watched the approach of the Indians. "Well look who's here," he said. "It's Robin Hood and his merry men."

"Oh my God!" Sheila blurted out. "ENGLISH!"

Big Chief Cross-in-the-Eyes set his coconuts down and grabbed her by the shoulder blades. Then, with his long, jaundiced fingers pressed into her flesh, he marched her up to the guard. Sheila craned her neck upward to see the expression on the chief's face as he pushed her forward. He was grinning.

When she was in front of the guard, the chief let go of her shoulder blades. The guard gawked at her. His face was so close she could smell his breath. He said, "You ain't no Injun!"

"Correct, sir. I'm Sheila Quintaine."

The guard made a snorting sound. He called back over his shoulder. "Hey Snorky! Would you mind coming over here for a second? You're not going to believe this."

"What is it, Jack?"

"What is it? There's these bright eyes staring at me. That's what it is."

"What are you babbling about?"

The other voice came from Indian huts behind the fence.

The guard said, "The Injuns are here."

"Okay, give them their bottles."

"They've got a visitor. It's a little . . . a little American princess."

Sheila watched the man the guard called Snorky walk from the Indian huts to the gate. He was a short, dark-complected man with a great bulbous torso and fat puffy hands that looked as though they had been inflated. He wore a powder-blue suit, remarkably spotless in the heavy, bug-filled air. The white collar of his shirt showed no trace of yellow. His powder-blue trousers had a razor sharp crease in them, both front and back. He also sparkled. He had an outlandish diamond ring on the third finger of his left hand, also a diamond tiepin and a diamond-studded watch chain. As he walked across the jungle floor, rays of sunlight sifting down from the cypress leaves found his jewelry and sent out blinding beams of light. He had a cigar. He had a gray hat. His eyes were black like the Indians'. The lids were only half raised. It made him look dull-brained. Still, Sheila thought that they were kind eyes. They were cheerful eyes. She looked around to see that the Indians had stopped in their tracks. Intently, they watched the man in the powder-blue suit. Under her breath she said, "He must be the Big Cheese."

Sheila told the man her story. He leaned down to be face to face with her. In this position, the fabric of his powder-blue trousers strained at the knees. The razor-sharp creases remained.

There was something wrong with his face. There were three deep lines as white as milk. The lines were conspicuous against the blue-black sheen of his shaved face. She saw something in the furrows of the scars, a chalky orange substance. It was like talcum powder. His scars made the one she got from the hurricane seem minor.

The man nodded kindly as she told her story. He gazed attentively at her with his black eyes, pausing only to check on the Indians. The Indians waited around patiently. They seemed pleased with themselves that they had found someone for her. Someone she could talk to. On the jungle floor, crickets, spiders, and roaches made cautious journeys. They crawled across the dirty toenails of the Indians.

The man had heard of Sheila before. Her story had made the second page of the *Tampa Tribune* less than a week ago. The story was about a mother and father whose daughter had been swept away in the hurricane. They believed she was still alive out in the Everglades due to an indestructible life preserver they had made for her.

"Did it say my father was an orchestra leader?"

"Yes, I believe it did."

"Oh."

"You miss your mommy and daddy, don't you, honey?"

Sheila threw her arms around the man's neck and began to cry. She was very embarrassed by the noise she made. She was not the kind of person to make these loud kinds of noises. Her throat and sinuses were wet and flabby. She was aware of the Indians drawing closer to see her cry. She could hear their feet in the underbrush. She clasped her hands around the man's neck at the clean collar of his shirt. Her tears stained his powder-blue suit. He really was a very fat man. He was a toad of a man.

As Sheila cried, tears of sympathy rolled down the man's face. The tears washed the talcum powder out of his scars. He patted his fat hands on her back. He took a monogrammed handkerchief from the pocket of his suitcoat and dabbed his eyes with it.

The man promised to take her home. He had a boat and an airplane. He could get her to Moore Haven in one hour. Fort

164

Myers in three. To Sheila, he was the comforting proof that God answered prayers and it did not strike her as unusual that a man with a fancy suit wearing diamonds lived in an Indian hut in the middle of the Everglades.

"The first thing we got to do," the man said, "is get you out of those Indian clothes. Don't get me wrong. The Seminoles are fine people. God was looking after you when you ran into them. But they're dirty, they smell, and they'd make a trashy little thing out of you."

"They cut up my shoes and made bracelets out of the leather," Sheila confided to the man.

Sheila was right about why the Indians were so good at baseball. They watched the Philadelphia Athletics practice in Fort Myers, the man said. He said that during the dry season the Indians often poled to the west coast. The journey took them a week. There, in Fort Myers, they set up roadside stands and sold cypress tomahawks, palmetto fiber dolls, drums, and moccasins. The Indians were considered a nuisance and a health hazard by the residents of the burgeoning town. The man said they were treated like Gypsies.

Sheila told him that she would like him to take her to Fort Myers. As far as she knew, there was nothing left of Moore Haven. He should take her to Edison's house. If her family was not there, Edison would know how to find them.

"Does he really only drink milk?" the man asked of the great inventor. "Or is that just a rumor?"

"It's the only thing *I've* ever seen him drink," Sheila said.

"You don't know who I am, do you, Sheila?"

She shook her head.

"You never saw my picture in the paper?"

"No."

"I'm quite famous in the town of Chicago. They call me a gangster there. My name's Alphonso Caponi."

"Al Capone," Sheila said.

He smiled.

165

16

Al Capone was a majestic thinker. He considered himself a patriot in the grand and noble tradition. The portraits of George Washington and Abraham Lincoln hung prominently on the wall behind his desk at his headquarters in the Lexington Hotel in Chicago, Illinois. Capone considered himself a kindred spirit with these men, not a criminal. No law enforcement agency, no religious leader, no rival gang leader, and no high-ranking government official could convince him otherwise. He was not a criminal; he was a kind benefactor, a loyal public servant, and a generous and unselfish businessman. To Capone, the story of America, from the Boston Tea Party onward, was the story of strong and dedicated men standing up against unjust laws. Prohibition was such a law. People needed liquor. They needed it as they needed food, clothing, or medicine. Whiskey was a necessity in life, an irreplaceable emotional outlet, an indispensable remedy in coping with the pressures of the age. The federal government, in banning liquor, had not only demonstrated its ignorance of the American people but its contempt for them as well. Capone was not guilty of such disrespect. He knew his fellow citizens; he loved them. He felt it his duty and privilege to fulfill their needs.

Capone's understanding of himself and his role in society included his failure to perceive his boyhood in Brooklyn as the element that distanced him from the American mainstream. There, in Brooklyn at the dawn of the century, he, as the son of an Italian peasant immigrant, had cavorted with the cruel and the vicious. He associated with young men who robbed, vandalized, pilfered, extorted, terrorized, tortured, hijacked, raped, and murdered. He had learned violence as Sheila had learned her mandolin.

Capone often retreated, by train, to south Florida when the rigors of the business world in Illinois became too great. He loved Miami. He called it the "Sunny Italy of the New World." In Miami, he was nearly welcomed. At least he was not thrown out of town as he was in Los Angeles. Eventually, he bought a home on Miami Beach off the Venetian Causeway. It was a mansion. He lounged around in silk pajamas, ate pasta, drank Chianti, threw grand parties, fished for grouper off his backyard dock, and golfed in tropical splendor at the nearby country club.

Capone bored easily in south Florida. He felt his business acumen was going to waste. He learned of the Bahamian rumrunners. He sought them out and conducted business with them. With the help of a U. S. mail pilot named Patrick McKinley, he had crates of the Bahamian rum flown into remote spots in the Everglades. Here the liquor could be stored without arousing suspicion or attracting the curiosity of his competitors.

Capone thought the Everglades was a wonder. He considered it a personal gift from Jesus Christ. With all his money and power, he could not have envisioned, created, or purchased a more perfect hiding place. How could competitors encroach on territory that was unknown, uncharted, and completely inaccessible? In these Everglades, the Lord had given him a gift indeed.

Capone was so enamored with his Florida sanctuary that he set up his own still at one of the hammocks where he had earlier stored Bahamian rum. He ordered copper tubing for his still from Sears, Roebuck in Chicago. He developed a coconut rum in the Everglades that his customers found quite delicious and which he distributed throughout the southeast at a 75% profit. Capone, through his agents, had supplied the rum which spiked the punch at the Moore Haven party the night of the hurricane.

Capone felt the Lord had blessed him with the Seminoles too. They were a docile people, cheap employees, and good customers. He could truthfully say the Indians, as the dependable source of his raw materials, were the keys to his business success in the Southeast. He, however, was careful not to touch them. He would not accept their gifts either: the dolls, the tomahawks, the bracelets, the jewelry. He thought their skin appeared sickly, particularly around the fingertips and the toes. He thought their crafts might be contaminated.

Capone looked at Sheila, saw the blue eyes shining in the weathered face, and saw his own son, Albert Francis. Albert Francis, nicknamed Sonny, was born in 1919, three years after Sheila and Skeezix. Sonny was a sickly boy who was partially deaf from an early mastoid infection. Capone raised him as a prince. He gave him every worldly advantage. He showered him with gifts. He sent him to the finest Catholic schools. He got a box seat for him at every World Series.

But Capone was deeply worried about his son. The boy showed no spark, no ambition, no determination. He ate, did his homework, played baseball, went to church, said his prayers — all with little passion, pride, or interest. Capone tried to refine the boy by arranging piano and accordion lessons. He hired the most expensive music teachers in Chicago but they could not motivate him. Capone took the boy to the opera house to hear the gorgeous Verdi arias. All he did was squirm in his seat. Capone feared he was raising a crude, dull boy with no appreciation for nuance and beauty.

Capone looked into Sheila's bright eyes and thought ruefully on his own son. How he envied the father of this girl! How his chest must swell with pride! Here was a girl with talent and ambition, a girl with fire and intelligence, a girl with a guiding force and a purpose in life. How had her father managed to put the spark in her eyes that he had not been able to put into Sonny's?

Capone thought of Sheila's predicament. What if his son was lost in the Everglades? Capone was convinced that Sonny would not have survived. And it was not because of his poor health. It was because of the spark that was not there.

"I have a son about your age, Sheila," he said. "I could never get him interested in an instrument."

"That's too bad."

"Could I ask you something?"

"Of course, Mr. Capone."

"Did your father force you to practice the mandolin?"

"Maybe a little at first."

Capone nodded with great concentration.

"But he always knew what was best for us. And look where we are today."

"I know," Capone said. "You and your sister are child celebrities."

"Ha-ha. I don't know about that!"

"I need to get something straight, Sheila," he said. "Just for my own benefit."

"What is it?"

"Did you ever practice out of fear of what your father would do to you if you didn't practice?"

"Never."

Capone was a great music lover, particularly of opera. He enjoyed the popular music of the day as well, the music he so often heard in the speakeasies—the Charlestons, the fox-trots, the fandangos, and the rags. Popular music, however, did not affect his soul the way opera did. Opera came down on him like a clean rain and washed away the burdens of his life. He knew many of the standard arias note for note. In the shadows of darkened Chicago opera houses, Capone often lounged in the

169

balcony with a heavy day's growth of beard and a loosened silk tie. Grinning dreamily, he mouthed the words in Italian to *La Traviata, Aida,* and *Pagliacci.* According to Al Capone, the Italian romantic composers—Puccini, Verdi, Rossini, Leoncavallo—could do no wrong.

Capone also had a great love of the mandolin, which he played. Though he could not read music, he managed to pick out little melodies by ear, having what trained mandolinists called "an acceptable amateur tremelo."

Capone played the gourd or bowl-back mandolin. It was the type of mandolin he grew up with in Brooklyn. It was the type of mandolin which produced the tender melodies he had so often heard in the evenings floating out the tenement windows on the odor of marinara sauce. He had seen the new Gibson mandolins with their flat backs, f-holes and extended fretboards. He marvelled at them. He marvelled at the ingenuity, the technology, and the sophistication involved in their production. He, however, was not convinced that the new mandolin was an improvement over the old.

Capone was only vaguely familiar with Kirk Quintaine's Progressive Mandolin Orchestra. Long ago, he had read in the *Chicago Tribune* about a mandolin orchestra leader who employed his young twin daughters. Had he known the type of music the orchestra played, he would not have approved. He would have considered it a travesty playing ragtime music on an instrument whose identity, whose roots were in Italian folk melodies.

Sheila had heard of Al Capone. He was notorious. His name was synonymous with lawlessness, anarchy, and Prohibition. From Minnesota to Florida, his name came up in nearly every adult conversation she had heard. As recently as the engagement at Edison's home the night before the hurricane, people were talking about Al Capone. She remembered four of Edison's guests standing on the porch of his home involved in a heated conversation about Chicago lawlessness when the great inventor himself broke in.

170

"Al Capone," Edison declared, "is a dim-witted greaser with the ethics of a jackal."

Capone was a major reason her father would not book an engagement in Chicago. Her father turned down many prestigious opportunities there because of Capone and the terror he represented. She remembered how he regretted having to turn down a double billing with the Chicago Symphony Mandolin Orchestra at Orchestra Hall. Her father said the town was simply too dangerous. There were thugs with tommy guns roaming the streets mowing down other thugs for the right to supply a certain speakeasy with gin. Insanity! As much blood flowed in the streets as booze, her father said. He said those tommy guns had fifty rounds a clip. She didn't know what that meant, but it certainly sounded menacing. The worse part was that innocent victims were being caught in the crossfire. Even poor little children were being gunned down, her father said, taken from their mommies and daddies before they even knew what life was.

Sheila had never heard a machine gun. The closest she had come to a weapon was the shotgun her grandfather used to kill prairie dogs in North Dakota. Even that did not seem so dangerous, it was just a little jolt when he pulled the trigger. It was not until she saw how the gun scattered the poor little prairie dog that she realized how perfectly destructive the weapon was. She imagined being shot by something so powerful—a shotgun, a machine gun, a tommy gun. She thought it must be like being chewed up by a dragon. It was beyond her imaginings.

Sheila had seen Al Capone's picture in the papers. While on tour, she saw his various mugshots prominently adorning the pages of every newspaper from Grand Forks to Atlanta. Try as they might, though, the newspapers could never manage to make him look evil. Capone appeared even less so in real life. Sheila was no more frightened of him now that she knew who he was than when he first swaggered out of the Everglades in his perfectly pressed suit with all the diamonds. He had the gentlest of eyes. She truly believed that this man could not hurt a flea. In many ways, Capone reminded her of Mr. Roscoe Boomhower, janitor for three decades at Thomas Jefferson Elementary in Bismarck.

Sheila had other feelings about Capone. They were feelings beyond the initial shock of his harmlessness. He had a power and a presence about him. She sensed that he was a man of his word, a man of honor and integrity. He was a man, she felt, who lived his life on principles, principles that were often at odds with the conventions of the day. Yes, he was like her father. She could put her arms around Capone's neck and think clearly on him.

Sheila was glad he was who he was. Her heart beat with excitement at the prospect of Al Capone returning her to her family. If he, the king of the Chicago underworld, could not rescue her from the Everglades, who could?

He said that he had an airplane. That was another exciting prospect. She could be in Fort Myers in three hours instead of three days.

Wait until Skeezix found out who her escort was! Sheila could not have orchestrated a more dramatic homecoming if she tried. She imagined the airplane, on pontoons, pulling up to Edison's dock on the Caloosahatchee River and Capone, in full sartorial splendor, leading her by the hand onto the pier. "That's Al Capone, isn't it?" Skeezix would ask in astonishment. "In the flesh," she would answer.

Now she asked him, "Mr Capone? Do you think I look sick?"

Capone leaned down so that his face could be level with hers. He put his chubby hands on her shoulders and gazed affectionately into her eyes. Half of his face was a grin. The lopsided look made her think again of Roscoe Boomhower, the janitor.

Sheila studied the white ruts in Capone's shaved face. I am three inches from Al Capone's scars, she thought with pride.

Above, wood storks lighted on the high branches of scrub pines. Several of them, with a lack of sense that Sheila found shocking, misjudged their own weight and the strength of the branch. So the branch broke off when they landed on it. It sailed down to the forest floor as the wood stork took to the sky in alarm. Many of the Indians, grinning, strained their necks skyward and watched the spectacle, watched the splintered branches sailing towards the earth. Others did not watch but leaned against cypress trunks and sipped their bottles of booze. Still others urinated behind trees, careful that she did not see them.

She sensed that the Indians were impatient with Mr. Capone and her. They wanted to be back in their canoes, on their way to Fort Myers or back to camp. Only Big Chief Cross-in-the-Eyes did not seem restless. He stood close by them with his arms folded, grinning and nodding his head. His ebony eyes often sought out Capone's, searching for a sign of approval or at least the proper recognition. After all, the chief seemed to be thinking, it was he who was responsible for this reunion.

Capone said to Sheila, "Sick? You don't look sick at all. Considering what you've gone through, you look darn good."

"How about my teeth?"

"Your teeth?"

"Yes. Don't be afraid to tell me the truth."

"I don't see anything wrong with your teeth."

"You're just saying that," Sheila said. "I know what's happening to them. They're starting to look like theirs." She pointed at Big Chief Cross-in-the-Eyes, who was grinning. "I already have a hole. I can feel it."

It was true. There was a hole in one of her top back molars. The tooth had finally succumbed to the milkless diet, the sofki, the pumpkin biscuits with honey, and the lack of hygiene. A particle of the tooth, from one of her new permanents, had fallen off. When it happened, she stuck her finger in her mouth and withdrew the bit of tooth. It was like a little flake of fingernail there on her wet fingertip. Where the particle had been, there was a hole in her tooth. Her tongue would not leave it alone. It constantly went in there to nudge it and inspect it. The tip of her tongue was sore and there was a mark on it exactly the size of the hole. Over and over and over again, her

173

tongue went to the hole in her tooth. Yes, it was there.

Capone said, "Sheila, let me tell you something. It would take you three years of complete neglect and abuse before your teeth would even start to look as bad as theirs. These Indians . . . they don't know what a dentist is!"

When Capone stood up, gunfire rang out from the bushes. He was hit. She looked up and saw his ear . . . what did it do? . . . it *exploded!* His ear splattered like a tomato pegged at a wall. Blood and shattered fragments of cartilage leapt into the air and fell in her hair and on the Seminole costume the Indians had made her wear. She noted that her ribcage was vibrating like a drum. This was how she knew she was screaming.

Capone managed to leap over the cypress slat fence and get behind it. In his mad leap for safety, she clearly saw his shoes. They were two-tone wingtips, chocolate brown and ivory. They were Nunn Bush brand and had rubber soles. In the meantime, the guard Capone had called Jack returned fire into the bushes, squeezing the trigger of his tommy gun, chipping off big hunks of wood from the cypress trees. The guard was crying like a baby. Tears streamed down his face. "Oh shit oh shit oh shit . . ." he said. "They got him."

The Indians fled from the danger at top speed. They bounded recklessly through the jungle of the hammock like chased deer. They injured the bottoms of their bare feet as they ran. They were bright and conspicuous in their strip clothing. When the gunfire began, Big Chief Cross-in-the-Eyes snatched her up like a sack of potatoes and ran with her. He held her on the side of him that was farthest away from the gunfire. He kept his head down as he ran. He panted like a dog. Because he was breathing so hard, it occurred to her that he might be older than she had thought. A younger Indian's breathing would not be so labored she didn't think.

"*Chief!*" she cried. "I can't breathe. I think I'm turning blue."

It felt like there was a concrete block on her chest. Had she been shot too?

Capone had to be dead.

17

Οn June 12, during the summer before their visit to Florida, a famous guest attended their concert at the Ryman Auditorium in Nashville, Tennessee. It was Lloyd A. Loar, composer, soloist, inventor, and acoustical engineer for the Gibson Mandolin-Guitar Company.

In 1926, Lloyd Loar was at the peak of his fame. The F-2 and F-4 model mandolins he designed for Gibson were of such surpassing quality and craftsmanship that learned musicians everywhere were hailing them as the artistic sequel of the Amati and the Stradivarius violins. Loar, in fact, was the first to apply violin construction principles to the mandolin. He applied the concepts of the tilted neck, the high bridge, and the extension tailpiece. He insisted on naturally dried woods for his mandolins and applied the Stradivarius principle of a graduated sounding board so that the entire body of the instrument vibrated and not just the area around the bridge. He also came close to the theoretically perfect fingerboard, falling only one and one-eighth inch short of the ideal ten and one-half inches. The result of his efforts was a mandolin so sensitive that it sang like a harp in the wind. Such was Loar's stature as an acoustical genius, that he, weekly, turned down positions from major universities across the United States to teach acoustical science.

Lloyd Loar also enjoyed acclaim as a soloist both on the mandolin and the musical saw. He was also a composer.

In 1921, he was awarded first prize for his violoncello solo in the contest for American composers held by the National Federation of Music Clubs. Loar was a musical inventor too. He recently patented an instrument called the mando-viola which threatened to make the standard mandolin obsolete. The mando-viola, which boasted five pairs of unison strings, encompassed, from its open low C to the twelfth fret on its E string, an unheard-of four and one-half octave range!

Lloyd Loar had only a vague familiarity with Kirk Quintaine's Progressive Mandolin Orchestra. Through business associates and fellow mandolinists, he had heard of the eccentric Indian jazz composer, his pretty wife, and his twin daughters in the second mandolin section. His most cynical mandolin acquaintances considered the use of his daughters in the orchestra as a cheap publicity ploy. Loar knew too that, through Gibson, Kirk Quintaine owned one of his signed F-2 model mandolins.

On June 12, Loar had business in Nashville. He had a free evening and decided to attend the concert. He purchased two tickets at seventy-five cents apiece. The seats were in the twelfth row, right center stage.

He came to the concert in casual attire. It was a shock to his fans who had only seen him on stage in his tuxedo. He was dressed in white. He had a white cardigan sweater with a burgundy trim, a white open-collar shirt, white trousers, white socks and white loafers. His escort was a lady younger than himself who had spit curls and a black flapper hat. Before the concert began, the emcee introduced him. Loar rose from his auditorium seat and acknowledged the crowd's cheers by clasping his hands over his head and shaking them like a prizefighter in victory.

Loar's presence made her father nervous. Sheila could tell.

176

Her father opened the concert with his own arrangement of Thurlow Lieurance's "By the Waters of Minnetonka," an Indian love song. The arrangement featured the mandobasses imitating Indian tom-toms by tapping the faces of their instruments with their fingertips. With Loar in the audience, her father could not keep the tempo down. The orchestra raced away with it.

Sheila could see Lloyd Loar perfectly from her position in the second row of the orchestra. Her eyes moved between the notes on her page, her father's baton, and Lloyd Loar in the twelfth row of the auditorium. Loar's light brown hair was combed straight back with no part. He seemed to enjoy her mother's vocals. He smiled during "Iola." Sometimes he looked right at Sheila. Sometimes he looked right at Skeezix. He did not look at his escort. After the fifth number, Loar rose from his auditorium seat. He grabbed his escort by the hand and left. His white shoes made a clattering sound up the aisles of the auditorium.

It was a merciful departure. The concert went downhill quickly after he left. The people did not enjoy Indian jazz. They began to shout for Sousa. One man in the balcony cried out: "CAN THAT WAMPUM MUSIC, BIGHEAD!"

The hostility from the audience was compounded by some mountain folk in the center balcony. They had cleaned themselves up for the occasion in hand-me-down clothes and meticulous and severe hairstyles. The men wore trousers with high hems. They wore long-sleeved shirts buttoned to the top button. The women wore long gowns with flower prints embellished with lace so that they resembled draperies. They reeked of dime-store cologne. The mountain folk had come down from the Cumberlands to hear banjo and jug music and were none too pleased to hear the highfalutin music of a string orchestra. They were rude. They ogled her mother.

Sheila felt the audience was very close to throwing things at them: tomatoes, bottles, papers, fruit.

Later in the evening, the orchestra reconvened at the hotel's dining room where they had a late-night supper of Tennessee specialties: smoked ham, sausage gravy and biscuits, turnip greens, and lemon icebox pie. The men in the orchestra sat around the dining room table with their bow ties unknotted and hanging limp over their tuxedo shirts. They put their faces down close to their plates and made clinking sounds with their forks on the china as they shoveled in the food. The women in the orchestra showed more decorum in their table manners. Some had, however, let their hair down or loosened the straps of their shoes. Emily Jackson, mandobassist, poked the ham on her plate with the tines of her fork while, under the table, only her toes were in her shoes so that the reinforced heels of her stockings were exposed. Her mother had taken off her knee-high moccasins completely and ate her supper with bare feet underneath the table. She still had her makeup on, though, and her Indian gown. Sheila had always loved the gown. It was spectacular. It was full-length brushed deerskin with an entire foot of buckskin fringe at the hem that brushed the floor where she walked.

Sheila sat next to Skeezix in the dining room. They ate their supper. Sheila watched her father. Tonight's concert was one of their biggest failures ever. And it was not only that Lloyd Loar had walked out after twenty minutes. Their music had been rejected, absolutely and unanimously rejected. Not one soul in the Ryman Auditorium had been converted to Indian jazz. Yet, watching her father, he did not seem bothered by it. His cheeks were flushed, it was true, but they always turned that shade of scarlet after a concert. He ate well. He had two pieces of ham. He sat in the center of the dining room table and conversed with the men on the usual topics: Lyon and Healy vs. Gibson, tuning problems, loose pickguards, the inconsistency of new strings, buzzes, and universal notation.

But very early in the morning she saw her father on the fire escape outside their hotel room. There were bats flying around out there, or nighthawks, she wasn't sure which. A gleaming crescent moon hung in the center of the sky. Its light bathed the Tennessee Valley, enlivening the Cumberland River on the eastern horizon. Her father still had his tuxedo on.

"Daddy?"

"What are you doing up, Skeezix?"

"I'm Sheila."

"Sheila."

"Are you crying?"

"No."

"Yes, you are, Daddy. You're crying."

"No, I'm not."

"Well then, you *almost* are."

"GO AWAY."

"No, I won't"

"Okay, stay then. If you're going to stay, stay."

It was a hot night in Tennessee. Her father's tuxedo was soaked in perspiration. The effusions trailing from his sideburns ensnared the moonglow and shone like silver streams in the night. The flying things she had seen before were not bats. They were nighthawks. The nighthawks swooped and darted in the air, chasing moths. The moths spun around like tops in the blueberry sky until they suddenly disappeared in the beaks of the birds.

Her father said, "I wish so much that I could play the music that the people want to hear. It would make things so simple. So easy. I wish so much that I could take out my Carl Fisher order form and send out for the stock arrangements, the surefire crowd pleasers. *Guaranteed* to put a lump in your throat. *Guaranteed* to make your breast swell. *Guaranteed* to set your toes to tapping. I think I would be a very good crowd pleaser. I think I would be one of the best. The problem is I just can't bring myself to do it. I don't know what's wrong with me. I'm hell-bent on playing music that audiences hate."

"We had a bad night, Daddy. That's all."

"I just . . . I just . . . I just can't do it. As soon as I pull out a stock arrangement, I don't stand for anything anymore. Yes, I do. I stand for earning a wage. I stand for putting bread on the table. I stand for being a working musician. That's what I stand for when I pull out a stock arrangement."

"You know what, Daddy? I don't think Lloyd Loar walked out tonight because he didn't like the music. I could see him from where I was sitting. I could see him perfectly. His escort got sick. That's what it was. Lloyd Loar was smiling when he was there."

"Was he?"

"*Yes.* He *liked* it. He especially liked Mom's singing."

"I appreciate that pack of lies, Sheila. It was a very thoughtful gesture. Ha! His escort got sick, huh? You could have dreamed up something better than that."

"I didn't dream it up."

"You know that I know that you're lying, so let's not talk about it."

"What do you want to talk about?"

"I want to talk about music. There's a music out there that's *righter* than any music that's ever been done before, a music that's more beautiful, more meaningful, more exciting. I can't do anything else in my life but to go looking for it. The silliest thing of all is that I don't ever expect to find it. I don't ever expect to find that glorious, hidden music. But, as I grow older, it matters less and less. It's the *search* that's the important thing. Can you understand that, sweetheart?"

"No, Daddy."

"I can't either," he said. "It's a pitiful life, but it's mine."

"Daddy, I don't *ever* want to do any music than what we're doing now."

Inside the hotel, the orchestra slept and dreamed. Soon, the purple dawn rose over the Cumberland River.

She began to transcribe the Seminole's music, their work songs, their celebration songs, their dance songs, their lullabies, and their religious songs. For paper, she used the skin or the bark of the banana tree. At the base of each giant leaf, there was a thick, tough section that, when dried out and cut

180

into rectangles, made a suitable parchment. She used quills for her writing implements, the quills of ibis, heron, egret, or spoonbill. The water birds shed their feathers about the camp and it was a challenge, every morning when she rose, to wander through the camp and find the very best quills. For ink, she used the residue from the soft-shelled turtle. When a soft-shelled turtle was boiled, a black scum rose to the surface of the water it was boiled in. The scum made an excellent ink. She collected it in one of the Indian's discarded booze bottles.

Transcribing the Seminole's music was a gruesome task. The intonation was unearthly. The Indians sang in a nasal grunt. This was not music. It was an *abuse* of music. Then, to compound her notational problems, the Indians frequently shouted and howled in their songs. She transcribed it as glissandi. How else could she notate it? Truly, the Seminole's music defied transcription. Still, she persevered.

She began each song with a melodic contour, moving her quill across the banana skin in a wavy connected line. The hills and valleys of the line reflected the rise and fall of the pitches. It was difficult. Pitch was not her forte. She did not have perfect pitch. Neither did Skeezix, though their audiences liked to think they both did. Since Sheila had no musical instrument for verification, her pitch transcription was nothing more than an educated guess.

She thought in terms of her mandolin as she attempted to write the notes. She knew ascending and descending fifth intervals because of the open strings on her mandolin. She knew half-steps because of the frets. She also knew their tuning note A and G below middle C. G below middle C vibrated her skull in an unmistakable way.

Her only salvation in writing their music was the presence of sequential patterns. This, at least, gave her a frame of reference. In "Song for a Sick Baby," she transcribed the first section with the tones F, E flat, C, and B flat. The same intervals appeared in the second section as B flat, A flat, F, and E flat, the pattern in duplicate, down a fifth.

Rhythm was even more insidious. She prided herself on her rhythmic skills. She could punch out ragtime syncopations with the best adults in the orchestra. Give her any dot, any tie, any rest, any combination or variance of sixteenth note and triplet and she could, usually, play them at sight. Unfortunately, her ragtime knowledge was to little or no avail with the Seminole's music. The major problem was that the pulse beat constantly shifted as did the beats to the bar. It was baffling. It was aggravating. Sometimes, she threw her quill down in frustration. She transcribed the beginning of "Song of the Medicine Man's Dance" with a measure of 7/8, followed by a measure of 4/8, followed by a measure of 5/8, followed by a measure of 3/4, followed by a measure of 2/4, then followed by another measure of 3/4! Another problem was the Indian's fondness for taking a standard eighth note triplet, subdiving it into sixteenths, then sounding only a sparse and illogical sample of the sixteenths.

She knew her transcriptions were not accurate. Her hope was that they were accurate enough so that she could, on a later date, recall them for her father. Her father would notate the Seminole's grunts with total accuracy. His transcriptions would be like capturing butterflies then pinning them to a board.

On the back side of her banana skins, she often jotted words. The words were extra-musical things that might help her recall the song at a later date. In "The Cypress Swamp Hunting Dance Song," she wrote:

Movement of dancers is outlined by four posts, at corners of a square. Fire is in the middle of the space. Dancers start at west end move toward the south, then east, then north. The remainder of their turns are around the four posts. In definite order. Passing by the southwest and southeast posts, the dancers circle the northeast post, approaching it from the east. Then they circle the southwest post, then go to the northwest post, moving around it to the east side of the square where they pass around the southeast post, after which they go north, pass around the outline of the square and return to their original position.

Sheila referred to their musical instruments on the back page of the "Corn Dance Song."

The Indians used coconut shell rattles to keep time to the music. Some of the women wore anklets made of small turtle carapaces strung together. The carapaces are sealed and filled with what sounds like little pebbles. When the women dance, the turtle shells sound in rhythm to the song.

Big Chief Cross-in-the-Eyes played a water drum. It was a black kettle half-filled with water and covered over the top with a buckskin head. He beat the drum with one stick about ten inches long with rags wrapped around it. Also, one of the Indians played the cane flute. Shrill and hideous. Transcription—*IMPOSSIBLE*!!!!

Sheila kept her banana bark under the platform where she slept, wrapped in a Seminole apron. Each morning when she woke, she pulled the apron out from under the platform and brushed crickets, spiders, grasshoppers, and little frogs off of it. On rainy nights, she kept the bundle of music on top of the platform and used it as a pillow. The bundle kept getting bigger and bigger and bigger like a bloated mosquito. The Indians had a lot of songs.

"My father," she told them one day, "is going to take this music here, add some jazz to it, and put it into one of his compositions. Then our mandolin orchestra will play it all over the country. Doesn't that make you proud?"

It was difficult to tell to what extent the Indians understood what she was doing. Surely, she felt, they must know that she was capturing music with pen and paper. She always hummed when she wrote the notes. She always hummed and she always tapped her toe. The Indians loved to watch her tap her toe. Sometimes, they gathered around her in their strip skirts and ebony hair. As the sun beat down on the thatched roofs of their huts, they gazed at her. Their eyes moved between her tapping toe and her quill.

The children especially loved to watch. They had more time to do so. They were not required to do chores. They played all day. Sheila did not like the Indian children. They did not have poise, composure, or discipline. They did not realize the importance of what she was doing. They were easily distracted. They would often gather around to watch her write music then suddenly dart away to play with the dogs or throw rocks at alligators or engrave pictures into the marl earth with a stick.

The Indians did not make judgments about her activity. They neither approved nor disapproved of her transcriptions. Sometimes they supplied her with her banana barks for the day. Sometimes they did not. Big Chief Cross-in-the-Eyes seemed happy that she was writing music. Unlike the others, he tried to understand what she was doing. She wondered if, with his crossed eyes, he saw the notes on the page as double images.

The banana bark on which she wrote, though an acceptable parchment, was nonetheless porous and oftentimes gave way to the pressure of her quill. It was irritating in the heat of transcription, while she was pinning down an elusive Indian rhythmic figure. The tip of her quill punched through the paper with an audible popping sound, rendering the bark useless. She expressed her fury with one word. Day in and day out, the word rang through the camp.

"Drat."

Drat, she would have to start all over.

Drat was the first English word the Indians learned. She was astonished the first time she heard it. In a muddy stream of Indian speech, the word shone like a pearl. Drat. Astonishing too, the Indians knew how to use the word. When a woman burned her finger on a hot kettle, she said it. When a man made a carpentry error with his log canoe, he said it. When an elder lost a molar to decay, he said it. When a child had an earth picture ruined by a careless dog, he said it. Drat. The Indians correctly associated the word with frustration.

Sheila transcribed over one hundred and seventy Seminole songs in the course of twenty-five days. She transcribed over one hundred and seventy work songs, celebration songs, hunting songs, dancing songs, legend songs, sport songs, religious songs, lullabies, and chants. She notated the songs one to a page with detailed notes on the reverse side containing information to aid her recall. Then she broke down.

It was a long night in November. She could no longer keep her mind on her music. She could not think for one more instant on "The Skunk Dance Song," or "The Song for a Sick Child," or "Seminole Lullaby #14." She could only think of one thing. She might *never* be rescued. The full horror of that thought struck her all at once. She might *never* be rescued. She might spend the rest of her life with primitive strangers who did not clean themselves, who let their children run wild, and whose music was a sick perversion of every standard she had ever been taught. She might spend the rest of her life sleeping on a platform while her parents and her sister enjoyed the comforts that America had worked for over a century to ensure its citizens. She might spend the rest of her life in a jungle that, for its sheer inaccessibility and uncharted wildness, might as well be the Matto Grosso of Brazil. She might spend the rest of the 1920s, the 1930s, the 1940s, the 1950s, the 1960s, and on up in a monotonous climate filled with bugs, her hair turning white, her face growing wrinkled.

Already she was changing. She could feel it. She was growing up. Her skull was shifting to make room for her enlarging brain. She could feel it. The bone between her elbow and her wrist was elongating to prepare her for adult arms. She could feel it. Her cheeks were filling out; she was getting fat because of the starchy foods. Her hair, a dark brown, was getting lighter because of the constant exposure to the sun.

There was a shock of hair in back that was actually turning blond! There was more hair on her arms: long, curly hair, starting at her triceps and moving down to her wrists. Her teeth were decaying at an alarming rate. The molar with what had started out as a tiny hole was half-gone now, disintegrated. Sometimes she lay down on her platform and listened to herself changing. She could hear nature taking its course in her body. She could hear herself growing up.

She cried and cried and cried that night. The Indians would never again go to Fort Myers. After the gunfire at Capone's hidden still, they were afraid to leave their camp. They were afraid to so much as travel a half-mile to the nearest neighboring village. If the Indians had any interest in reuniting her with her family, it was destroyed after their brush with death at the hands of the white man.

Her father would never give up on her, that she knew. He would scour the Everglades for her until he was an old man, until he had a white beard down to his knees like Rip Van Winkle. If she could tell him anything, it would be first that she loved him, and, second, that he should give up. He was a man of too great a talent to spend the rest of his life searching for her. Nobody knew how vast this swamp was. He might die before he found her.

As for dear old Mr. Edison, he was a great inventor and a kind and humble person. He had treated Skeezix and her with great respect and affection. Still, he was only a man, not a god. He could not pluck her out of the swamp at will. And the great contraption she envisioned him inventing for her—an aerial, telescopic, heat-sensitive person finder—was only, she knew, a product of her imagination. Mr. Edison was old; he had a few precious years left. He must devote himself to inventions that would serve all humanity and not one lost girl in the Everglades.

So her hope was gone and she cried. She could not stop crying and she kept the Indians awake. In the night, they grumbled in their Indian tongue. Finally, the old woman came forward. It was the old woman who had treated her wound after the hurricane. She pressed Sheila's head to her shoulders and comforted her, stroking her hair and singing soft lullabies.

"Get your diseased fingers off me, old lady!"

Sheila's mouth dropped in horror. She had never, never spoken to an adult so rudely.

18

Thomas Edison was milking his goat outside the Glades County Courthouse when Skeezix found the letter.

The letter was on his pillow at the head of his Red Cross cot. It was folded in three equal sections and lay open on the pillow. The torn envelope that contained the letter was on the floor.

Skeezix didn't pick up the letter to read it. She left it on the pillow and glanced down at it from a standing position. She looked casually around the inside of the courthouse to see if anyone noticed her. This was eavesdropping and her mother and father would not approve.

The letter was from Mina Edison. It was filled with hateful things. Skeezix's stomach churned as she read. Skeezix imagined Mrs. Edison writing the letter at the dining room table of their home in Fort Myers as mockingbirds flitted among the bougainvillea outside the windows. Mrs. Edison was younger than her husband. She had not been friendly to Sheila or her when the orchestra played at their house. As she read Mrs. Edison's words, she recalled the woman's behavior that night. She recalled her behavior distinctly.

Nov. 1, 1926

My dearest husband Thomas,

What, for the love of Pete, are you still doing in that godforsaken town of Moore Haven? Can you answer me that? Surely you can no longer nourish the hope that Sheila Quintaine is still alive. I am reluctant to say this, but say it I must: That little girl's bones were cleaned by the vultures long ago. That bit of unpleasantry may be difficult for you to accept, but the sooner you accept it, the better off you'll be. To nurse a fantasy that the little darling is out in the Everglades somewhere subsisting on berries or being cared for by savages is *pure folly!* Worse yet, to build up that family's hopes with such tommyrot is cruel torture. Don't you see, you only prolong their agony.

I must say, Thomas, that your insistence on this rescue extravaganza for *one little kid* forces me to question the condition of your mental faculties.

Skeezix once again looked around the courthouse to see if anyone was watching her read the letter. She pushed the first page aside and began page two.

Need I remind you that you are the greatest inventor the world has ever known? Your public, the great masses of humanity, anxiously awaits your every advance. How can you let them down, these millions and millions of souls, by frittering away your golden years on a futile search for a lost child?

You are no spring chicken, Mr. Edison. Your days of greatness are numbered. I would think you would consider spending your time wisely in the pursuit of a crowning achievement, and not on some doomed rescue mission.

The most painful part for me is wondering whether you would devote all this time and energy to one of your own children or grandchildren if they had been lost like

189

Sheila Quintaine. I lay awake at night wondering about this. You know that it is a very painful subject for me and I have shed more than one tear with my doubts. Please come home. You've been gone a month.
Your loving wife,
Mina

P.S. I know how you like to leave things around. Please don't let "The Brain" get her paws on this. Keep it hidden.

Later, it dawned on Skeezix. *She* was "The Brain" that Mina Edison referred to in her letter.

Edison did not seem affected by the letter. Perhaps he did not read it, Skeezix thought. More likely, her words rolled off him like water off a duck. Skeezix sensed that Edison ignored his wife. He came back into the courthouse with a pail brimming with goat's milk. He poured some of the milk into a glass and drank it warm. He told the group of his latest brainstorm. He was sending for a kid from St. Louis, a barnstorming pilot. Edison said it was his best idea so far. He spoke rapidly. His ancient, blue-veined hands trembled with excitement. His blue eyes beamed. His face turned red. Flecks of foam sprayed from his mouth as he spoke.

"I've been reading about him," Edison told the gathering of musicians and rescue workers. "He's an aerial wizard. He's a barnstormer, a wing-walker, and a parachutist. He was with the Army Air Corps. He's done some stunts that are unbelievable! He can grab a flag off the top of a pine tree without slowing down. Now is that precision flying, my friends? I should say so. I figure a man of his ability could comb the entire Everglades—down low—in just a couple of days."

Skeezix glanced down at the letter on Edison's pillow. It was exactly as she had found it though, most likely, Edison would not notice anyway. She watched his old hands shake as he spoke of the young pilot from St. Louis. For a moment, she forgot Mina Edison's nasty words.

190

"He's been to Florida before," Edison continued. "Two days after the hurricane, he flew a reporter from the *St. Louis Post Dispatch* down to Miami. He flies day or night, it doesn't matter to him. He has no fear because he's an expert parachutist. He's doing a mail route now, from St. Louis to Chicago. I think a kid like him would jump at a challenge like this."

"That is a definite plus that he's been to Florida before," Broadus Gantt said. "How much were you going to offer him?"

"A hundred dollars," Edison said.

Paddle fans creaked overhead. Raymond Osceola picked up a cockroach by its antennae and smiled at Skeezix. The cockroach struggled wildly against its confinement, the coffee-colored legs fluttering audibly in the damp room.

Broadus Gantt did not see Osceola's prank. He listened intently to Edison's plan. Skeezix knew that he felt responsible for Sheila's predicament. On that fateful night, he had lost her in his attempt to save her. Gantt was as determined as her father to find Sheila. Unlike her father, however, Gantt always had a cheery countenance, a positive attitude. Never had she seen his eyes fade with doubt. In this way, he was more like Edison. She thought for a moment on Broadus Gantt. He was a high school classics teacher who owned an Egyptian banjo of pure gold.

Lindbergh arrived three days later, on a Tuesday night. He wore a dark brown leather jacket. He wore a visorless cap with a chin strap. He wore flying goggles with an elastic band that clung to his skull. He walked up the steps to the courthouse slapping mosquitoes on his hands and face. The rescue party stood outside the door to greet him.

"Are the mosquitoes always this bad?" Lindbergh asked.

"No. They're often worse. I'm Henry Ford."

Skeezix thought Lindbergh smelled. He smelled of the higher altitudes, a region she imagined above the clouds where the air was fresh and cold and often turned into solid matter in the form of ice crystals. Lindbergh was a thin man with a somber face. His skin was tanned and weatherbeaten. His brown eyes were chocolate pools sunk deep in his leathery face. She looked at his hands. They were the hands of a day laborer. His hands were black with grease. There were arcs of dirt under his fingernails.

Lindbergh went through and greeted each rescue worker personally. Edison flashed his dentures at him and called him son. Ford said he wouldn't get up in one of those flying machines if his life depended on it. When Lindbergh got around to Skeezix, she introduced herself.

"Mr. Lindbergh, I'm Skeezix Quintaine. My sister is the one we're looking for. I don't know if Mr. Edison told you, but she's my twin. She looks almost exactly like me."

"Oh," Mr. Lindbergh said.

"So . . . *this* is what you're looking for." She pointed to herself and smiled. She smiled at him the way she smiled to the audience when she was introduced on stage. It was her professional smile.

"It's nice to meet you, Skeezix."

His hand was cold like she thought it would be. When he wasn't looking, she checked her hand to see if any of his grease had rubbed off on her.

Lindbergh joined them for supper. He ate six cans of the Vienna sausages. She counted. He tried some of Edison's goat milk and said it was creamy.

Edison asked him question after question after question. Lindbergh was flying a Curtiss Oriole with a ninety-horsepower engine and a hundred-and-ten-gallon gas tank. On his trip from St. Louis, Lindbergh had had to refuel in Murfreesboro, Tennessee, and Valdosta, Georgia. He had landed the airplane in a sugarcane field near a line of Australian pine trees. It was a half mile from the courthouse.

"We think she's in a Seminole camp," Edison said. "There's many of them out there in the swamp. One of the problems is they live in these little huts called chickees. From the air, they probably look all the same. Another problem is that they have probably dressed her up like an Indian, so it's gonna be hard to distinguish her. That's what we're up against."

"If I can have Skeezix in the cockpit with me—"

"No, she's not going up."

"—then I could always see what it is I'm looking for."

"She's not going up, Mr. Lindbergh. It's as simple as that. I've lost one daughter. I'm not losing another."

What was it about this man? What *was* it? Simply, he was a fanatic. He was an intense fanatic. His leg jiggled all the time. His left leg. He had so much nervous energy. His body, the thin, boyish frame, could not contain it all. The energy leapt off of him like electric sparks and gave a charge to anyone who got too close. In this way, Lindbergh was like her father. But with people they were different. Her father was keenly aware of people's reaction to him. No one escaped the scrutiny he gave their reaction. Her father often thought long and hard about the people who liked and disliked him. She sometimes caught him frowning into the night with his great chin resting in his hand. He was thinking about them. Lindbergh was the opposite. He was oblivious to people. He forged ahead, never distracted by their opinions. There seemed to be an invisible and impenetrable wall around his skull. When questions were asked of him, he answered them in a way that made it seem as if *he* had asked them. And when her mother raised her voice in protest to Skeezix going up in the plane with him, he went on with the discussion of his plan as if she had sat there silent.

"Well, I'm going to bed," Lindbergh said. "I suppose you'll want to get going bright and early tomorrow."

"The sun rises at 5:40," Edison said.

"You're the boss."

"You're goddam right I am."

Lindbergh leaned down close to Skeezix so that she could see his clear eyes. "Crotchety old goat, isn't he?"

She saw Lindbergh again much later. It was 3:30 A.M. He was outside on the courthouse steps. With his dirty fingers, he was trying to extract a coconut from its husk.

"I couldn't sleep," he told her.

"I couldn't either."

She sat down next to him in her nightgown.

She had gotten some pimples in the last week or so. She was painfully aware of them now, sitting next to Lindbergh in the night. The pimples were on her forehead. She had about eight of them. They were nasty little volcanoes about to erupt. She felt them tenderly with her fingers.

"I sure hope we find my sister tomorrow," Skeezix said.

Lindbergh was breathing hard. The husk would not let go of the coconut. She looked above them to the fronds of the royal palm trees around the courthouse. They were still against the night. The fronds did not so much as flicker. In those trees, she sensed the yellow eyes of enormous owls searching the ground below for rats. They were out here, the rats, sneaking around in the dark on their four little paws, testing the air with their fine whiskers.

"These people are musicians," Skeezix told Lindbergh. "They're meant to play music for people, not trudge around in a swamp all day. They're miserable. My mother is sick. She has a temperature. I felt her forehead tonight. It must be a hundred and two or three. Sometimes I feel her hand. Her wedding ring is hot. She hates me to do it, to feel for her temperature. I say, 'Mother, I know you're sick.' She has sinus problems. She has a lot of phlegm in her throat. She really needs to see a doctor."

Lindbergh finally wrenched the coconut from its husk. The fibers of the husk, like string, lay scattered by the courthouse steps in tufts, yellow in the moonlight. Lindbergh tried to crack the coconut on the side of the steps as if it were an egg. It split longways and he lost most of his milk. The coconut milk lay in a clear puddle on one of the steps and he said, "Darn! I *wanted* that." Inside the courthouse, she heard snoring. That, and the whining of bedsprings. It might be her father in there tossing and turning. She had begun to hate the inside of the courthouse. It smelled of mildew, unchanged bedsheets, and lost hope.

"My mother still won't look at me. I mean really look at me," Skeezix said. "I guess because I remind her of Sheila. Sometimes I'll catch her shaking her head with this look on her face. It is a look without any hope at all. It's as if she has made some mistake so horrible that not even God can forgive her. My mother and father rarely say anything to each other, and, if they do, it's never very friendly. They don't touch anymore. My father always used to put his arm around her after supper. He never does that anymore. They both seem angry but never at anything in particular. They're just angry. You know, Mr. Lindbergh, my mother used to have the most beautiful skin in the world. I know you wouldn't believe that now, but she could have been on a magazine cover. Her skin was so milky-white and smooth. But now, look at it. It's weathered and wrinkled and she's getting this little blue vein by the side of her one eye. The worst part is that she doesn't care. She doesn't take care of herself anymore."

Lindbergh yawned. He complained about the weather. He hated the Florida air. It was so thick you could cut it with a knife he said. This air, so hot and heavy, was unhealthy for the lungs. It was not meant to be breathed by humans. It was meant to be breathed by the reptiles, the bugs, and the odd-looking birds that ruled this hostile world. He continued working at his coconut. With his dirty fingernails, he dug at a half-inch layer of snow-white meat that clung to the shell.

Skeezix said, "I don't think my mother believes that Sheila is still alive."

Lindbergh glanced at Skeezix to see a tear rolling down her face. He threw up his hands.

"Look at this now. She's crying."

Lindbergh sighed as if he had been outrageously persecuted. What had *he* done to be singled out for this cruel torture at the hands of an importunate child? He licked coconut shavings off his fingernails and shook his head. He shook his head in extreme distaste. Skeezix sensed in her stomach that it was not from the coconut but from her behavior.

"We'll find your sister tomorrow," Lindbergh said. "So quit crying, all right? I came out here for some peace and quiet, not to listen to you boo-hoo. Boo-hoo. Boo-hoo."

Skeezix rubbed the tears from her face with the sleeve of her nightgown. "All I wanted was a little sympathy, Mr. Lindbergh," she said. "A little sympathy."

Edison slept late the morning he told Lindbergh the sunrise was at 5:40 A.M. He slept in a fetal position on the top of the covers of his cot while sunlight pierced the room through the Venetian blinds. The harsh rectangular sunbeams struck the great inventor all over his sleeping body and pried at his very eyelids.

Everyone gathered around him and watched him sleep. Skeezix counted twenty-seven people. There was Leroy Fink, Valentine T. Peck, D.E. Lichtenfels, F.W. Clancy, H.H. Pickering, Winthrop DuQuesne, Xavier Tesch, H. Russell Truitt, her mother, her father, herself, Broadus Gantt, Al the Pinkerton guard, Silas "Buster" Nobles, the sternwheeler captain, Ford, Lindbergh, and ten Red Cross workers including Lennie and Raymond Osceola.

There was a question as to whether Edison was alive. While he slept, there were lapses where his chest did not move for as long as fifteen seconds at a time! It grew deadly silent inside the courthouse whenever this happened and she could hear the dragonflies bumping the screen windows, roaches scurrying in the shadows, and mockingbirds singing outside. Then Edison would gasp, jolt, or twitch and a collective sigh would resound through the courthouse and people would resume to chat, to drink their coffee, or pass the time in their own way.

"All right! All right!" Al the Pinkerton guard finally yelled. "Let's break this up. Can't a man sleep in peace? How would you like everyone staring at you while you were sleeping?"

The last question was directed at the Indian relief worker in the cowboy boots, Raymond Osceola. Al the Pinkerton guard

196

had taken an instant disliking to the brash Indian, and, as the weeks wore on, their association only deteriorated.

"Let me tell you something, Al," Osceola said. "If I had invented the electric lightbulb, I would *expect* people to watch me sleep, eat, shit, whatever I did. It's the price of fame, fella."

"You know what the price of a big mouth is, Injun? It's a broken jaw."

"Ooo, big man with a gun."

Osceola turned to his fellow Red Cross workers for support when Lindbergh stepped in and broke up the impending fracas. He grabbed Al the Pinkerton guard by the arm and led him away. He whispered something in his ear. Skeezix saw Lindbergh's hand clenched tight around Al's upper arm. The pilot's knuckles were white from the tension.

Of all the people watching Edison sleep, Lindbergh was the most impatient for him to wake up. It seemed that way to Skeezix anyway. He shook his head in disgust, sighed, jiggled his foot, looked at his watch, looked out the window, yawned, swatted mosquitoes, paced the mud-caked floor of the courthouse, stood up, sat down, stood up and sat down again.

When Lindbergh wasn't looking at Edison, he was looking at her mother. Skeezix had several theories about this. Perhaps he stared at her out of curiosity alone. That was her first theory. After all, she was a novelty, the lone woman in the group. Then again, perhaps her mother was simply more pleasant to rest his eyes on than the other musicians. This, even though her beauty was a fraction of what it had been. Skeezix's third theory was that Lindbergh was staring at her mother to decide if she was ill, as ill as Skeezix told him last night.

She would not approve of him. He might be destined for greatness, but she would not approve. The mother she knew before Sheila disappeared would not approve of Charles Lindbergh. He was dirty and aloof. He was not kind to people.

"Are we going to wait around all day for him to wake up?" Lindbergh finally yelled. "Good Lord. Someone shake him. It's half past eight. We've already lost half a day! I thought this was the guy who never slept."

Ford took Lindbergh aside. He defended Edison in a quiet voice as if he were afraid of waking him. Skeezix marvelled at Ford's diplomacy. He showed sympathy for Lindbergh's impatience. He did not hold his dirty fingernails against him.

Ford said to Lindbergh, "Edison might have burned the midnight oil when he was a young man, but he's nearly eighty years old now. He needs his rest."

We younger people must show understanding, Ford said kindly. We too will be eighty years old someday.

19

Edison opened his eyes to the world at ten minutes after ten. The courthouse erupted in spontaneous applause. The only people who did not applaud were Kirk, Lily, and Lindbergh. They were not good-natured about Edison's extravagant sleeping habits. Lindbergh owned an old Elgin pocketwatch that he kept zipped up in the right-hand pocket of his flight jacket. For the past hour, he had gazed at the watch in disbelief. The watch was a heavy silver timepiece that took up all of his palm. On the ivory face of the watch, roman numerals were finely etched in black.

"He may be a genius," Lindbergh said, "but someone should have waked him up. We've lost most of the morning now."

Lindbergh slipped the watch back in his flight jacket.

"I suppose now he'll have to go milk his goat."

Edison was ready to go at thirty minutes past ten. He led the search party to Lindbergh's plane on the outskirts of town. It was a half-mile walk from the courthouse and the mosquitoes were everywhere. Skeezix walked between her parents, holding one of each of their hands. Edison halted the journey abruptly several times to search for parrots he believed he heard in the tops of the trees.

"Wait. Listen. Don't you hear?"

199

The entire search party stopped and craned their necks to the sky. Squinting in the sunlight, they peered into the crowns of royal palm trees for parrots.

"What is this parrots?" Lindbergh cried. "The guy is stone deaf. How could he possibly hear parrots way up there?"

Lindbergh pointed to the tops of the palm trees. Before he could say another word, however, he chanced upon Henry Ford's doleful look of reproach. Lindbergh sighed and was silent.

In time, the search party reached Lindbergh's Curtiss Oriole.

Half the town of Moore Haven was there. The majority of the townspeople had returned to reclaim their property and assess their damages from the hurricane. In the process, they heard rumors of celebrities coming into town to search for Sheila Quintaine, the lost member of the Amazing Mandolin Twins.

The townspeople milled about the vicinity of Lindbergh's plane. Some were actually on it. Two men in knickers and two-toned shoes sat on the silver fuselage, straddling it as if it were a horse. A red-haired teenage boy with freckles sat in the cockpit and spun the steering wheel. Two women sunbathed on top of the wings. The women had spit curls and wore bathing suits that revealed the milk-white skin on their legs. A dog was in the passenger seat. Someone had put it there and it was afraid to get down. It was a dalmatian and it beat its spotted tail on the seat and smacked its lips nervously. At the front of the plane, countless young boys took turns spinning the giant wooden propeller blades. Near the ground under the cockpit, two old women in Sunday dresses sat on the giant Firestone wheels.

Some of the townspeople sat on the ground near the plane, in the shade of the Australian pine trees. They sat among the fallen red needles and egret droppings. They brought picnic lunches with egg salad sandwiches wrapped in wax paper. They had dill pickles soaked in vinegar. They drank Coca-Colas out of opaque green bottles. They smoked Chesterfield cigarettes. They played mumbly peg. They spun yo-yos. There was a pinochle game. Two people had ukuleles made out of cigar boxes. Someone had a blue kite in the air.

Lindbergh raced ahead of the search party. His mouth was open in disbelief.

"WHO GAVE YOU PEOPLE PERMISSION TO TOUCH MY PLANE!!!!"

The people on the plane did not pay Lindbergh any attention. Neither did the other townspeople. Their eyes were fixed on the old man in the center of the search party. Even the dalmatian was focused now. The kite sank from the sky.

"It's him. It's Thomas Edison."

In the meantime, Lindbergh singled out individuals lounging about his Curtiss Oriole. He threatened them with bodily harm. Edison stepped in and silenced him with a quieting motion of his hand.

"Good morning, everyone!" Edison called to the crowd. "Beautiful morning here in Florida, isn't it? We're thrilled that you came out to greet us. I wondered if I might ask a little favor of you? Could you possibly clear the runway? Could you do that for us? We've got some very important business to take care of today and that would really help us out."

A young man with a scalloped hat walked up and touched Edison on the sleeve. "He's just a man," he said. Al the Pinkerton guard grabbed him by the collar.

"Don't you ever touch him again."

The offender had a HERBERT HOOVER FOR PRESIDENT campaign pin stuck in the top of his scalloped hat.

Lily Quintaine won out over Lindbergh: Kirk took Skeezix's place in the plane. He sat next to Edison in the passenger seat, where the dalmatian had been.

Lindbergh cleaned debris out of the cockpit. It was the trash the celebrity hunters had left behind. Muttering angrily to himself, Lindbergh tossed out chewing gum foils, Coca-Cola bottles, sandwich wrappers, cigarette butts, and candy bars.

When he had cleaned the cockpit to his satisfaction, he showed Edison and Kirk how to use the parachutes in case of an emergency.

Lindbergh started the engine. There was a great black cloud of gasoline smoke. Ibis and egrets escaped to the sky. The water birds beat their wings toward the eastern horizon where alpine cloud formations rose from the sawgrass. Ford walked up to the cockpit. He was dressed in fresh linen; Lindbergh looked seedy in comparison. Ford shouted over the roar of the engine.

"NO TRICKS NOW."

"WHAT?"

"BE CAREFUL. JUST REMEMBER WHAT YOUR CARGO IS."

"WHAT'S THAT SUPPOSED TO MEAN?"

"IT MEANS LEAVE YOUR BARNSTORMING STUNTS IN KANSAS, LINDBERGH. YOU'VE GOT A NATIONAL TREASURE ON BOARD."

Edison looked old and fragile in the morning. There was no color in his cheeks. His eyes were dull. The skin on his ancient hands was mottled and crusty and the bulging veins underneath were purple. He had a black wool scarf wrapped tightly around his neck. He braced for colder temperatures in the upper altitudes. Soon, the Curtiss Oriole was out over the sawgrass.

Kirk looked at Lindbergh. He could feel the tension drain from the pilot's body. Lindbergh seemed more natural in the air than the egrets flying below them. Kirk had a certain sympathy for Lindbergh. He recognized in the young pilot something he had begun to call "fatal dedication." Through no fault of his own, his work had become the shining star in his life and everything else hung below it like old and dull Christmas ornaments. It was a curse. He couldn't take a breath without thinking about his work. The young pilot had many years of misery ahead of him. He might never learn the value of leisure and family.

Kirk swallowed. He looked down at the sawgrass. The

alligators looked like little black maggots from up here. Kirk's face was cold in the wind. He felt his clean, clean face. He had shaved very carefully this morning in the event that . . . . The airplane's engine was very loud and he found it difficult to think.

He had kissed Lily on the cheek before he got on the airplane. Her face was warm and pink and, in her eyes, there was yet a residue of peace that she found only in her dreams. The daily dread had not fully set in. For Skeezix, he had a pat on the shoulder. He tried to look at the pimples on her forehead without her noticing. My God, he had thought, my daughters are growing up. My *daughters* are growing up. Yes. That's what he had thought. It wasn't my daughter is growing up. It was my *daughters.*

Kirk had not chosen hope or despair; hope had chosen him. It was not in his power to give up. Sheila was out there. She was alive.

In 1918, when Sheila was two years old, she had a bout with pleurisy. She was in and out of the hospital the entire month of September. At the same time, Kirk experienced an explosion of growth as a composer, arranger, performer, and conductor. After years and years of study, he had learned the secrets of the mandolin orchestra and was applying them successfully to his own progressive group. He had learned to score for the six components—mandobass, mandocello, mandola, first and second mandolins, and harp guitar—to create a unified orchestral sound. He had learned the published arrangers he could count on for competent scoring: William C. Stahl, A.J. Weidt, Albert Bellson, Herbert Odell, Lloyd Loar. He had learned the minimum number of musicians needed to achieve a full orchestral sound. Seventeen. Double or triple that was even better. The more mandolins, the grander the sound, though a hundred-piece touring ensemble was not feasible. He had learned to tune. The perfect fifth interval had been permanently imbedded in the convolutions of his brain so that he could tune quickly and accurately without device. He had learned when to replace strings (mandolins every six weeks, mandocellos never!). He had learned how to arrange the orchestra on stage. He had learned to conduct a lightning-fast Trio section. He had learned to insist on dynamics even during sightreading.

Also during Sheila's illness, he had come to important conclusions about the visual element of the mandolin orchestra. First and foremost, the mandolins needed to be shiny. They should actually twinkle under the spotlight. If that meant periodically removing the strings to polish those hard-to-get-at spots then, by God, it must be done! Also important was elevating the mandocellos and harp guitars on stools so that their visual grandeur was not lost in a sea of mandolins. It was important that the instruments were held in the "two o'clock position" so that the headstocks were at eye level with the audience. This gave the audience full view of *The Gibson* pearl inlay at the top of the headstock and also any fancy filigree work on the tuning pegs. The carrying cases for mandolins should never be seen by the audience and must be kept neatly behind stage. In regards to dress, he insisted on black tuxedos with white bowties for men and black floor-length evening gowns for women. Patent leather shoes were another requirement. For stage decoration, it never hurt to use a giant American flag for a backdrop, especially in patriotic regions of the country. Also, the strategic use of a potted plant often added a festive air. Boston ferns, dieffenbachia, and bamboo trees were suitable for such purpose.

In September of 1918, Kirk was beginning to be recognized for his mastery of the mandolin orchestra. In the August edition of *Cadenza* (Boston) magazine, it was written: "Kirk Quintaine's Progressive Mandolin Orchestra is one of the brightest stars in the plectral firmament." Also, on September fourth, the *Grand Forks* (North Dakota) *Gazette* wrote: "Kirk Quintaine is developing one of the finest mandolin orchestras in the U.S.A. His meticulous attention to every detail of performance results in a marvelous night of entertainment for the listener. Perhaps more notable, however, than his first-rate orchestra is a style of music that Quintaine is credited with inventing himself. Quintaine calls it 'Indian jazz' and it's a combination of ragtime syncopation with traditional North American Indian folk melodies. This listener, for one, has never heard anything quite like it."

Kirk slept happily the night the review was published. Still, he had greater music in store. This music would bring him worldwide fame. In September of 1918, Kirk was writing a composition he felt would be the crowning achievement of Indian jazz.

The piece was called "The Buffalo Hunt Rag." It was the musical retelling of the Plains Indian story about driving buffalo over precipices in Wyoming rather than hunting the giant beasts. It was full of jaunty ragtime rhythms, menacing Indian bass, and irresistible melodies. "The Buffalo Hunt Rag" even employed the programmic use of the mandobass players thumping the faces of their instruments to imitate the buffalo's crash from the sky. Everything he had learned about Indian and ragtime music was in this song. Yes, it was Indian jazz, and, to a certain extent, it expressed what he had expressed before. This time, however, the music was more certain. More succinct. More confident. More memorable. "The Buffalo Hunt Rag" would become an American classic in the company of "Yankee Doodle," "When Johnny Comes Marching Home," "Maple Leaf Rag," and "St. Louis Blues."

As a piano composition, "The Buffalo Hunt Rag" could stand on its own. But the true genius of the piece, he felt, was its instrumentation. He scored it for flat-backed mandolins, the American version of European violins. Dvorak himself would recognize "The Buffalo Hunt Rag" as the true voice of the New World.

But something happened.

Sheila's illness stopped the composition dead in its tracks.

On a Saturday night at 11:30 P.M., they rushed Sheila to the hospital for the fourth time that month. She was having breathing problems again. Little Sheila rested her head on Lily's shoulder on the passenger side of the Model T. Sheila was so weak, she couldn't lift her head. While the good citizens of Bismarck lay in their pajamas between the sheets of their beds, Kirk raced down the dark city streets in the Model T, running the stop signs, looking out for policemen. Back at home, "The Buffalo Hunt Rag" lay on the desk in his study, notes still drying on the manuscript paper.

He squeezed his hands around the steering wheel and shook his head in indignation and rage. Why? Why was she so ill? Why couldn't they make her better? Why had he been singled out for this persecution? Why? And then, six blocks from Bismarck General, the thought entered his brain. It was such an evil thought that he, at first, did not acknowledge its entry. Later, he admitted the thought but would not allow it to come forward where speech might turn it to stone. He wished . . . He wished . . . He wished she were gone. There. That was it. He wished she were gone. Perhaps his heart knew that the yearning for Sheila's death was not real; still, the thought was in his brain. He was being tyrannized by a sick child. And, in his mind, he rebelled.

At the hospital that night, she grew worse. Her tiny lungs shut down. Only a small portion of her bottom right lung worked. Kirk looked at Sheila's chest. He watched the little lung's desperate attempts to oxygenate. He watched the little rib above the working portion of her lung rise and fall. Then he moved his eyes to her face. There were purplish circles under her eyes. He watched Sheila with sorrow and pity. But mostly he watched her with rage. He raged at her suffering.

Later, he wanted to see if she was strong enough to speak. He talked to her.

"Can you say hi to Daddy?"

"Hi, Daddy."

She tried to smile. The smile broke his heart. At four A.M., she began to respond to the doctor's treatment. Kirk collapsed on the hospital chair next to her bed. The bed lamp threw shadows across the gleaming institutional floor. In the distance, he heard the quick steps of nurses.

Early in the morning, he looked out the hospital window. The autumn announced itself in a gust of starlings. He had come so close to the truth. His children were the only good and real things in his life. The love he had for his children was deeper and more powerful than any he had ever known before and it grew every day. He was honored and blessed to have them. They were a miracle of renewal in his own fading youth. His daughters were the true masterpieces in his life not his Indian jazz rags. Sheila and Skeezix were worth a thousand of those.

Why then, the truth known, had he walked away from them at every opportunity?

In the cockpit, Lindbergh scanned the sawgrass below them. He swept the landscape with his eyes, from left to right, from right to left. He had found six Indian villages in the first hour. He told Kirk he could spot them from five miles away by the crowns of the coconut palms jutting above the hammocks.

"THAT BOY HAS GOT SOME EYE ON HIM," Edison shouted above the engine's roar.

When Lindbergh spotted an Indian village, he circled the Curtiss Oriole over it several times as Kirk and Edison leaned over the silver fuselage. They peered down at the copper faces gazing up at the plane. Kirk often asked Lindbergh to go down again, to go down lower. Lindbergh never objected.

Edison said, "Just remember, Quintaine, the Indians might have tried to make Sheila one of them. She might be all dressed up in the Seminole costume. Her face is probably brown from exposure . . . ."

"What are you trying to tell me?"

"She may not stick out like a sore thumb. That's all."

"I know my own daughter, Mr. Edison."

"I know ya do, son. I know ya do."

The seventh village was Big Chief Cross-in-the-Eyes'.

"She's not there," Kirk said.

"You want me to go down one more time?" Lindbergh asked.

"Yeah, one more time."

Lindbergh banked the plane sharply to the left and went down again. This time they were so low that Kirk could almost pick the coconuts off the trees. This low, he could actually smell the Indian's wild humanity.

"Wait. WAIT. WAIT! IT'S HER! IT'S SHEILA! LOOK!"

"WHOOOOPPPPEEEEEEE!!!!"

In a gesture of triumph, Edison wrenched the scarf from his neck and flung it into the air. It floated slowly and rhythmically down to the ground as if it were Aladdin's carpet. Kirk and Edison embraced. Kirk felt Edison's old clavicle bones under his coat. He felt the cool surface of Edison's dentures against his cheek. He felt Edison's old fingertips pressed into his back.

"SIT DOWN, GODDAM IT, YOU TWO!" Lindbergh shouted from the cockpit. "ARE YOU TRYING TO GET US ALL KILLED?"

Edison, overcome with excitement, began to cough the violent and desperate cough of an old man. Recognizing the danger, he quickly sat down on the passenger seat with the back of his skull resting on the fuselage. He caused his hands to go limp at his sides.

Lindbergh landed the plane south of the village, mowing down a long path of sawgrass, killing birds and reptiles.

Kirk was out of the plane before Lindbergh shut the engine off. He raced across the swamp. There was blood on the palms of his hands from pulling back the sawgrass. He tripped and stumbled and sank. There were parts of the swamp that were waist-deep. The water penetrated his trousers and he felt it cool in the secret recesses of his body. Dragonflies circled his steaming head. They were miniature pilots, like Lindbergh.

The wooden propeller blades of Lindbergh's Curtiss Oriole twirled slowly in the November breeze. They caught rays of sunlight and tossed them back over the sawgrass. Kirk reached the bank of the Indian village before the propeller blades had come to a complete stop.

When he first saw her, she was standing among the Indian children with a cloud of gnats above her hair. He looked at her in shock. He saw himself in her like never before. There she was, him in all his pain and awkwardness. Was it really fair and wise to inflict this pain and awkwardness on an innocent? Was it really fair and wise to give them life? Of course it was. It was the only fair and wise thing.

Sheila dashed across the camp. She flung herself at her father. She held on and would not let go.

"I bet you thought we gave up on you," Kirk said. "Do they ever bathe these dogs?"

They jumped up on Kirk as he embraced his daughter, yellow dogs, black dogs, big dogs, little ones, dogs with old gums, mother dogs, fierce yippers. With their muddy footprints, they, each one of them, recorded themselves on the back of Kirk's shirt.

The Indians stood around the leaping dogs. They were in their bare feet. They stood around the thatched roofs of their huts like statues. They were dressed in their brightest finery. Each ebony eye was frozen on Kirk and Sheila.

"Daddy?"

"What?"

"Why are you bleeding?"

Edison and Lindbergh made their way from the plane across the sawgrass to the camp. Several times, Lindbergh had to carry Edison over the rough parts. He carried him like a baby. He put one arm under his back and the other under the crook at his knees. Grim-faced, Lindbergh carried the great inventor across the Everglades. He kicked up water with his boots. Alligators, turtles, and frogs scrambled away in a panic. Overhead, ibis and egrets beat their wings across the sky. When Lindbergh carried Edison, the straps of his flight cap bobbed alongside his head like odd pigtails.

Edison said, "I wish Mina would have remembered to pack my galoshes."

When they finally arrived in camp, Sheila stared and stared at Edison.

"What is it, Sheila?"

"I kind of expected you."

Edison turned to Kirk. "They took good care of her. You can tell."

"They fed her well," Kirk said. "I'd say she's gained twenty-five pounds."

Edison went around the camp and greeted each Indian individually. He flashed his dentures at them and nodded with great exaggeration. He had little toys for the children which he produced from the pockets of his coat. They were miniature cameras with little shutters that didn't really work. After he gave the toys away, he went off alone. He explored the Indian camp by himself. He peered at every little Seminole artifact. Rarely did a piece of flint, a necklace, a comb, a broom, a pot, a doll, or a biscuit escape his attention. He studied the Seminole artifacts with the trained mind of an inventor. When he reached the kitchen hut, he dipped the wooden spoon into the pot of sofki and sampled it. He tipped the sofki spoon to his lips and tilted his head to the thatched roof of the hut.

Meanwhile, Kirk introduced Sheila to Lindbergh.

"How do you do," Sheila said.

"You look like your sister," Lindbergh said. "But not that much. Do any of these Indians speak English?"

"Not a word," Sheila said.

"Which one's the chief ?"

"Him."

"That's the chief ?"

Big Chief Cross-in-the-Eyes went to the hut where Sheila slept. He knelt down and pulled the music out from under the platform. He presented it to Kirk.

"You did this, Sheila?" Kirk asked.

"The best that I could," she replied. "It's their music."

Lindbergh yawned. He swatted a mosquito on his wrist and said, "If you people don't mind, I've got a mail route to run."

"They'll take us to the airplane in their canoes," Sheila said. She was the first one in the canoe. It was Big Chief Cross-in-the-Eyes' canoe. She sat down on the jagged, chiseled-out cypress bottom.

"You know what I'd like tonight, Daddy? A pair of underdrawers. I haven't had a pair of underdrawers on for two months."

Kirk got in the canoe. He sat behind Sheila. Lindbergh and Edison got in a different canoe. They took off. The dogs chased them for a while then turned around and trotted back to camp. The Indian poling Lindbergh and Edison's canoe was someone she had named Eskimo Face. He was younger than Big Chief Cross-in-the-Eyes. They glided across the swamp. The sawgrass made a continuous scratching sound against the bodies of the canoes. The Indians grunted with each pull of their poles. Their brown forearms tensed.

Sheila said, "I'd like to have a bed. A bed with a mattress and clean sheets. I'd like to have some milk. Some coconut macaroons. Some doublemint gum. Some socks. I'd like to have some real soap. I'd like to have some fingernail clippers."

The day had begun to fall towards the night. The white sunlight had changed to yellow; it poured through the holes in the mahogany trees and sabal palms in the hammocks. In the sky, the moon sat to the right of the sun, pale as a memory. Big Chief Cross-in-the-Eyes' strip shirt took on a new brilliance. A raccoon clung to the branch of a gumbo limbo tree. Through masked eyes, he watched the canoes as they drifted by. Gallinules and coots flew in front of them, landing in a spray of swamp water. Then, just as quickly, they took off again, assaulting the peace with their honking and squawking. Edison, seeing that Sheila had begun to cry, nodded and smiled in sympathy from the other boat.

"I'd like my toothbrush. Some toothpaste. I'd like to eat with a fork and a knife. I'd like a pillow. Some real paper and pencil. I want to see my mother. And Skeezix. I want to play my mandolin."

Kirk said, "I love you, Sheila."

The next day they went to the Kenilworth Lodge in Sebring to pick up the ladies of the orchestra: Mrs. Evelyn Thompson Witt, Ella Griffith Bedard, Violet May Cooper, Emily Jackson, and Beatrice Templeton. The Kirk Quintaine Progressive Mandolin Orchestra, once again complete, loaded its mandobasses, mandocellos, mandolas, harp guitars, mandolins, lone xylophone, and a truckload of the best music ever written onto a northbound train. They began their journey to the Dakotas.